Hermes in Paris

PETER VANSITTART
Hermes in Paris

PETER OWEN
London and Chester Springs

PETER OWEN PUBLISHERS
73 Kenway Road, London SW5 0RE

Peter Owen books are distributed in the USA by
Dufour Editions Inc., Chester Springs, PA 19425-0007

First published in Great Britain 2000
© Peter Vansittart 2000

ISBN 0 7206 1106 7

A catalogue record for this book is available from the British Library

Printed and bound in Great Britain by MPG Books Ltd, Bodmin, Cornwall

To Hugh Schon, and in memory of Elvira

Romulus' town was then in all the vigour of youth, while Carthage had reached that degree of corruption at which States are incapable of supporting either the abuses which enervate them or the remedy which might regenerate them. To Rome, then, belonged the future. On the one hand a people of soldiers, restrained by discipline, religion and purity of behaviour, animated by patriotism, surrounded by devoted allies; on the other, a people of merchants with dissolute manners, unruly mercenaries, discontented subjects.

– Napoleon III, *Life of Caesar*

FOREWORD

Some readers may like to be reminded of the historical background. The year 1870 is remote, though Bertrand Russell, Bernard Shaw and H.G. Wells were then living. The French Revolution had not extinguished French Monarchy. The First Republic, after war and Terror, eventually subsided into the Empire of Napoleon I, followed by two successive kings – brothers of the guillotined Louis XVI – then, after revolution, by their cousin, Louis-Philippe, of the younger, Orleanist branch. He was ousted by yet another Paris revolution, 1848, which installed the Second Republic under the Presidency of Prince Louis Napoleon Bonaparte, granted not by proven ability but by skilful propaganda, nostalgic songs and his evocative name.

The Prince-President had to swear his loyalty. 'In the sight of God and before the French People represented by the National Assembly, I swear to remain faithful to the Republic, One and Indivisible. I will regard as a national enemy whoever will illegally attempt to challenge what France herself has established.'

Inwardly, however, he had a lifetime's pledge to the Bonapartist Idea, an efficient, modernizing Empire with Great Power policies and his own additions of social reform. In December 1851, shortly due by law to retire, and pleading emergency rights, he dissolved the Republic by a *coup*. Mismanaged, perhaps by his half-brother Auguste de Morny, this entailed some two thousand victims of street-fighting, with hundreds more gaoled, deported, exiled. To the unforgiving, Louis Napoleon for ever remained the perjured Man of December.

He soon proclaimed the Second Empire, styling himself Napoleon III, to acknowledge the 'reign' of Napoleon I's son, now dead. The Empire was confirmed by male plebiscite, Bonapartist democracy, himself retaining dictatorial powers.

Before 1848, he had not been regarded as a consequence, and two farcical attempts on Louis-Philippe's throne assured him ridicule. After Louis Napoleon's electoral triumph, Thiers, displaced Orleanist minister and historian, remarked that the real rulers would allow the Prince women and money, then lead him by the nose – the kind of misjudgement repeated by German notables in 1933. Marx considered that France had made two mistakes: in believing Louis Napoleon a genius and believing him an idiot. In exile after the *coup*, Victor Hugo sneered at him in *Les Châtiments*:

> Ruined by debauchery, dull of eye,
> Furtive, pale of visage
> This night robber who lights his lamp
> With the sun of Austerlitz.

Officially, he was the son of Napoleon I's brother Louis, sickly King of Holland, and Hortense, daughter of Empress Josephine. Hortense was beautiful, impulsive, a fiction writer, painter, composer – she wrote the Bonapartist hymn 'Partant Pour La Syrie' – and sexually voracious, described by her husband as a Messalina who breeds.

Gossip, habitually ungenerous, relished beliefs that Louis Napoleon's real father had been either Admiral Verhuel, Dutch diplomat, René de Villeneuve, courtier, or Count Flauhaut, illegitimate son of Talleyrand, who survived until 1870, the very day of

Sedan. The tireless Victor Hugo assailed 'this child of Chance, whose name is a theft and whose birth is a fraud'.

Whatever the truth, the youth who, beneath a modernizing outlook, retained some Corsican superstitions, astrological, fatalistic, became certain that Fate had made him Napoleon's heir, justified by the deaths of 'Napoleon II' and his own elder brother.

Corsican – Italian – in origins, he was scarcely an obvious Frenchman. Raised in Switzerland, tutored by the republican Lebas, son of Robespierre's loyal colleague, schooled in Bavaria, speaking with Swiss-German accent, known in London society, he always thought in the grandiose terms of an international meddler. He refused the Presidency of Ecuador, contemplated joining Polish nationalists against Russia, served with Italian rebels against Austria and the Pope. Captured, he escaped from Austrian prison, helped by his mother's charms, wiles, bribes. 'The name we bear', he insisted, 'demands us to aid a suffering people imploring our assistance.' This generosity of spirit was to underlie his foreign policy: venturesome, challenging, risky.

In books, *Napoleonic Ideas*, *Political Dreamings*, *The Extinction of Poverty*, he assiduously revised his uncle's thoughts, presenting them as novel forms of civilian glory, humane, rational, technological, up to date. 'The Empire is Peace.' Throughout, he held vague concepts of a European federation, with permanent Council and international Court of Justice, free peoples bonded by laws, peaceful co-operation. 'La sainte alliance des peuples.' Disarmament would promote goodwill, outlaw war. He had visions of promoting a Europe of interlocking circles: free trade, a currency union, all disputes settled by friendly discussion at international conferences. Such notions expressed his personal amiability and hedonistic, unsystematic mind. He wished his people – all peoples – well, was more generously intentioned than Palmerston and Bismarck and shrank from the 'blood and iron' severity favoured at least by Bismarck.

Politically too indecisive, he was an accomplished seducer: he spoke little, his taciturnity rendering him mysterious, though Bismarck dismissed him as a sphinx without a secret. 'An odd little chap,' Lord Clarendon added; 'it's impossible not to like him.' *The Times* of London obituary diagnosed him as strange, meditative, inscrutable, dark to others – often, doubtless, to himself.

Ruling a volatile, restless people, he had to provide more than idealistic meanderings at taxpayers' expense and, despite reiterations about peace, he was soon at war. Avenging the French disaster of 1812, he joined Britain in the Crimean war and in sacking the Summer Palace in Peking, 1860. He commanded, amateurishly but successfully, to expel Austria from Tuscany – though, to appease the Catholic vote, had to defend Papal Rome against his Italian Nationalist associates. He precipitated French involvement in Indo-China, completed the conquest of Algeria, increased French influence in Syria, Somalia, Madagascar, the Caribbean. Then, with dreamy opportunism, fed by false information about Mexico and the American Civil War, deferring to the optimism of his wife, Morny, the Bourse and self-styled 'experts', he established a Mexican Empire, with guaranteed French protection, under Archduke Maximilian of Austria, 'the Archdupe'. The demands of the victorious American North and the spectacular ascent of Prussia forced him to renege on the promised protection, abandoning Maximilian to execution by Mexican republicans. This demolished much of Napoleon's prestige, already impaired by his miscalculations over the Austro-Prussian war, in which he had reckoned on becoming arbiter after a stalemate: swift Prussian victory was everywhere considered a French defeat. The republican journalist Rochefort, a declassed nobleman, jeered at the Minister Rouher for styling the Mexican venture the most imaginative idea of the reign: 'Not Maximilan's reign, of course.'

Unlike most rulers, Napoleon III had mixed with men and

women of varied social status. His first attempted revolt subjected him to a brief American exile, the second to six years' imprisonment in the unhealthy Castle of Ham, where he fathered two sons on an obliging laundress and clog-dancer, sensationally escaping disguised as a workman, Badinguet – a name hilariously foisted on him by enemies – a plank on his shoulders, cheap pipe in his mouth, 1846.

In and out of prison he remained an assiduous writer, his imagination compared by Palmerston to a rabbit warren. He wrote on unemployment, the need for experts in power, the advantages of a Nicaraguan inter-oceanic canal, on the Swiss army, on artillery, sugar-beet, the lessons of English history, on Julius Caesar, archaeology, town and country planning, education, mutual aid, cheap credit, gas, chemistry, economics, railways. Lacking brilliance, he possessed some shrewdness, obduracy and sensitivity to common opinions. 'It is always necessary to astonish the French; never leave them the last word.' 'The nation is a slave who must be persuaded that he is on the throne.' 'Statistics have a certain eloquence, with which all false theories must clash.' Slightly more than a theoretician, he designed cannon, military rockets, iron warships, model farms and houses, land banks, was to initiate schemes for urban planning and rural reform.

Dictator throughout the fifties, he faced difficulties. His cosmopolitan amiability competed with the French desire for glory and his sympathy for militant Polish, Italian and Prussian nationalism was shared by few of his subjects. He desired a France contented with philistine pleasure, economic prosperity, cheap credit, yet was expected to retrieve the continental supremacy won, then lost, by his uncle. Faced by multiple contradictions, he remained opaque and unpredictable. Courtiers repeated his little jest: 'The Empress is an old-style royalist, Morny a constitutional monarchist, I myself am a socialist, the only Bonapartist in France is Persigny, and he's mad.'

The Empress, Eugénie, a Spaniard, was beautiful but never popular and with a growing and unwise appetite for politics. Her husband was harassed by too many Corsican relatives, mostly greedy and unscrupulous. The most intelligent were his cousin, Mathilde – a link with the world of Flaubert, the Goncourts, Saint-Beuve, Taine – and her brother Prince Napoleon, 'Plon-Plon', disposed towards republicanism, hating the Empress, resenting the young heir, Prince Imperial. When their father, Napoleon I's brother Jerome, once irritably told his nephew that he had nothing of the great Napoleon about him, the Emperor replied, 'My dear fellow, you are mistaken. I have his family!'

The Second Empire had ten successful years. Napoleon III appeared dominant abroad, Paris again a centre of diplomacy and splendour, of international congresses, exhibitions, parades, fêtes, women's fashions. He himself invaded Italy to free the north Italians of Austrian rule and won victories at Magenta and Solferino. The Universal Exhibition of 1867, a glittering riposte to diplomatic setbacks, attracted fifteen million visitors, including most European rulers. Paris itself was rebuilt, with wide, airy boulevards, parks, trees, the Bois tamed for lakes, arbours, vistas, an English Garden. Slums were cleared for large tenements, acres reconstructed for hotels, department stores, hospitals, banks, Les Halles, railways, a grandiose opera house. Crèches, co-operatives, canals, pension schemes were encouraged, also state loans and insurance. Water supplies and sanitation improved, Cherbourg was modernized, hulks abolished, unions and the Press granted increasing freedoms as the dictatorship relaxed. All this was pushed through by the Imperial will, regardless of individual rights.

The sixties showed decline. Ill health debilitated the self-indulgent ruler, whose choice of ministers was largely limited to mediocrities. Morny – suave manipulator of the misnamed Legislative Assembly, sugar-beet millionaire, speculator, dramatist, connoisseur of women and race-horses, skilful fixer of plebiscites – died prematurely, as did the military reformer, Marshal Niel, essential for the future. Overworked, Napoleon fumbled badly in foreign policy, too readily relying on gratitude for his support of the new Italy and expansionist Prussia.

At home, the more benefits the urban population received, the more it demanded, while economic prosperity had begun to falter. Napoleon recognized the insecurities of his position. His dynasty, unlike those of rivals, was inorganic, parvenu, never a matter of course but dependent upon votes and personal theatre. This he strove to make appear an asset: 'I candidly accept before Europe the status of parvenu – a glorious title when obtained by the free vote of a great people.'

By 1865, however, his tone was less optimistic, and he wrote in his biography of Julius Caesar, designed to justify his own methods of government:

When at the summit of general prosperity, dangerous utopias arise without roots in the nation, the slightest exercise of force extinguishes them; but when, on the contrary, society in deep torment, from needs genuine and urgent, demands reform, the success of the most violent repression is only brief; the repressed ideas incessantly reappear and, like the fabled Hydra, for one head slashed off, a hundred replace it.

He also uttered a classic complaint of authoritarian reformers: 'Dictatorship can only be a temporary regime, and yet a parliamentary system destroys the government that founds it. So then what do you do?'

His reforms – planned with the liberal Morny, later with an erstwhile republican, Emile Ollivier, won over by his personal charm – increasingly seemed reluctant concessions to opposition stirring in the cities. In 1869 he persuaded Ollivier, admirer of George

Washington, to head a new ministry, with a brief to 'crown the edifice' with a more constitutional 'Liberal Empire', which Theodore Zeldin considers could have proved one of the most interesting political achievements of the century.

The germ of this story began over fifty years ago, when I encountered the novels of Emile Zola and Alfred Neumann, to whom I now repay a debt.

ONE

Paris, 2 January 1870, the day blue, crisp, unseasonably warm. Hermes sits at his favourite table outside Café d'Olympe on rue de Castelnau, in one of his periodic revolts against contemplative stillness. Today he is visible to all, having laid aside the broad cap that often makes him anonymous, sometimes unseen. Beside him lies a yellow cane with serpentine mouldings topped with a gilded ram's head. Under silvery hair, his narrow face is smooth, long-nosed, pale as fairly expensive notepaper, his thin lips slightly amused, though the eyes, of indeterminate colour, are expressionless beneath heavy lids. In brown, modish cloak fringed with blue fur, his satin cravat dull crimson, perfected in Morny style above a mauve waistcoat, he is a dandy, incapable of displaying surprise, distress, anger. Noting him, slight but with ambiguous presence, it is easy to understand that for years, when a gathering abruptly falls silent, people have joked that 'Hermes has come.'

Sociable enough, by some fluke of personality, he is simultaneously solitary: affable, he is also teasing. Attentive to his needs, though at another table, are 'the three Graces' girls speaking only amongst themselves in a strange tongue. Like him, they are night creatures, favouring darkened pavements, thieves' kitchens, backwater taverns at crossroads or in the remains of woodlands.

Under a sun freed from last week's gales and snow, they can all watch the constant procession, cheerful, purposeless, stung into fresh being by the New Year promise. It is a live frieze of Parisians: young uniformed elegants from Saint-Cyr, shabby students, wealthy cosmopolitans from Hôtel de la Paix and rue de Rivoli, cigars at the ready, Latin Quarter philosophers, pork-shop cooks with barrel-like torsos, varnished hairdressers, ringleted heroines in long tinted skirts from Montmartre studios, Montparnasse brasseries and cabarets, *lorettes* in bright, gauzy scarves, dancers from les Bouffes Parisiens, Variétés and small, flashy La Chapelle brothels, primly hatted *souteneurs*, beggarly pickpockets, a mock-Juno or two in scarlet flannelette and pertly slanted yellow bonnets too young for them. Lordlings in violet capes and fancy hats from Saint-Germain and Saint-Honoré, forgoing their carriages and, blotched with desire, jostling with malcontents from seething eastern suburbs, Saint-Antoine, Saint-Denis; skeleton ragamuffins, declassed and ruined gentry from inflammable Belleville, all are on parade. Women's hats are tilted forward in fashionable mode, their coloured ribbons streaming behind like reminders of summer. You can trap a cheap, sidelong glance from a soft Bon Marché midenette or ogle a Dove of Venus or soubrette from Théâtre Lyrique or Folies Nouvelles, honey-pots for the tourists whom the Empire so encourages, to revel in its towering masterpiece, the New Paris. Red-cloaked gendarmes seem off-duty, grinning and chattering as if truly human. Secret police remain secret, doubtless sniffing dossiers in the Central Political Bureau, that unpopular sinew of the regime, headed, of course, by Corsicans. Progress on the recently completed boulevard is slow, obstructed by massed pedestrians mingling with phaetons, cabriolets, victorias, landaus, broughams, barouches, dog-carts, simple fiacres, char-a-bangs and omnibuses, wide berlines gilded and crested, coachmen in cocked hats, flicking whips from on high, bawling orders or insults, blowing horns, footmen standing behind, rigid in wigs and knee-breeches, while, within, illustrious personages condescend to inspect the Vendôme Column, the Seine, the distant towers of Notre-Dame, freshly planted trees, stark and black against the clear sky. Tall wheels, small wheels. The flow is endless. Rush-light poets, threadbare journalists, urchin jockeys from Les Buttes, nondescripts with eager girls on their arms, all enthusing over this golden afternoon, gift of the capricious times, and occasionally throwing a coin to what Herr Marx, in London, no great flatterer, has termed lumpenproletariat.

Hermes, as if recollecting something piquant though trivial, looks up at the lofty, belaurelled N on a pediment, encircled by stone bees. For joyous mortals streaming towards nowhere it signifies intensity of being, enhanced vision, poetic in its guarantee of happiness. The letter is inescapable, carved above the banker's portal and beneath the fishmonger's roof, behind the judge's head and, never far from the altar, soaring high as the Column topped with the French Hercules, Bonaparte, demi-god, embodiment of supreme human effort. N, its familial bees and violets outrivalled only by wrathful Napoleonic eagles, is a telling reminder of past and future: mortals are obsessed by their own invention, Time, and N is both topical polemic and password to nebulous infinity. Hermes himself sees things naked, shorn of nostalgia and griefs. Gods, nuances of being, universal membranes, concern themselves with memory only as periodic twinges, though he indulges himself in rather more. Earth is an ever-refilled museum of artefacts that change only outwardly, the atomic core undisturbed. He contemplates rows of dead chieftains, princesses, slaves, broken shards of empire, chips of inspiration, overthrown by decay and necessity, withered by touch of immortal light.

The present ruler, who had begun his December *coup* by smashing the drums of the National Guard – Hermes' touch – has declared that great causes demand a historical figure to personify them. Once adopted, he can rely on his crimes being forgotten, only his great deeds remembered. At this, Hermes winks at a cat scared of the multitudinous wheels, feet, voices. It returns a stare of green hatred, so that he winks again.

Brazen music begins, first faint, now noisy, as the crowd parts in uneven suction for striding feet, drums, flourish of trumpet, opulence of flag and horse, the trudge of soldiery still bronzed from Algeria and Mexico.

Ah, Mexico! Hermes' beaked, tallowy face is allowed a grin almost vulgar, though unobserved by Gallic faces, simple as cowbells, at surrounding tables.

So, a Paris gala, the air rainbow, partitioned by dragoons in green tunics, white surcoats, carabineers with gold breastplates, a dense array of silver lace, polished froggings, heavy shakos, further dabs of colour added by crimson epaulettes, scarlet kepis. Officers with puppy faces swagger as they had outside Troy and Carthage, at Marathon and Zama, though those applauding may be yearning not for some overwhelming triumph but for whores from Mabille's circus or the flesh markets of rue Doudeauville, a flash tenor from the Opéra, even . . . but hush! The military march forward. Blue cloaks of the Line, long Arab cloaks of Spahis, blue and scarlet with green turbans: Zouave braid, Hussar stripes, Lancer pennons, Chasseurs d'Afrique light blue. The tramp and blare is further dedication to N, here garish, circled with swollen leaves, there austere and lonely, signatures of the times. Horses clatter, spurs jangle, plumes lie back in the wind. At intervals, in contrast, are smudged bootblacks from Pont Neuf, priests' dingy skirts or the blurred white and red velvet of a Saint-Simonite futurist.

Hermes remains detached. Uninterested in mortals' private flesh he considers their expressions, motives, angles of existence, but colours are an unnecessary addition to which he rarely treats himself. Colours are warnings, temptations, threats, distractions, preying on these mood-harassed lives, but for him, free of all but himself, colour is a flaw, exclusively terrestrial, an irregular gloss on airy nuances. For him, only two are distinctive, black for mortals, white for the divine. Black, save in China, contains ignorance, fear, death, *moira*, Fate; white is undeviating assurance, speed, nakedness, purity of outline. Even Aphrodite's eyes had been white: down here, those of the Empress were famously sapphire blue; no compliment, for the more ambitious the mortal the more blatant the imperfection. Hermes sees not colour but pattern.

Hours are passing, but he needs no watch. From sibylline priest-esses and Hector, tamer of horses, to Empress and Minister is a mere sigh. Whatever their uniforms, mortals are in bondage to roles of hunter and hunted, easily reversible, in what they call politics. These Gauls shout for Caesar, as yesterday they chanted for rain, jumped high for corn, crept to witches, washed spears in blood, danced in circles to invigorate Apollo.

The din loudens, stimulated by the last battalion; hands lift like doves for the barouche of an undoubted civilian, Mlle Hortense Schneider, Offenbach's sometime star, a marvel, a scandal, conceal-ing beneath sparkling petticoats what hacks calls *passage des princes*, four of them allegedly exploring it in one night during the Universal Exhibition. 'How I adore the soldiers,' she trilled so enticingly in *La Belle Hélène*, Uniforms, plumes, boots, music, eagles, sleeping swords, are they reassurance, threat or gaily dappled romance? They certainly recall victory in Russia, like boulevard de Sébastopol, in Italy, like Pont Solferino. Surely, all is so visibly in order, under the supreme leader, heir to the great N, Hercules on his Column.

Hermes, twitching an eyebrow for another coffee, which he will not drink, contemplates no almighty N, only human pride. His pre-rogative is that of a guide from appearance to essence, though never regarded as wholly serious, and he periodically forgoes the onus of office. Lapsing from absolutes, he is at ease in the mortal world of travelling salesmen with their droll stories, merchants exchanging sinuous mendacities, also of renegade priests, plausible rogues, all back door, side-alley modes of livelihood. He had chuckled when, in Paris for the Exhibition, the old roué ex-King of Bavaria had been greeted by the Emperor.

'May I be permitted to present to Your Majesty these gentlemen, my ministers?'

The Bavarian's scowl was exquisite, operatic, a black medley of curled lines. 'Certainly not! It would bore me into my grave!'

The Emperor, let it be said, gave his usual good-humoured laugh, the ministers bowed disconsolately and retired in a huff.

The coffee arrives, but he is attentive only to bonnets, top hats, forage caps, the excrescences on heads vain, timid or indeterminate; furred greatcoats are animal disguise against the covetous and famished; reptilian shoes hide what has long lost fleetness; delicate canes are extended claws; gold watches brute proclamations of superior strength, strength more over others than over that unimaginative concept, Time.

The day is short, dusk approaches, gas lamps throwing a glow over Paris. Under the yellow flares, faces flit between the human and the bestial, like hybrids dear to men's imagination and, indeed, worship: the dog-headed, horse-bodied, fish-tailed. Darkness ordains reversals, making abnormality normal, the obvious very subtle. What Earth considered progress is mere swapping of misunderstandings. Agamemnon succeeds Agamemnon, shadows cast shadows in another circular dance.

Safe from street packs and drilled automatons, in lairs behind thickened walls, where artificial light is perpetual and hours, indeed seasons, are erased by routine, gentlemen with chimney-shaped hats and pale, scented gloves would be collecting as if at a water hole, conferring, calculating, rootling for news, gambling on the future, debating the significance of Sadowa and Mexico, which had tilted Europe askew.

Hermes, in his own way, is listening, always entertained by whatever goes awry: an ill-balanced marriage, a gullible child, a sententious but ludicrous lawsuit, adroit swindles, sea disasters, the breaking of oaths, pompous worship of nonsense, a Caesar arriving too late for his Triumph or tripping on the red carpet, a coronation where the nervous Archbishop places the crown on the wrong head, revolution, when the Minister of the Interior flees to the interior. A great statesman addressed the entire Diplomatic Corps in all its metallic and braided finery on a text of reconciliation: the notables sat entranced, such eloquence, such sentiments, such finesse, but, nearing the peroration to outsoar all else, irrevocably to establish reconciliation as a smooth matter of course, the speaker's wife, standing very erect beside him, dropped dead, and the widower's heartfelt expletive ruined the occasion. A duchess at Arras, opening a new public library, was inadvertently handed the wrong speech, thus beginning, 'As I sit here, under the wondrous oaks of Fontainebleau . . .'

In such is Hermes' delight.

Nearing the end of his session in Paris, he would welcome some drama, to delay the jaded fatigue that ultimately ensues. Now, as the day cools, he loses interest in this slow-moving populace, preferring to trace shadows and hints, the transformations of twilight. Quicksilver of nature, he is at his best in half-lights, which require ampler dexterities. Here in Paris he already has some repute as a night-time boulevardier, persuasive teller of traveller's tales, a fellow apt to appear unexpectedly, vanish without warning. Some suspect he is a Prussian spy, a key-hole fellow, or nimble swindler, professions appropriate to shadows. He can be glimpsed, cloaked, dainty-footed, on that narrow footpath adjoining Gare du Nord at the identical instant when others report seeing him descend from a cabriolet outside the Madeleine wearing bizarre, unidentifiable decorations or lounging around garish Montmartre trailing three sulky nymphs.

Known as an exquisite carver of meat, never losing at cards, he has a bulging purse which he never seems in need to open.

At a loss to assess him, people usually distrust his sly manner and lop-sided grin, while entertained by his glib anecdotes and clever tricks. At an expensive party he produced a quick-fire mechanical cigarette lighter, shaped like a triton, apparently of his own invention. At another, he entered one door attired like a general, withdrew, at once appearing in the frock-coat and stars of a diplomat.

Seen closer, his features, neither young nor old, are slightly seamy round eyes and mouth, have a cool, dandyish stare, sometimes overbright unless shaded by the broad-brimmed cap. Now, languid, bored, he is roused by a news-urchin with impudent cries and gamin flourish. He flips a coin, a newspaper is tossed at him which he expertly catches between two fingers.

Le Moniteur, government sheet, nicknamed 'Le Menteur'. Its headlines smooth away his listlessness, his sallow face creases, with a concern less than benevolent, that of a rich banker, courteously, even stylishly, refusing a loan to an old friend. Then, as he reads further, it is almost boyishly cheerful.

At his New Year reception, the Emperor, surrounded by his new ministers, 'the Honourable Men', addressed the besashed, bemedalled, besworded Diplomatic Corps in words that M. Reuter instantly dispatched to all the world's capitals: 'The year 1870 can, I am certain, only consolidate this general agreement between France and the other Great Powers, and tend to the increase of Peace and Civilization.'

TWO

IN a quiet square off the Sixth Arrondissement near Parc de Jemappes, a night prowler, peeping into a certain ground-floor apartment, could survey comfortable domesticity. From a brisk fire and well-polished lamps, lights darted over red chairs, a faded Japanese screen, a polished oval table on which were neatly stationed plate-silver candlesticks and epergne loaded with dark red and yellow waxen fruits; brocaded cushions, Venetian-style shutters partly concealed by slightly frayed pink curtains under papier-mâché pelmets speckled in green and white. Artificial roses were arranged very carefully in marrow-green vases. A curved red-lacquer cabinet was moulded with swans' necks, gryphons, Empire bees, and vaguely suggesting a tent. The treasures within were manifold: pincushions in shells, an antique gold watch, chessmen, a Chinese doll, small brass bowls, books with titles obliterated by age, a stuffed humming-bird on a bracket, some Restoration and First Empire coins and, like flimsy sun-rays, some painted fans, an ostrich egg on an ivory tile, a musical box, black, dotted with mother of pearl, a row of grey fossils, a paperweight of snow within a glass dome. Opposite, above the escritoire, hung family silhouettes, oleographs of woodlands, villages, a spire, a picture of the Empress in white crinoline cut from a fashionable journal and framed in mock-gold.

Stiffly seated on one side of the fire, black suited with mauve cravat, Etienne, a bony, long-haired, spectacled government servant, was holding a book, though upside down. On the other side, on a sham Louis XV oriental divan Etienne had bought at cut price in rue le Lappe, draped in a fluffy English tea-gown, also upright, plump, full-breasted, smiling, Amélie was sewing at a small table. Under a lamp, their son Emile, pupil at a junior school, Saint-Denis, preparatory to Lycée Fenélon, was at homework, or pretending so, though at this moment gazing at the family portraits on the small upright piano which none of them could play. From within, Henriette, the cook, slammed a door. Etienne winced, looked severe, then, as Amélie continued to smile, he shrugged and said nothing.

At forty, a few years older than Amélie, Etienne already had some seniority at the Education Department, supervising several rows of dutifully stacked clerks, inky behind the ears, respectful to the coming man. Earlier, seeing them embrace at the door, delicate flowering of affection, Hermes gave them his small, imprecise smile, then examined Emile whom he had first seen yesterday, in the park, and noted as a boy serious, probably withdrawn, possibly of interest. He now smiles again, though such a smile is unreliable. Like the Emperor, another guide of souls, Hermes deals in puns, nuances, double meanings. He has earthly favourites, but his favours disconcert. One so favoured is the Beloved, an old man of impoverished Saint-Antoine, lair of the red wolf of revolution, area of violence. He had inherited an estate but sold it, thereafter distributing his income to others, though, lately, backed by Hermes' attention, with benefits apt to disappoint. On the Emperor's fête day he gave a street banquet to assist social harmony, which ended in republican brawls; he taught dancing to the blind, but last week his most promising pupil, at practice, had tripped over a carelessly placed bag of artichokes and broken her neck. He had led protests, well advertised by the Left, against the removal of street cobbles, not from indignation at the disappearance of weapons handy during insurrection but on behalf of children, immemorially rolling marbles, nuts, curtain rings between the stones. Devout revolutionaries grinned as he explained that in children's imagination was the real Republic. Arrested for 'sedition', he was rescued only by direct intervention from the Emperor, prompted, people said, by the Prince Imperial, though, to the Beloved, he was less a live boy than an imprisoned doll.

Emile is surely more interesting than his parents, for, like Hermes himself, he loves streets as he does stories; indeed streets are stories, with marvellous beginnings, and endings to be supplied by the watcher. In this gleaming New Paris much survives from the perilous and disreputable: tribal vendettas, spectral presences, Stygian beliefs – amongst which is a peasant notion that buggering a healthy child cures venereal distempers.

The fire stirred. Etienne laid aside his book, Amélie's pretty face looked well between curls. Both then turned towards Emile, hunched over his exercises, then rising, trim head bowed. He was ready for bed.

'Did school go well today, Son?

'Yes, Papa.'

'Emile, would you like a hot drink?'

'No, Maman. Thank you.'

'Goodnight, Son.'

'Goodnight, Papa.'

'Goodnight, my darling. Give Maman a kiss. There. Sleep with angels.'

She sighed, though inwardly. Emile was departing, and Etienne like perhaps, most husbands, was often going out, even after his return from the Department.

THREE

O F gods the most fully conscious, Hermes nods to himself, mar-shalling a cast, marionettes not of the most amusing quality but sufficing. Maître Ollivier, dwarfish Thiers, Count Bismarck and King Wilhelm – for the Germanic tribes are restless again – Benedetti, Gramont, Rochefort, clownish Persigny, the Emperor, indeed the Emperor and Loulou, Prince Imperial, Child of France, Child of Hope, hopeful demi-gods pouring their souls into flame. He has now drawn another from the pack, Gambetta, Léon Gambetta.

Of the Empress, so beautiful, incessantly talking yet withal dumb, little can yet be staged, save for a few rumours to be freely scattered. She has leading lady prerogatives, scarcely those of Hortense Schneider, for her talents are less perceptible. Human beauty does not concern Hermes, wit and intellect do not concern the Empress. However, around her lie ingredients for comedy, short but exquisite. A swaggering Empire, a toy Napoleon who wades rather than strides, counterfeit nobles, a stage army marching to frivolous tunes, a panorama with Midas, Thersites, Helen, Icarus, but no Achilles in sight.

His fatigue is gone. He is content. Gods, though immortal, can decline into torpor, be locked in scholars' books, sleep unendingly in esoteric regions, be etherealized into dream and metaphor, but he retains lively spirit through humour, through curiosity, which may falter but never die.

Let the curtain rise. New Year, first scene, though a god is independent of years, devices by which men attempt to dispel their vagueness of being. An empire can flourish and perish within a blink or, like Etna, survive with periodic explosions.

The comedy begins. So hear, in the Assembly, the lines of the Emperor's new hireling, Emile Ollivier, Minister of Justice, chief of the Honourable Men:

'Today in Prussia, Italy, Austria, Bavaria, in every tongue and in all rites, prayers are being offered to the God of Battle, begging for human hecatombs. We in France do not add our voice to such blasphemy. We hold no brief for any God of Battle. We believe in a God of Justice and Peace who holds in His hands the hearts of princes and nations, and controls them at His Will. We will implore Him to preserve the chief in whose grasp our fate is placed, from over-hasty decisions and unjust designs.'

Just so. Ex-republican, distrusted by that Spanish Conservative the Empress, Ollivier rose once more to rebut insults, accusations of betraying principles of office.

'As early as 1857 I declared my opposition to revolution, which can only entail national disaster. I begged the government to give France Liberty, and now the Emperor, having done just this, I devote myself to the task of securing the triumph of Liberalism.'

The Liberal Empire! Contradiction? Apparently not. Stamps of acclamation from Right and Centre smothered discord from the Left, several factions in this drama led by Gambetta, another lawyer, slender, black-bearded, sonorous, flamboyant, Stentor from the south. 'I protest . . .' but his furious outburst was swiftly rebuked by the President. Nevertheless, he was a young man whom the future was unlikely to ignore, with a mistress, lustrous Léonie Léon, much discussed but seldom visible.

Hermes, connoisseur of human oddity, has made another choice discovery. One of those sniggering at the rhetoric of the Honourable

Man is a certain Charles-Luc de Massonier, youngish journalist, aspirant poet, café intellectual, usually poised between indignation and hilarity and, at present, ready to submit an article on Ollivier's speech to whichever editor desired to topple the Empire. Over-hasty! The Emperor? He was the most irresolute statesman in Europe. Unjust designs! From the Man of December, of massacre, secret police, of Mexico? Liberal Empire! Crudest of deceptions.

Charles-Luc had achieved a small foothold through personal enterprise, having, as an unknown scribbler, composed a pamphlet, *The Necessity of Fire-raising*, printed on violet paper, beginning: 'Humanity has a record of servility. Greece and Rome explored the extreme limits of freedom, we ourselves are doing the reverse, despoiled as we are by government agents, even of the right to exchange ideas, even in conversation . . .'

This was before the removal of press censorship, and, though only five copies were sold, exclusive of those bought by himself, he was prosecuted. Hearing the indictment in silence, he chose to con-duct his own defence, thereby initiating his first entry to fame, pro-visional as love and as thrilling. At first nervous, he quickly gained confidence from his own cleverness. He read out the passage in question, then paused, holding the court in some suspense, gazing up at the Imperial portrait as if expecting some comment, shook his head in disappointment, paused further, an actor very deliberately reaching for the key line, then off-handedly revealing that the entire pamphlet had been culled from Tacitus nearly two thousand years previously. Odd that the Caesarean Emperor had not spotted that. The fresh ploughed fields of yesteryear, he thought, reserving this for another occasion.

The court joined in a shout of laughter, even the august judge, enveloping all Paris and, to be just, even the Emperor had smiled in his pleasant way. 'Gentlemen, every age enjoys a Tacitus. Ours may not prove the least of them.'

Charles-Luc had hitherto proved very little but thereafter signed himself 'Tacitus', commenting with eloquent relish on the passing charade: Sadowa, Mexico, the Exhibition, the defective bladder of the mountebank Caesar camped in the Tuileries, the death of Morny. The Emperor's bastard brother, by another whim of Hortense, Morny – the co-author with Persigny of the '51 *coup*, millionaire leader of fashion and horse races, stage manager of December, of Mexico, smuggler of valuables in the diplomatic bag, writer of playlets and farces, a worthy man of the Empire, who, asserted the Tacitus of our time, kept by his bedside caskets containing pictures of his women, naked, a flower between their legs – had rivalled his exalted brother in the race for women and francs, with the unruffable calm of the professional amateur.

Still without access to foremost journals, Tacitus had ascended to the position of at least being mocked by them as 'M. Unnamed Sources', 'Herr von Reliable Informants', and was always ready with an article, a verse, gossip for lesser publications. Like his principle target, he was physically unimpressive. His fatty neck encroached on a chin, beardless, already jowled, above hunched, desk-ridden shoulders and supporting doughy features, eyes now cautious, now enflamed with suspicion behind thick, slightly darkened spectacles in which, the spiteful and envious remarked, he resembled a Turkish judge.

Tacitus thrived on irregular bouts of self-esteem. He was no hack, from the dank, violent schoolyard and dangerous riverbank: he sought the stars, to scrape their gold, imagery very decidedly, very poignantly, his own. To be a poet was his pride; almost all other poets were merely poetic. Exceptions were few, though Baudelaire had managed to write:

> The poet resembles the prince of the clouds
> Haunting the tempest, mocking the bowman.

Exiled on earth, besieged by jeers,
His huge wings prevent him from walking.

That was well enough, though he himself could have written, or
at least thought, much the same.

Life today was mouldy, excellence despised, mediocrity crowned,
the Vendôme Column symbolized a greasy pole, a comparison he
had used several times.

However, there is more to be appreciated by Hermes, lover of
feints and forfeits, ironic parrying of animal aggression, sly taunts.
With his genius frustrated by publishers, editors, critics and fortunate and unscrupulous rivals, at his wife's expense Tacitus was contriving revenge. Under another pseudonym, he had advertised the
founding of an anthology for which he invited contributions from all
dedicated to purity of language.

Instantly, contributions leapt at him from every province: son-
nets, of course, to the moon, to Bacchus, to the girl next door; dia-
tribes against Empire, against Republic, against the modesty of La
Reine Victoria; extracts from novels, diaries, manifestos, declarations of intent; a ninety-page description of a machine that
hummed, showed the time and emitted blue flames; lyrics of green
rivers, enchantment, Corinth and Syracuse, Auvergnat villages and
Alpine peaks; an engineer's survey of sky looped blue and grey
between mansions around place de la Madeleine. A soiled page of
scrawled verse arrived from that newcomer Paul Verlaine, fattening
his muse on absinthe, boys, wet-dream reveries, chocolate-box
fancy. 'The long sob of autumn violins.' Indeed. A fuck to such
whimsy. These literary curlicues imagined themselves Columns.
Any scribbler could claim to have heard stars croon, or creak like
unoiled wheels, or to have seen goddesses strip for an apple. One day
he would devour the apple itself. Already he had dived into strange
depths, climbed heights extraordinary but not fantastic.

Contributions continued. From Academy Immortals, from authors famous, notorious, proscribed, from those with private presses and unrecorded sales, from inventors, generals, moonstruck labourers, demented skivvies in bedrooms like deserts, together with assiduous compilers of stupidity, vanity, error and sheer muck.

To each, high and low, with muttered oaths and obscene exclamations, he dispatched a refusal displaying all offensiveness at his disposal, and had already assembled a volume, huge, remarkable, though unpublishable, to which he added verses of his own, thus consorting with the great and would-be great. Privately, he entitled it *Lame Pegasus*. These days, for pleasure, he read no literature save his own, thus preserving intact his individuality and imagination.

Even this was insufficient to absorb Hermes. Tacitus, however, had an existence more devious than it appeared. Unknown to fellow journalists, who recognized him only in shabby frock-coat, soiled linen, patched boots and dented hat, and who knew of his insalubrious attic near Gare de l'Est from which he had addressed an open letter to the Empress beginning 'The People of France have asked me to declare that I have not chosen my hunger and wickedness', he secretly possessed, by grace of that well-endowed though bed-ridden wife Adelaine, a considerable establishment, further out in leafy Saint-Germain-en-Laye, with two polite little daughters, respectful servants, expensive library. Docile as farmyard ducks, the entourage knew nothing of Tacitus, only that Monsieur was a man of affairs who sometimes sacrificed time and industry for idealistic or charitable purposes. Adelaine, never well enough to visit Paris, grieved at his account of the malice, misunderstandings and libels incurred by his unfailing good nature.

Such double-life gratified his appreciation of existence, his Hermes-like distinction between *seems* and *is*. His reputation for penury entailed further misconceptions. A committee of compassionate ladies subscribed to fill him a hamper of necessities –

butter, sausage, white bread, laxatives, medicinal fruit, wine, soap, a large hunk of cheese, wrapped in a substantial blanket – had discovered his grander address and, arriving, had been perplexed by being greeted by an ornate steward who, unaware of 'Tacitus', disdainfully dismissed them and their basket.

Meanwhile, though superior critics still instructed him, in bad prose, how to write, his pieces were making some headway in the smaller, more scurrilous political sheets. Ignored by the widely distributed *Charivari* and *Naune Jaune*, Tacitus exposed or mocked current scandals with a vindictiveness excelled only by Henri Rochefort, scourge of Honourable Men, Mexican heroics, ecclesiastical savants. He enjoyed writing as he did women and food: the most trifling column could settle old scores and provoke new ones, startling those for whom ideas were mere fodder for evening hours.

Tacitus' habitual reference to the Emperor as 'the ex-President' had become his trademark. Ceaselessly propagating revolution, he was by no means addicted to personal acts of terrorism, recoiling from even thoughts of blood: blood oozing, clotting, blackening in sunlight, dense with flies.

Journalism had become a rival Empire – obedient to no wily Emperor whose own lies stiffened the tongue, whose N flaunted against heaven – its cohorts of Caesarlings jostling for favours from a voracious public. The Goncourts had observed something impressive about the lack of personal judgement exhibited by the enlightened Parisian, a slave to the opium of his newspaper. Journalists from five continents gathered in Paris with the assurance and opportunism of window cleaners. Readers could be benighted by new freedoms of choice. Such well-cushioned editors as Villemassant exercised controls as powerful as any Prefect. The Left was split between *Marianne*'s support for a parliamentary republic and *La Sociale* advocating socialist dictatorship. Foremost writer of the extreme Left, the Irreconcilables, *Enragés*, the Dangerous Ones, men of darkness, was Rochefort, with witty mockery of the stage-set pageantry of Prefects, Honourable Men, Throne and Altar, judges, attorneys, librarians, teachers.

After some months of Brussels exile, to sink its debts he had replaced his blood-red *La Lanterne* with *Marseillaise*, equally abrasive, rapid-firing at all bastions of the Empire. During his absence, *La Lanterne* had been smuggled into France within thousands of plaster busts of the Emperor, which aroused Hermes' antic grin.

Le Vengeur was dominated by Felix Pyatt, sneered at by Tacitus as an imitation Hugo, vanishing during whatever crisis he had helped ferment. Tacitus was sometimes allowed to write a piece for *Cri du Peuple*, whose editors were fiercely obsessed with legends of the Revolutionary Paris Commune. Its competitor, *Réveil*, was the organ of Delescluze, Ulysses of the '48 Revolution which had installed the perjured Prince-President who, mindful of the times, had vainly suggested a Ministry of Ideas. The hero was now careworn by imprisonments in Paris, Marseilles, Corsica, Cayenne, amongst those with faces like perspiring chalk, stained by vile food and rotted drink. *Le Siècle* stridently opposed the regime but, in one of the agreeable contradictions of the time, had for its chief shareholder the Emperor. Against these, barred to Tacitus, were the conservative and moderate: *Moniteur*, *Figaro*, *Constitutionel*, *Soleil*, *l'Evénement*, ridiculing and unravelling myths cherished by the Left: the viciousness of the Bastille, the virtue of the Incorruptible, the importance of the Commune.

All sections of the Press hinted at yet another Empire, lurking underground far distant from the official opposition worthies, tiny Thiers who could be swallowed by Persigny's top hat, operatic Gambetta, respectable Favre and Ferry. Such militants despised liberal and socialist lily-men in rue des Gravilliers with their eloquent but timid London conferences, allegedly financed by crafty Bonapartes.

They were pallid altar-boys beside Rochefort and Delescluze and the Cyclopean fire-breather Rigault, mouthing the necessity for sexual promiscuity, obedient to the example of the Imperial Court. 'Prostitution', Rigault murmured with gentle ferocity, 'is socialist dogma.'

All Paris had laughed when Rochefort, in *La Lanterne*, asserted his loyalty to Bonapartism, the goblin-faced journalist selecting for praise the reign of Napoleon II as a reign without taxes, inordinate expeditions to foreign parts, acquisitive ministers, wholesale deceit. 'Without question, he once ruled, for today we have Napoleon III.'

The secret societies were modelled on the Terror. Carbonari – of which the Emperor had been a pledged member – Famille Saisons, Droits de l'Homme, Babeufists, Blanquists, doubtless half-imaginary yet said to net half Europe with revolutionary cells, issuing death sentences like playing cards. Blanquists apparently possessed their Société République Centrale, combating the rival, equally dangerous Club de la Révolution.

At the back of them all, screaming 'Vengeance', was the Ancient of Days, 'the Old One', Auguste Blanqui, perennial leftover from savagery, beard green from damp prisons. Where he was, in or out of prison, almost no one knew, but his placards, instructions, articles, regularly appeared, implacable, unappeasable. A Hades creature, Tacitus privately considered, with death on his brow and darkness around him. In print, however, Tacitus lauded the Old One as worthy of profound respect, though, for most, Blanqui caused the impact of a bomb. Tireless, he denounced the Napoleonic Idea, the mighty N, but no more vehemently than he did Orleanism, Catholicism, Mutuellism, Liberalism, State Socialism, Capitalism, Marx, Parliaments, Empires. They were all wrong. He wanted explosion for its own sake, a sort of art which scatters its debris without care of its effect. Each man for himself, women likewise, children nowhere. Let revolution get to work, mindful of the mighty Robespierrian principle that there are times in a revolution where no one has the right to be alive. Natural selection would eradicate weaklings, traitors, scavengers and the neutral.

Tacitus, man of wrath, avenger of the People, nevertheless shuddered like the rest. Dutiful father, he was not very healthy and overburdened with work. Natural Selection might have its eye on him.

Another ancient, never writing, never seen in public, but willing to be interviewed even by such minnows as Tacitus, was the Citizen Lambert, aged ninety-five and who, imagine it, had been Recorder for the Revolutionary Tribunal which had sent King and Queen, Hébert, Danton, Desmoulins, Robespierre, Saint-Just, finally its own chief, Fouquier-Tinville, to the knife, the last vainly repeating the everlasting refrain, which Hermes had heard in Nero's Rome, that he had only obeyed orders. Citizen Lambert had actually watched the death-carts, saluted the Committee of Public Safety, squared up to the vast revolutionary process.

Thus, in the amphitheatre of time, print and swift delivery had replaced heralds, oracles, sorcerers, as mentor, arbiter, dispenser of tidings good or bad, not with whispers in darkened rooms or ambiguous verses but in blaring headlines, trumpeting editorials, columnists pouring out daily rations of wit, innuendo, bilious opinion. At its base, gross with rumour, caustic rant, ambition, despair, were anonymous figures who kept close to the wall, whom Tacitus, disdainfully drawing aside, regarded with fascinated disgust: hangers-on, government spies, pothouse incendiaries, perhaps an occasional frustrated genius like himself. Editorial offices were frayed with false grins, unreliable generosity, rejected overtures.

Tacitus, embroiled in it all, was dissatisfied, not only with the Empire, editors, publishers but, very deep down, with himself. He must sometimes admit that Saint-Beuve was more scholarly, Flaubert more admired, Rochefort's poisoned sallies more applauded. His own poems were mushrooms striving to push through cement, scores of them awaiting the light, stacked in his head, itself a crypt with a key still mislaid.

By day, this worthy fellow badgered editors, waited in outer offices, harangued idle ladies or sauntered about the New Paris, *rentiers'* hive, notebook in hand, huntsman seeking prey. He was familiar with freshly minted hotels, department stores with three thousand rooms piled with exotic tribute from all continents, together with cheap soaps, jugs, ribbons, all conceivable *articles de ménage*; he enjoyed describing the forms, the obnoxious parades, the conspiracies being hatched in elegant salons and decorous libraries, residue of a France swinging between monarchies and republics, shedding regimes like a courtesan briskly disposing of lovers.

Occasionally received in higher regions, like that of Thiers in place Saint-George or even aristocratic palaces, he was granted only such favours as were due to a useful lackey; he was tempted to reveal himself as Monseigneur Charles-Luc de Massonier.

More often, he was stalking the lower depths, listing cholera and typhoid statistics, extortionate landlords profiteering on the latest confiscations, compulsory purchases and evictions demanded by the rebuilding, corrupt officials and road contractors. Given a column, he could chart much that upstart urban planners ignored: back-alley abortionists, purveyors of contaminated mercury, hospitals with medieval drains. He could put two and two together, with surprising results, the essence of effective journalism. He memorized crooked lanes, fetid mews and courtyards, nests of sedition as carefully as he did the new boulevards, so necessary to authoritarian rulers with a taste for artillery.

Primarily, he cherished the theatre of Paris, constant whatever the regime, the arena of print and map makers, engravers, cobblers, barbers, and booksellers behind their cramped stalls where he enjoyed the contrast between a soiled Catullus for one sou, a ragged

Villon for two. He would halt, savouring not only his talent, his latent power, but acrid smells of basement coke-ovens, the grins of gardenia madames above huge, brimming panniers, the gutter exchanges between a pawnshop Jules and barfly Simon, his ears agog for snippet and hearsay. Always at ease with such as the tarts from Galérie des Variétés, he would swap jests with The Galaxy, former chanteuse, whose song 'Wherefore Wandereth thou, Delilah?' had swept through cities like a Landes conflagration, but now, rather late, she must rely only on whoredom. To beggars he gave a wry smile, though nothing else, arguing that revolution would soon reverse their prospects, but he would wink at the ladies trailing long skirts hinting at the unseen flash of legs, and occasionally hire one. Poetic needs were catered for by snow on roofs, a song from a dark cellar, a glimpse of the Seine, which flashed a metaphor, 'wrinkles on dirty silk'.

Even shadows can create history, as that misbegotten child of fortune the ex-President knew so well: though himself only a scarecrow hoping to deceive birds but merely scaring children.

A Tacitus is most at home not in Saint-Germain-en-Laye but, awash with cognac or absinthe, in the throbbing political cafés, Lilas, Bossiers and the like. Gambetta himself, renowned not only for brave republicanism but for his silver bath in which could be imagined delectable Léonie Léon, was to be tracked down at Procope, or Union in the rue Monsieur-le-Prince, shrugging away Rochefort's gibes at 'the Ladies' Hairdresser'. On boulevard de Temple, at Café Deffieu, one could mock English and Austrian swells nibbling Bordelais crayfish wrapped in sauce of the moment, at idlers savouring *babas au rhum* in Café Voisin, Brébant's was fiery with young zealots with money to throw away, from rue de Tournan; Maison Doré with its imitation baroque mirrors, welcomed gourmets who sought associations with voluptuous Nero. In such territory might be seen Gustav Courbet, loather of monarchy, who acknowledged himself as master-painter without ideals or religion and who had scandalized prim socialites of the Empire by exhibiting a carefully composed portrait of female pubic hair.

Further east were more furtive refuges for Jacobins, Fenians, expelled Masons, First Internationalists with messianic hopes despite the collapse of bronze-workers strikes subsidized from Belgium and England. Methodically, Tacitus noted their demands: abolition of pawnshops, industrial funds, mortgages, of titles, armaments, of overwork in night bakeries. Verily, the Kingdom of Heaven was at hand, where privilege would be reversed, the People storm Olympus waving the banner of Proudhon: 'Property Is Theft.'

Not all of this was ideological. At Parnassus, pubescents of both sexes could be rented by the hour. Corinth had private rooms where all was permitted. Here could be found artistic portfolios. Tacitus could open one and there, displayed naked on a billiard table, under the satyric gaze of the ex-President, sprawled Empress Eugénie, all orifices blazing, surrounded by leering Honourable Men – Ollivier, Persigny, Plon-Plon, Rouher, Boubaki, Gramont, poking her with red-tipped cues. Overall, a trick or two awaited Paris. Closing his eyes, Tacitus, in fear, in wonder, saw elves of destruction crouching in plutonic caverns, preparing the conflagration of the City of Light. There would be another New Paris, a desolation of lopped trees, scorched ruins, abandoned boulevards, controlled by unseen Committees of Public Safety, enfeoffed to the darlings of Terror. Safe in his big coat he shivered deliciously and saw to it that his household staff were strong and well paid. A face, glaring, screwed up, briefly seen under a lamp, the snatch of a proscribed song, a graffito scrawled on a church angel, were tiny signals of bubbling convulsions which the Herculean N strove to bank down.

FOUR

HERMES seldom laughs but he has a versatile repertoire of smiles, amply rehearsed as he follows the Tacitus of our time further into haunts of comedy.

Often, after midnight, avoiding the tensions of domestic bliss, Tacitus would complete his round at the Café Madrid, nocturnal even at noon, hub of the infernal, where gathered the Dark People; avenging angels, fire-raisers, poised to dismiss God by a show of hands or cheaply produced manifesto, dissolve law by a demonstration, send packing the Empire and install . . . ah! There, disputes flared, feuds were rearmed, blood could flow. Some habitués were suspected government provocateurs and spies, several so blatant that they were scarcely noticed.

The place was wide, very high, reeking with cheap cigars and liquor. Candles fretted with drip stood on blotched tables, competing with oil-lamps hanging from shadows massed under cracked lofty beams. Through the jittery haze, faces glowered, grinned, went fixed as if paralysed, backed by yellowing Montmartre posters, old musichall bills, stained prints of Revolutionary occasions: the storming of the Bastille and Tuileries, Danton rousing all France, Robespierre at Thermidor, bleeding and speechless on a table, Saint-Just, handcuffed, nodding at the framed Declaration of the Rights of Man. 'Nevertheless, it was I who got that done.' Such treasures still invited toasts to long-dead martyrs: Félix Lepellier, bawling at

Marat's funeral that Denunciation is Mother of Virtue; to Baudin.

All these men and women, patched by murky atmosphere, at long tables, shadowy recesses, dim alcoves, would remember that great day in '48 when the Republic decreed: 'In the name of the French People, Monarchy in all its forms is abolished without possibility of return', though within a few days it had elected a new master, President Louis Napoleon.

Amidst raucous disputes and rhetoric, each face was a library, showing indignation, failure, premature fatigue, illness, insobriety, stern endeavour, self-belief by which their owners imagined themselves Catilines, Mothers of Gracchi, Marats, Héberts. Wit could flicker like snakes' tongues, abuse growl, fraternity be pledged, almost instantly revoked.

His resolution intermittent, Tacitus arrived unostentatiously, greeted by his usual cronies, rather few, with winks or handclasps. All was as usual, at one end steam arose as if from underground cauldrons, making those on benches visible seemingly through tissue.

Depression, however, immediately settled over him, a damp mist obscuring a clever remark he had prepared. There, enthroned, attended by his toadies, was Rochefort, tall, skinny, in a long black cloak, with huge forehead, bumpy, as if strewn with knuckles, high-boned, black-bearded, hair like undergrowth, cartoonists' delight; Rochefort, wild man of the woods, Mohican, *L'Intransigeant*. Like Tacitus himself, the fellow had been born a grandee, Comte Victor Henri de Rochefort-Lucay, though, unburdening himself of such trash, he was plain Rochefort, a name to shake palaces, known throughout France, from the Grand Almoner's chapel to the slums of Marseilles and the workshops of Le Creusot. His sallies were repeated everywhere. 'The Empire has 30 million subjects. Not counting the subjects of discontent.'

Rochefort, living with his small daughter, named after Camille Desmoulins' wife, in a shabby flat, prosecuted, gaoled, exiled, always resurfaced, producing his paper on time, for thousands of readers. Last year's elections had swept him into the Assembly as republican Deputy for the Seine Section, refusing the oath of allegiance, tolerantly overlooked. Hero of the streets, he yet disliked crowds as he did Jews, imperialists, the rich, the hypocritical.

His table here was always the most crowded, by those who both admired and feared him. His smile was sharp sunlight on ice; he had the awesome certainty of unshakeable identity.

Thinking of *Lame Pegasus*, ignoring his young, rather unwholesome, companions, Tacitus covertly studied Rochefort, though he never approached him. The ill-disposed had assiduously reported Rochefort's quips about the Tacitus of our time. He had called him a poet exploding with words but with nothing to say: poetry, he continued, is disciplined vision, not verbal juggling. Worse, Rochefort had submitted nothing to the Anthology, thus dodging the onus of scoffing rejection. Now, oblivious to chatter, compliments, even his half-empty glass, Rochefort, Deputy, editor of the inflammatory *Marseillaise*, was writing, very fast, as if shooting down opponents, tomorrow's fulmination, baiting Court, Senate, Bourse, the Archbishop, Jew financiers, military chiefs, and exposing the most cherished secrets of Honourable Men.

Rochefort had seen him but deigned him not even a nod, and Tacitus shifted his gaze, only to see someone worse. At another table, deep in the phantasmagoria of fug, of unfinished eyes and noses, coarsened skin, was Raoul Rigault, small as Thiers, wretched body topped with too large head, shoulders stiff as a coat-hanger, pin-sized eyes unblinking behind thick rimless spectacles, hair dropping over his collar, beard ragged. Revolutionary desperado, he too enjoyed stalking through Paris, when he would deface street names, chalking his own replacements, so that rue Maréchal Niel became overnight rue Hébert, avenue Richelieu renewed itself as avenue Proudhon. Rigault liked to repeat the words of Hébert, the Communard, 'Lord of Paris', victimized by Robespierre: 'To be safe, we must kill everyone.'

Rigault, noxious creature, recruited street urchins to hover at the doors of ministries and bureaux and scrape up information. He was said to be funded by unknown sources and to be organizing a counter-police of blackmailers and terrorists, so that many shrank from his control of the scum of Paris.

At this distance, he appeared a continuous shrug, his laugh a metallic clink, and he too affected not to recognize Tacitus, who at last responded to a youth, untalented but at least eager for his respect.

'Your drink, sir? Green heaven?'

'Green acid.'

'Just so. Your health.'

Tacitus sat with arms folded, mouth closed, remembering what Saint-Just had taught and the ex-President had learnt, that power belongs to the impassive, the laconic. Rochefort would write himself into oblivion, Gambetta blow his head off with oratory, but he himself would outlast them all.

Glancing at him, another man, stocky, still young though greying, thickly moustached, with large, black, critical eyes, abruptly left the table, leaving him affronted and somewhat uneasy. The fellow was Georges Clemenceau, physician, radical Mayor of Montmartre, lover of painting, student of philosophy, journalist; affable, cynical, apt to refer to politics as imbecilities, who had written that the right to slander ministers should be unlimited: at very best, ministers were the geese that saved the Capitol.

Tacitus' resentment at Clemenceau's departure was tinged with relief. The doctor was not a marionette to be dangled by fashion or a passing charismatic; nor could he be beguiled into *Lame Pegasus*. His depression increased. The atmosphere was surly, one of blighted eyes and heavy mouths, while Rochefort still wrote, Rigault still stared at his visions of bloody consequence. Most others were still disconsolate from the collapse of the recent Baudin riots.

Baudin? A victim of the '51 December massacre, forgotten for years, then disinterred as pretext for disorder. Suddenly everyone remembered him leaping a barricade, defying the guns, at once shot down, but showing how that a hero dies for principle. Saint Stephen of the revolution.

A huge memorial demonstration had rocked Paris, then faltered, withered away. Despite republican electoral gains, all was now stalled. Even bankruptcies in high places had not prevented the regime recovering wind, and now it was running too smoothly. Parliamentary rights, press rights, union rights, were being lavishly bestowed by the Liberal Empire, completing, apparently, the last stage of the Napoleonic Idea, rounding off N.

'This blackguard of an Emperor . . . he loves games.'

'Particularly with women.'

'They say he enjoys blind man's buff. That explains his foreign policy.'

Tacitus, accepting another drink, had nothing to say but could see outlines of an article, forthright yet subtle, energetic yet reflective, that might outpace Rochefort and overshadow Rigault.

He did not underestimate that bow-legged, parrot-nosed, eagle-haunted *crapaud* in the Tuileries, *flâneur* with his stage-villain moustaches, who was most certainly a master if not of foreign policy most certainly of theatre. He loved parading as a Venetian nobleman at masked balls: that mask could hide vacuity, more likely deviousness, cunning, the seducer's purpose, an elusive identity. Like Moses' God he was whatever he chose to be: alley-cat Don Juan, pseudo-Hercules, pocket-Prometheus, with a flair for metamorphosis that would have flummoxed Ovid himself. Theatre, Tacitus could see his opening sentence, was humanity's guiding impulse. The Empire sustained itself by a glittering Peace Congress, showy review, International

Exhibition, an Imperial traipse through loyal provinces, so that Herr Marx, safe in musty England, could declare that Liberty, Equality, Fraternity had degenerated to Infantry, Cavalry, Artillery.

Rejoicings at a successful republican by-election could be promptly stilled by the sight of the ex-President on horseback holding before him on the cropper his hatchling, the Child of Hope, Napoleon IV. N yet provided sensation, mindless, deceiving, but, like fireworks, exciting. Last October, the Empress, agleam on her yacht, had led official Europe to open the Suez Canal, masterpiece of her cousin de Lesseps, a fairy-tale pageant, proclaimed as another gift of the Empire and further embellished by Eugénie's patriotic tears.

Ignored by Rochefort and Rigault, slighted by Clemenceau, seated amongst callow printer's devils who would renounce all beliefs for a kiss by some Duchesse de Quelque Chose, Tacitus resigned himself to the hubbub, too gloomy to find energy to depart, becalmed between Olympus and Hades, though contriving an expression suggestive of secrets too momentous to be disclosed.

'But have you heard?'

'Heard what? I hear everything.'

'Well then, I need not bother.'

'No. I'll hear it again.'

'It's only waiting to be confirmed in *Le Temps*. A rag used in every shit-house in Paris. Incidentally, did you know that *shit* and *science* originated from the same root-word? It follows . . . anyway, there'll be another plebiscite. An appeal to the People.'

'That's nonsense. He won't risk it.'

'He's spent his whole life risking as much.'

'Ugh! He's a rehash of everything despicable, his neck creaks, his woman stinks of Spanish turnips, he employs that clown Octave Feuillet. One can scarcely say worse.'

Faces quickened, moved into light, were rank with dismay and suspicion. Tyrants love plebiscites, the spurious democracy not of intellect or virtue but of mere oafish numbers, pliable ciphers.

Rigault had sidled away but Rochefort remained, perhaps concocting some venomous joke about plebiscites. Damn Rochefort.

On all sides, following a toast to the famous silver bullet somewhere being prepared for the Imperial assassination, Tacitus heard ridicule of the Emperor. His gutteral accent obstructed even *Eugénie*, an elegant name, the syllables of which should be delicately positioned, not delivered like a cough. His own names were as various as his clothes. Man of Blood, Man of December, Prince Fortunatus, Augustulus, Badinguet, New Caesar, M. Moustachu, Napoleon the Little, Hugo's choice. In London, he had chased women, as Captain Jones. In New York, as Mr Robinson, he had bought a Swiss passport. He had sported one sash of the President of the Thurgau Shooting Club, another as President of the French Republic, had been on the run in Italy attired as a Tuscan footman, escaped French gaol in a stoneworker's blouse; would appear in the black coat, green waistcoat, yellow trousers of a St James's dandy, the buckled tunic of a London special constable, the blue evening dresscoat and white waistcoat of a Piccadilly gambler. Butt of the caricaturists, he was mocked as parrot, fox, dejected cockatoo, duck, toad, cut-price Attila, Richard Cromwell, false coin, slaver, Judas, serpent, spider, an *arriviste* puzzled that he had arrived, doctor persuading the healthy that they were sick. In Offenbach's sardonic *Orfée aux enfers* he was lustful Jupiter, changing himself to a fly for immoral purposes. He was a constellation of negatives, without the eloquence of Lamartine or Hugo, the intelligence of Thiers, dynamo racket of Gambetta. How had such a mountebank ruled France for twenty years? On legs, the ex-President was a gruesome reminder that even shapelessness has shape: on horseback, he was the New Caesar, martial, even dangerous.

An unkempt youth, his ill-shaven face awash with flattering

smiles, shoved Tacitus another drink. Displeased, suspicious, Tacitus nevertheless accepted it, murmuring, in return, 'Under certain circumstances, a glass contains the ocean', morosely offered, respectfully accepted.

The ex-President, the conspirator, had fluked a long run of luck, now due to expire. Tacitus could fill a fine page of *Lame Pegasus* with excruciating Imperial prose. For once, the Academy had shown excellent judgement in refusing admittance to the author of *The Life of Julius Caesar* to what it liked to call its august portals. Napoleon was said to be writing a history of constitutional England, or a futuristic novel, extolling the technocracy, meritocracy, mechanical miracles of an ideal republic. What a busy little mind! Someone, some Marie Behind the Bushes or, more probably, an Irishman, had compared the Imperial head to a rabbit warren. Eyeing a fleshy girl arguing with a couple of pretty boys, one with a starched, lilac waistband under a velvet coat, its dirty sleeves once turquoise, he was unaware that he too was being watched, through eyes not of this world.

A career worth pondering, this deuce of a Badinguet without talent or industry could nevertheless purloin a nation, rearrange a continent, win battles, trample on populations, pose as a glamorous, mysterious creature of the moonlit lakes and forests of Fontainebleau, strangely born, though scarcely of a virgin. Tacitus could whistle 'The False Louis', street rhyme about Queen Hortense:

> With Verheuil, she keeps still,
> With Flahaut, what you will.

An English poet had called Louis Napoleon 'the Son of Man, but of which man?'

Drink enlarging his perspectives, Tacitus saw himself as Thersites, despised, hated, outcast, but clear-eyed amongst absurd heroes, the fossicking rabble, tidal flow of pavements and lonely beds. Then despondency slumped back. Damn Rochefort!

Another shaft from *L'Intransigeant* still wounded:

> There are writers who write because they have something to say, and those who write because they wish to write. M. Tacitus would scarcely demur at being classified with the latter. Most of our poets lose inspiration and rely only on memory. Our friend never possessed inspiration and remembers only a few tags. Such people are at the kindest valuation, poets frustrated by being illiterate. It is not that these poetasters and critikins are misunderstood; they are understood only too well. Each of their publications unmask them, in the manner of a police arrest, not for criminality but for lunacy.

Looking about him, *farouche*, but locked in a haggard moment, he swore revenge on Rochefort, while lifting his glass to the downfall of the harlequin Empire.

FIVE

'MILLIONS! Millions!' people exclaimed, massed outside the great park of the Tuileries. Despite bursts of sleet they were good-natured, if ribald, under the giant, illuminated N. For this, the first ball of the year, every window of the palace was lit; green, gold and scarlet footmen lined the approaches with flaring, medieval flambeaux, which made them figures of tapestry, upstaging some of the guests. Above, on the terrace, beadles were ranging in plumed hats, brocaded baldrics, high boots, themselves backed by blue orderlies garishly lit by tiny electric lights of all colours. 'Millions,' the crowd sighed again. Noble equipages emblazoned, coroneted, heraldic, continually passed through the gates, beyond which, near enough to be recognized, princess, ministers, excellences, duchesses alighted amongst the torches. They were not all of best vintage, for many old families, forgotten, or sulky, held aloof from the ill-bred Empire despite the lustre of the universal N.

Standing amongst Parisians, all classes delighting in pageantry, was Etienne. He had lapsed into a personality unknown to the gaunt Department office, with its dutiful clerks and rows of files. Prim husband of Amélie, proud father of Emile, methodical, disciplined, rising man, he was now eager as a schoolboy, telling himself that for a smile from *her*, a murmured plea for a kiss, he would destroy the world.

The rising man had an obsession too banal, too thoroughly clerkish, to attract Hermes, who left him to himself, without comment.

Her was not beloved Amélie but a lady he had never met, who knew no more of him than she would of a Rhône waterfly. *La Particulerie* was Countess Lisa Pizezdzienes, fragile as Vermeil porcelain, in the circle of Princess Pauline von Metternich, the ugly, vivacious wife of the Austrian ambassador, intimate with the Empress. He had seen the Countess in a theatre box on a gala occasion and was immediately entranced. Now he saw her name, her picture, in Amélie's smart journals filled with reach-me-down features of Court gossip. He began reading novels, even poetry he imagined her enjoying, so that Amélie regarded him with even more respect. In dreams and reveries he rescued her from a ring of fire, a sinking ship, a demented horse. He signed a document saving her from ruin, she knelt before him and wept.

Now, having assured Amélie that business would keep him late in the Department, he waited, cold and wet, in hopes of a glimpse of her. He knew she would not come, she was in Budapest, but perhaps, perhaps . . . a vast silken bed, she undressed, slowly, languorously, exhibiting luscious curves and crevices, white mounds, a patch of dark moss in a streak of firelight . . . occult in boundless suggestion.

Cheers and whistles greeted the Duke and Duchess de Persigny in a carriage sufficient for a large family. Florid, bulky, nose slightly askew, eyes moist, reddened, seeming to be working loose, handing down his voluptuous doxie, the Duke grinned to the cheers, ignored the whistles. He was a familiar stalwart of the Empire, its chief towncrier back in those inauspicious days of farcical rebellion, debts and imprisonment. Times had changed, he no longer held office but remained, noisy, excitable, in the Imperial entourage, frequently abused by Tacitus as 'The Sergeant', for he had begun as obscure Sergeant Fialin before awarding himself a viscountcy.

The pair lumbered up the palace steps, slowly, painfully, to an outburst of song, barrel-organ operatics:

> The size of her seat
> Is scarcely discreet
> La Persigny, *v'la!*

The rest, while disgusting, was mostly forgone, though Hermes could have supplied it, perhaps was doing so, though most voices were happily chanting:

> Duke Persigny, Persigny O,
> Lost his nose at Solferino,
> Back they put it, upside down,
> When he sneezes, O the clown!
> Sneezing at jokes by Mynheer Shatov
> He perpetually blows his hat off.

Duke Persigny jokes continued after the pair had been followed by Baron James de Rothschild, upright and smiling, as if he held a mortgage on Paris, scarcely inconceivable. As for the Duchess, she was deluged with lovers; all Paris counted them, enjoying the story that when the Sergeant complained in public a young aristo intervened, saying that he would not have his mistress insulted.

In imagination, the crowd followed the illustrious into the Tuileries, past scarlet equerries, green and silver Officers of the Hunt, brown and gold ushers, ascending to Elysium, the Pavillon de l'Horloge, through a brilliant avenue of Swiss Guards, feathered, metalled, halberts slanted.

Without warning, as if by magician's cliché, in braggadocio display, fireworks were exploding above the palace, more millions, the tinted chips and flares spreading into the clusters of Bonaparte bees and violets that flew, halted, trembled, then shook themselves into an enormous N played upon by a novel electric searchlight, and suspended for an instant over Paris, France, the world. It dissolved, then, spirited from a constellation, emerald, scarlet, sapphire, blue as Eugénie's eyes, there blared the Imperial hymn 'Partant Pour la Syrie', treacly but not wholly forgettable.

Groans and plaudits resumed for the roll-call of the Empire, flocking into the immense, illuminated structure: Bassanos, Esslings, Montebellos, Murats, Cambacerères, a Ney, Prince de la Moskowa, puppets of history, under the eye of Hermes. Also, Duchess de Morny, widow of Auguste, he of the *coup*, of Mexico, of Longchamp races. With her ambled Princess Walewski, relict of the late Foreign Minister, sired by Hercules himself on his Polish countess. The Princess was alleged to have allowed her favours to the Emperor, a tribute to His Majesty's taste.

Cheerful greetings were thrown at Countess de la Pöeze, so thin that Rochefort called her a needle seen sideways. Then a Mouchy, a Talleyrand, M. Viollet-le-Duc, so busy weighting France down with restored cathedrals, Dr Conneau, the Emperor's lifelong physician, fellow-prisoner at Ham. There the powerful Gallifet, there Marshal MacMahon. M. Dumas had been seen, without camellias, M. Gounod was said to have arrived, along with Count Benedetti, the Corsican, darkly self-assured French ambassador to Prussia.

Jeers proclaimed the arrival of Plon-Plon, the Emperor's cousin, Prince Napoleon, coarsened replica of Hercules; an intelligent radical, he had risked his intelligence in the Crimea where he was reputed to have shown cowardice, so that shouts of 'Craint Bomb' now made him glare and mutter. More Imperial relatives were inextricably mixed with Bourse magnates, lords of transport, hotel princelings, directors of agricultural colleges and electrical combines. One saw magnificos from the Bureau Arabe, the State Library, the Comédie Française, perhaps MM. Gautier, Sainte-Beuve,

Delibes and a few of the artistic *gratin*, for the Emperor had founded a Salon des Refusés, thereby demonstrating contempt for conservatism, insensitivity to painting, compassion for losers or flair for the unexpected.

History was on the prowl, for there, between the flambeaux, kissing a polished, sparkling hand, was old Flahaut, another bastard, Talleyrand's, and perhaps . . . but no. He was swiftly enveloped by a cohort of stars, crosses, sashes, of heroes of the Crimea, Italy, Algeria – Péliessier, Leboeuf, Boubaki, Canrobert, pacing to the roll of unheard drums, the tread of grandeur, and statesmen, Ollivier, the Honourable Man, creator of the era of serenity and ideas, Rouher, once christened by Rochefort as 'the Man who said that All's Well in Mexico'. All were applauded for their glitter and dignity, though the din subsided into hostile silence for Baron Haussmann, with whom the Emperor had designed the New Paris and who received the blame for prodigal acquisitions and dislocations. Behind him, pleased with himself, was Antoine Agenor, Corsican careerist, now Duke de Gramont, singled out by Hermes, pleasantly amused, for particular attention. Tonight, however, he was barely noticed, for beneath further eruptions of fireworks another spectacular N, again hailed by artificial light, cheers were resounding for the hero of East and West, Ferdinand de Lesseps, whose Suez Canal, the Empire's feat of the century, had slapped the complacent face of England. Hermes' light cane might have saluted him, and also Monseigneur Bauer, tall, smooth, dapper in violet soutane of fashionable cut, murmuring 'Good Evening, Good Evening' as if bestowing absolution, a specimen whom a Hermes delights to collect. Formerly a Magyar atheist, political conspirator, photographer, artist, salesman, he was at present, thanks to the gay-go-up of the times, Imperial Almoner, Apostle Proto-notary, Confessor to Her Majesty. Hats were doffed, some knees were bent, until another silence announced the arrival of the Prussian Minister, heading other foreign notables: Metternichs, Grazianos, Schwarzenbergs, Kraczynskis, Mercy-Argenteaus.

Fanfare made visible, the bright gold N hovered on the night, a talisman, enduring amidst the rainfalls of sparks, while a band played lively melodies from Auber, Gounod, Hérold, Meyerbeer, Waldteufel and from Offenbach's *Orfée*, which brought gods down even lower than Earth. Some singing seemed to rhyme with the delicate filigree above, formations of dazzling, ethereal bouquets, waves, cornucopias, white, scarlets, greens, purples, in arcs and circles and soaring, exploding ascents in constant rebirth.

Within, hours were suspended, moments were vast, tremulous as raindrops, a whisper, a wink, momentous as a treaty. The great windows, trimmed with gold leaf, curtains drawn aside, gleamed with the radiances without. Woven with intricate simplicities, though, Hermes must notice that, inexpertly hung, the Gobelins and Syrian hangings, in doubtful juxtaposition, yet gave medieval or paradisaical vistas, above which, through scents and cigar fumes, glimmered the naked allurements of Boucher ceilings. One passage reflected Meissonier's battlefields, heroic, tragic, another, the smiling ladies of Vigée Lebrun; an ante-room, where brilliance drooped, a doubtful Rubens, a presumed Andrea del Sarto were almost submerged in foliaged, will-o'-the-wisp half-lights which dulled the jewels and decorations, made eyes and mouths cruel or cunning, before moving back into the electric glare, through dense globes of hothouse lilies, roses, camellias.

Space was labyrinthine, always tempting one deeper, weighted by heavy, upholstered sofas, solid curtains, massive statuary, making ramparts against the streets. Lustrous mirrors were rimmed with a fantasia of cherubs, leaves, grapes, flutes, echoed by the fleeting expressions, exquisitely designed hairstyles, almost naked breasts, of humans edging towards infinity.

Light-blue and white Cent-Gardes, the Emperor's Chosen, lined the curved, balustraded Grand Staircase, their heads flashing silver like cruets tufted and upturned. Scarcely mortal, motionless, they stared ahead at the measured ascent of world notables, each name a carillon. There was no uniform style, only jumbled, broken patterns. Skirts were hobbled, bustled, hooped, multi-panelled, very full, like bell-jars, or looped in a fashion once set by the Empress and much derided by the old aristocracy for degrading ladies to ballet-dancers. Long moiré gowns flaunted against short gowns of emeraldine satin, ivory-white satin, crêpes of frothy lace, Alençon and Valenciennes, geranium-pink velvet bobbed with crocus yellow, tulle trimmed with pale moons, cornflowers, fish-scales, shawls of lilac silk glistening within confections of tiaras, pendants, bracelets, brooches, puffed sleeves and bare arms, black frock-coats, golden coats, resplendent knee-breeches, trousers creamy, trousers striped blue and grey, flamboyant cravats of Americans and Jews, while, like leaves rustling, were the fans newly created by Duvelleray spreading tiny pictures of Japanese gardens, lakes and groves and scrambled with the wisdom of the Bonaparte Hercules. *Courage is like Love, it feeds on Hope.*

Ladies, and numerous gentlemen, were sprayed with jewels from Vechte, Payen Dotin, Froment-Meurice, the very latest, as if to exhibit would-be purity, like chastity adrift in a brothel. Beards and moustaches changed shapes yearly, imitating the ruler; dresses swelled, dwindled, deferring to Mr Worth, the Empress's favourite couturier. Red and gold automatons, the Court Chamberlains, incessantly bowed, to the fluffy and tulled, the frogged and epauletted, the over-courteous and the manifestly drunk. Robed, impassive Arabs tall in white and crimson, bouncy Italians, stern, soberly tailed and shirt-fronted English, Hungarian generals sashed and cross-sashed, Austrian noblemen in rainbow uniforms, Russian diplomats, South American hidalgos. A few rich, light auburn wigs, to honour the Empress. Opalescent chandeliers gently swayed with the murmurations beneath, their crystalline brilliants reflecting the multitudinous colours of Northern Lights or the gala fireworks.

Hermes would be at home here, as patron of secret dossiers, deceiving gestures, usurers masquerading as princes, smiling bankers and trusting borrowers disguised as *penseurs*. All could venture far, without very much movement, approaching Salle d'Apollon, Salle du Trône, Salle du Premier Consul, Salle Louis Quinze, Salle Blanche, Galérie de Diane, each with its particular colour, evanescent and, another compliment to the Empress, foggy with Peau d'Espagne. Mistaking a footman for a guest, a Portuguese gentleman confided that he felt as if encased in a Neapolitan ice-cream.

The Salle des Maréchaux was a Napoleonic tableau: beneath massive gold and ivory baldachin, it was loaded with more Meissonier panoramas, First Empire medallions, representations of Murat, Ney, MacDonald, Berthier, Davoust, eagles and sphinxes clustered round Hercules in Egypt, their bronze aura inflexible, their outlines gaunt in outdated uniforms, legendary dramas, their faces, from arctic distance, disdaining the modish chatter, whispered assignments, the sagging shirt-fronts, carefully designed *décolletages*, the bedizened collars and sleeves of legendary campaigns. Their grim presence would tweak long-buried hints of actual bloodstained corpses piled at Eglau, frozen limbs inexorably stuck in the hard Beresina, the haggard standards of Waterloo. Even the most loyal Bonapartist entered only to escape.

Throughout, under whatever ceiling, all was spendthrift with subtle handshakes, finely graded inclinations, covertly appraising glances, marvellously chiselled compliments, the trained gyrations of Europe. Many must have appreciated Jupiter's injunction in *Orfée*:

> Keep up appearances,
> 'Tis all that matters.

Affected by sham classical trappings, the painted Venuses, Ganymedes, Helens, the magic of rings, jewels, simplicity itself could seem a riddle.

Tonight, gestures and banter were livelier, the ladies more animated, the gentlemen more languidly composed than they had been last year, after Baudin riots, electoral setbacks, war-scares over Luxembourg and Belgium, prompted by the porcine, insolent Prussians. There had even been fear of revolution, what the Emperor would call 'certain moments'. Remember, he had, in earlier times, been forced, as he put it, to carry his own baggage. But at this witching moment guests took light from their own pearls, opals, sapphires, diamonds fixed on ears, encircling throats and arms, dangled from wrists. The Emperor's New Year speech had exorcized spectres, winter itself had drifted away in the glow of violets heaped beneath the Arc de Triomphe, and the sea was grey, not with desolation but with ironclads designed by who else but the Emperor.

Separated from this fancy-world, some of the Imperial Family were grouped in the Green Salon staffed by a distant Corsican relative, Count Felix Bacciochi, First Chamberlain, and entitled, though by Tacitus, the Imperial Procurer. Pallid against green walls were busts stationed at different levels of the Napoleonides, Kings Jerome, Louis, Joseph, Joachim Murat, Prince Lucien, Princesses Caroline and Pauline recently joined by His Elegance Auguste de Morny, Marco Millions of the Empire: bald, eyes heavy-lidded, his faint smile that of an expert poker-player and as if calculating the expense of this butterfly evening. Very considerable. Its value? Very little. At one end, highest of all, Empress Josephine looked across at her daughter, Hortense, both smiling, almost grinning, lovers of life.

Here, even the devoted bloodhound Persigny was excluded. The Family had ignored the supper where too many guests had struggled for too few places, vainly presenting invitation cards to inexpressive flunkeys. On plump divans, stiffly gilded chairs, saying very little, like effigies staged by dark, watchful Bacciochi, sat live Bonapartes. A deep, tassellated armchair held Princess Mathilde, gowned with sumptuous reds and mauves, with a necklace of huge pearls and a cap, black velvet, yellow-feathered, slightly tilted, giving her somewhat raffish appearance. The Emperor's cousin, Plon-Plon's sister, disliking, perhaps despising the Empress, she had, long ago, been briefly engaged to the young, debt-ridden, unlikely pretender, Louis Napoleon. Her face, heavy, in Napoleonic mould, was still handsome, and, as friend of Flaubert, the Goncourts, Saint-Beuve, she was a useful link with the literary and artistic. Behind her, present only under protest, looking as usual as if barely recovering from a ferocious quarrel, Plon-Plon sat with arms folded, a doggerel version of Hercules. Younger scions sat mute, encased in their own wonder or overawed by their seniors, and the Prince remained contemptuously silent, his stable-boy humour, angry intelligence useless but unfailingly evident, like his pirate-king smile.

An adjoining salon was livelier, with talk of M. Verne, that spinner of lunar and oceanic wonders. Hoping to be introduced later to the Princess was M. Bürger-Thoré, art historian, ready to convince her of the genius of a Dutch master, Johannes Vermeer. Just departed was the acclaimed young actress, Bernhardt, likely successor to the deceased tragedienne, Rachel, another of the Emperor's mistresses.

The ruler himself, painted within a frame bumpy with gilt, gazed down from the walls of Galérie de Diane, reminding some of the late de Tocqueville describing Louis Napoleon's eyes as the thick glass of a ship's cabin which admits light but is impenetrable. The portrait made his glance a little sidelong, even shifty, as though here, in his own palace, he was lit only by candles, thus secretive, in which, brighter, there glowed Winterhalter's portrait of the Empress and her ladies. They were gathered in a moonlit glade, birch and willow gleaming against a crescent of azalea and rose-bud, the foreground sward rolled to perfection. Eugénie, seated, was Artemis, frosty in luminous crinoline, pale, tinged with blue diamonds in her hair, more diamonds, celestial dew, shining within the Parma violets at her breast: the others, virginal white, clustered beneath her as if in some ballet arrested by a Merlinesque note of music, the wavering light transforming them to nymphs, bouquets of lilies, swans, dedicated to the goddess.

Leaning forward on a jewelled stick, old Flahaut was enthroned beneath the portrait with, so to speak, a few assistant relatives. White-wigged, with parched, depleted face, he might be drifting on memories of other courts, other times, or half-listening to the famous Prosper Mérimée, who had introduced his lifelong friend and quasi-pupil, Eugénie, to the Prince President's entourage.

Several ornate statuesque figures were ranged before him, their colours varied as those in a marble. Ladies and gentlemen alike were deferential, expectant, as though the greatest story-teller could award them the kiss, the magic rhyme, the completed riddle, to restore their blood and energy.

Distantly, from the ballroom, sounded waltzes, quadrilles, competing with the extravaganza without and clips of talk overheard from the mirror-draped corridors.

A few minutes back, Mérimée, fastidious in starched linen, black tails, discreet decorations, had touched a few nerves by remarking that, in the Exhibition year, people had been scared without knowing why. He now mused that at supper he had observed several courtesans, recently ennobled, plying their trade like butchers. 'They too were selling fresh meat . . . or what appears to be fresh. Their smiles applied like paint, not, I would hazard, of the finest quality.'

Several titters, two respectful nods. Mérimée's expression was amiable though with a suggestion of courteous malice.

'A smile, well, we inherit that from barbarism. It can be a feint, a weapon, a bid for survival. But a wink is more shrewd, a gift of civilized living. It can be a warning, truce, treaty . . . a sign of conspiracy, a move towards seduction . . . a gesture from Fate.' Ladies smiled, indulgent, wistful, nostalgic, stroking their fans and perhaps striving to imagine the unimaginable, a wink from the Empress. While Mérimée paused, footmen passed through, their green and scarlet clashing against all others, while glasses foamed in broken-off ribbons of light. Mérimée would, like Hermes, not have taken the servitors for granted, he would be noting that, though their mien was quietly attentive, their eyes were those of betting men.

He sipped, he paused, he resumed. 'Fate, my dear ladies, though she may not exist, is always strictly herself, incapable of what I have called the pliancy of opinion . . .'

A Deputy, formerly a successful brewer, looked serious, touching his grey imperial gently, as though it were an impressionable rosette. 'Since you mention the subject, esteemed master, I am tempted to regard Fate as a dentist person, always in waiting, never to be entirely overlooked. Jewish, I dare say.'

Mérimée pretended to consider this. 'That's a comparison singular and, it may well be, apt. In regard not to Fate but to a certain enterprise that I can only refer to as Jewish, I went to visit that old Duke of our acquaintance, and without a proper invitation. He was, of course, lying in bed, looking exhausted, thoroughly drained, silent as a carp. Then, before I could begin, he was talking. Like one of those new machines cranked up. Nonsense, of course, sheer babble, incoherence, as you would expect. And there was I, unable to utter a word. Then, as if reminded of his age and condition, he fell asleep, leaving me to depart, my mission abandoned. I could not refrain from dispatching him a *billet*, thanking him for his hospitality. By return, I received an eloquently phrased missive on paper that might have cost a hospital, evincing his astonishment that I had arrived uninvited, had spoken so lengthily that he had been forced to remain dumb and that I had left without allowing him the honour of bidding me farewell.'

Further off, in a darkened recess, clustered antique ladies with resonant names but little else, whom the unkind whispered were hired to appear, conferring high-born lustre on the newest of Empires. Moving painfully, croaking out their small anecdotes, their flounces and mantillas were those of lost fashions. Only their fans seemed really alive, fluttering like painted doves and conveying untranslatable messages, for the fans of their girlhoods had had their own singular language: a lowering, a closing, a twitch could be invitations, suggestions, innuendo; through them assignations were confirmed, scandals confided, certain presences deplored.

Outside, fireworks still pranced and scattered, gaudy as Haiti, transfixing the winter crowds, saluting this grand night of the Empire. Within, the revellers danced towards midnight, quickened by music, the thrills of authority, also by intermittent awareness of those huddled beyond the gates, the inferior, the insignificant, the uninvited, who nevertheless had twice rushed this very palace and wrecked a throne. Most were chattering too fast, too clumsily, lacking the leisured formality of a previous dispensation.

More immediate was speculation about the Imperial Couple. Eugénie, whom the Siamese envoy had reported as the senior of the Emperor's wives, had not been seen, was reported indisposed, her absence, as usual, inviting much gossip. Once, at a masque in this very apartment with its glimmering blue and gold pelmets, brocaded curtains striped like tigers, breath had been suspended, gasps stifled, as she had stepped through an arch – hold your breath again – in the pastel shades and steepled coiffure of her obsession, Marie Antoinette, the doomed queen. Too many might have heard Mérimée's tale, as if instigated by Hermes, of a Spanish gypsy long ago telling the young tomboy Eugénie de Guzman de Montijo that an eagle would bear her aloft, then drop her.

Had the Emperor himself been seen? No one knew, or cared to divulge, though many hinted and compressed their lips. His Majesty, too, was prone to sudden, even improvised indisposition, and in a setting so labyrinthine that anything could be occurring, very close yet hidden.

The music had loudened, animated but at a distance inducing a peculiar stillness within the *salles*, pavilions under skies of unnatural hues ashine with impossible seas, unearthly groves, realms of sun-chariots, lascivious centaurs, fountains of lust, forcing eyes to strain upwards, to the empyrium, simultaneously a toxic grail and a plutonic bad dream.

To reach the Grand Salle des Fêtes, dancers had to pass a vast square of watery Chinese silks, satinwood cabinets, lion-footed, crammed with porcelain swans, midget Korean horses, decorated saucers thin as moth-wings, transparent as gauze, Mexican obsidian pyramids, daintily blue English bowls, neat Louis XV snuff boxes, Japanese scallop shells, tribute from Madagascar, Mauritius, Algeria, Indo-China, yellow jugs designed like fantasy locomotives, tiny watches displaying different times, so that Time itself was fractured, meaningless. Much was dusty, careless, jumbled as if in a street market, while creating an illusion of prodigal wealth and expenditure. Then, at last, the ballroom, a pagoda made limitless by scores of ovalled, Cambodian mirrors, within which dancers paced and shuffled, whirled, almost cantered, beyond the world. Wall candelabra resembled overflowing flower baskets, petal and leaf enveloping the electric lamps within. The orchestra played from an upper gallery, beneath which had been fashioned a rockery brimming with orchids, a waterfall throwing up rainbow tints, with butterflies, dragonflies, of brilliant paste clustered on black and roseate surfaces.

Here, too, little could be trusted as real. The sham-classical, the hybrid, pirouettes and bows, quivered, were extinguished, were reborn. Only the giant N and E, beribboned above the musicians and fringed with lilies, now beginning to wilt, remained stable, held in strange covenant.

Beneath windows tall as grenadiers, past the twirling, at times ghostly, reflections, the gardens too were illuminated, now that fireworks had ceased: orange trees, palm trees, gigantic fan-shaped ferns, minarets, domes, all installed for the night, honoured de Lesseps and his fabulous Labour.

The ballroom was overcrowded, so that dances might peter out in a confusion of false starts and collisions, consigning performers to elaborate hand kissings, bowings, curtsyings, those of novice players in a play imperfectly rehearsed, of disputable authorship, with a finale unknown, perhaps unwritten.

The watcher could identify diplomats from Madrid, Turin, Munich, a St Petersburg ballerina disdaining all requests, banshee Irish writers, English gentlemen chilly as Theseus. Also, unknown personages existing, so to speak, on credit. Many retired, defeated or exasperated by the scrimmage, freeing others, so that Strauss waltzes could surrender to rhythms more helter-skelter, the sweet elixir, spiral of melody, now heard in M. Delibes' polka, from his forthcoming *Coppelia*. The inscrutable Emperor, were he present, might have demanded – no, in his unassertive way, requested – the cancan, such being his taste. Or was he, stealthy listener, self-employed spy, actually amongst them, in one of his impersonations? Hans-in-Luck, who had become N, arbiter of Europe.

N transmuted the brittle exhalation of music, costume, champagne, regalia to some gossamer isle of sleeping princess and golden cockerel, crafty magician, eloquent quack, cackling witch and gingerbread house. Withered statesmen, time-straddled schemers, even Mathilde and Plon-Plon with wits like polished steel, might glimpse a flash of nursery vision: silver mermaid and silken ladder, Erl King and Baba Yaga. The Night Queen and Dr Coppelius were *on the way*. Inside the magnetic pull of dream, the realm of N and E was for a moment the wanton yet peerless kingdom of Prince Fortunatus and Cophetua, Florizel and Perdita, where dead and living embrace, cowherds pick up golden florins, dukes and duchesses, Morneys and Persignys keep open house; where at midnight the sun is most radiant, flowers are maidens, animals speak gnomic verse. Legends were woven into bright being as gods stepped down from tapestry in the alchemy of tunes. Strains from *La Grande-Duchesse de Gérolstein* were hilarious reminder of King Grisly-Beard in Berlin, royal Pumpernickel and his swollen Vizier, Count Bismarck, both of whom had respectfully accepted the Imperial summons to the Universal Exhibition. All Paris had laughed at the pompous Gérolstein generals and grandiloquent colonels, the good-natured satire and nimble tunes, and delighted in the charms of Hortense Schneider. Grand Duchess, Helen, Eurydice, she was the supreme cocotte, creature of melodious make-believe and calculated tenderness, parading in an aura of jewelled shadows.

Music slowed, quickened, then blared in all abandon, sweeping through the spellbound palace, the most brilliant bubble of the century, spreading to the ultimate recess where lay no monster or phantom but the Child of Hope, guarded by the Spanish faery, most beautiful in all the world, always awake even while sleeping, alert for the dreaded red chord of the Marseillaise that Hermes could whistle with the expertise of his long experience.

SIX

LIKE his father, Emile loved going out. Watching him, Hermes was content. Here was no tedious cherub or monotonous elf but a silent, not very graceful schoolboy, thin, unobtrusive, neither popular nor unpopular, with grey, clever eyes on a pale face under lanky hair into which Maman, with the pleasing aplomb of ignorance, regularly rubbed bear's grease, believing, erroneously, that it promoted health and, indeed, prolonged life. With gifts of foresight, Hermes doubted the latter.

Emile, too, enjoyed slinking, moving unobserved. He disliked being singled out in class, being named, ordered to recite or receive punishment. Like many, perhaps most, children, he felt complete in himself. Papa was kind but somehow far off. In the bedroom he became *someone else*, gasping, crying out, then murmuring as if to a cat, then a silence, very strange, as if the air had fallen down. Maman, always loving, always trusting, allowed him outside the house, easily soothed by a promise to return early after a visit to the library, the confessional, a school friend, to feed ducks in a Seine creek, all invention.

After school, after a kiss for Maman, and a conspiratorial smile at Henriette in her floury sleeves, splashed bandeau, he would often have nearly two hours before supper and homework to roam Paris. It was this that had attracted both him and Tacitus to Hermes, patron of travellers, guide of souls, and who delighted in giving Destiny a nudge.

Emile's Paris was two-fold, that of Maman and Papa, of the Emperor and Archbishop, and that of his private discoveries. The Emperor's Paris was Notre-Dame, Hotel de Ville, Tuileries, Senate, Assembly, the heavy blocks of offices, Papa's Department, the Invalides, where Napoleon lay buried, the new boulevards where Maman enjoyed huge, stifling stores, teeming crowds, the rich parade of carriages from place de la Concorde where the King and Queen had been, as Papa put it, murdered. 'Gros cochon', M. Havet, his teacher, called King Louis XVI.

Some impulse, nameless but urgent, now constantly beckoned. He was godchild, not only of Hermes but of riverside haunts, twisted side streets, rowdy back alleys, unlit passages, houses crooked as if lamed, uncannily silent, with open doors, tiny markets, stables, occasional pig-sty, overlooked by the busy, interfering Emperor. Protected by the unseen, he wandered them at will during these precious, late afternoons, seldom questioned, never molested.

Strolling through shoppers, beggars, loungers, he never forgot the Universal Exhibition on the Champs de Mars, the dazzling pageant at Longchamp, with the Emperor on horseback, between the King of Prussia and the mighty Tsar. Thousands of hussars, dragoons, lancers, in lines absolutely straight, had galloped towards them, swift as dervishes, all feathers and leather, reds, blues, scarlets, dust whirling. The three sat absolutely motionless, the soldiers hurled themselves on, were almost at their throats, then halted as if one, drawing swords, a single glittering upthrust, shouted 'Vive l'Empéreur', the massed stands rising to cheer.

The Exhibition had opened into another Empire of queer clothes, extraordinary colours, animals, weapons, treasures, foods. He had seen the Chinese giant, Chang Wu Po, heard black musicians strumming and throbbing, watched an abnormal machine gather rags, tear them to bits, wash them, reassemble them in a single shining cloak! Not then understanding exhibitions, he had thought that lions, eucalyptus trees, howitzers, the giant, the Tsar had merely wandered in from the streets. True, M. Havet, a thorough pisspot, a syrup of figs, thought him stupid. So, though, never actually saying it, did Papa. *Hélas!*

For Emile, the Exhibition had never closed, was alive around him. Paris itself was a giant, the Tuileries the head, the Barracks the shoulders, the Bois the body, hairy as M. Havet, the Column the cock, the boulevards the legs and veins. Faces could be dried-up lemons, moist apricots, apples bruised or shiny. Heaven and Hell were layers of the Exhibition, though with everything struck into stillness, under a sky very tight, as if pinned at the edges to prevent it flapping, from the gigantic electric fans. Electricity, M. Havet said, too often, was the future.

Streets displayed the extravagant, the unexpected, the curious. In rue Cerutti with its freshly painted hotels, the Emperor, when a boy like himself, shy, awkward, but somehow exceptional, had lived with his maman. Streets had a way of making visible the unseen, angels were possible, a horse looked decidedly human. Trains were fire, streaking over black arches where beggars brewed drink that stank worse than Henriette's overcoat. Near Parc Monceau, whose dark railings were tipped with gold, was a small fairground of striped tents, flashing towers, a grinding roundabout, gypsy-eyed pickpockets and ostlers who might wave a silver coin at him, their whispers like fingers caressing a lynx, so that he would bend over some stall pretending interest in amber bracelets, broken dolls, old books yellow as sick. Water-carriers drifted by, sporting green velveteens, painted women showed missing teeth, beneath soiled awnings wriggled Algerian belly-dancers, cooks offered marzipan, a boy in a red, cone-shaped cap juggled with a black and green snake, the freak-show of dwarfs, the armless, legless child, the thing with two ears on one side, none on the other. Maître Foulange, in mustard-coloured turban, mauve pantaloons, effortlessly swallowed fire.

From this jungle of noise and colour he preferred the cocoa-peddlers with their jingling bells, the black ladies like yellow tents, with trays of ice-cream, lemon, pineapple, lemon and currants. Then the skittle-alleys, tables of gingerbread, the shooting lots, where wild-haired men potted dummy Bismarcks, Lincolns, the soft-faced Ludwig of Bavaria, Thiers with spectacles, always cracked, and no chin. Fairs also had powers beyond little rifles, freaks, bags of cocoa: Marc-Henri, who shared his desk, had bought a caged bird in a fair-ground. Only he had the key but, next morning, the cage, though still locked, was empty.

The streets themselves were perpetual fairs, with water-sellers in cocked hats, blind men, dancing bears, organ-grinders with monkeys, lovers being ugly behind a statue or fountain, old soldiers with faces like dried-up oilcloth ready to thrust a hand into your trouser pocket, however little there was to find. The reek of vegetables and dog, the clamour from taverns, the smell of a man damp from running. Pavement artists changed stone to sunsets and jungles. Jews in glum black and strict tall hats might pass, of whom Papa said they lived in unparalleled luxury, though out of doors they did not seem to.

Following his nose, he found Gruesome Street where M. Troppmann had hacked his people to fragments and got sliced for his trouble. Henriette's newspaper had a cartoon, 'The Imperial Troppmann', showing the Emperor dripping with blood. The murders had thrilled everyone at school, like a holiday. What a story, Troppmann killing the whole family. Pictures displayed a table beneath black-robed judges, piled with little boots, bloody pinafores, a terrible axe, faces stained by badly managed burial. You imagined Troppmann as outsize, a hunk of oozing ham, hands like torn galoshes. But no, in the picture he was small, scared: told he must die, he had bowed, as if grateful. Papa had left early that morning. Had he joined the crowd at the guillotine and whispered about it in bed with Maman?

Troppmann must now be in hell, which M. Havet described as perpetually trying to kiss your forehead in the mirror.

Off rue de Choiseul, doll-makers stitched and hammered, painted and ripped, as if sacrificing midgets. Back streets offered sights more various than those fairground Worlds of Wonder, peepshows giving little more than girls' bottoms or undressed ladies with unpleasant patches of hair. Puppet shows made him wonder what toys did, after night closed down, leaving them free. He had chanced on the Gateway of the Damned, a crumbling arch dark even by day. King of the World, he would stand on Solferino Tower on top of Montmartre, surveying all that was his. In the Parc Lully-Rameau, where an old man chirping like a bird sometimes bowled a hoop, a small wood was Dragon's Lair, guarded by a thin stone figure with feathered feet and snake-entwined staff, who, if you waited long enough, occasionally winked. He would stare at it in a sort of prayer, the mood in which he used to comfort a new toy, missing its friends left in the shop. He still had the uncomfortable notion that if you looked at a dog, a star, or a stone, then spelt it backward, you might one day alter it.

With Maman he visited grand parks further west, where gods and goddesses, like the puppets, waited for night to deliver them. Slender fountains tinkled gently, as if they had once been girls. The yellow globes of light along the Champs-Elysées transformed faces to lepers, queer angels, sickly flowers in Papa's *Illuminations d'Orient*. At Versailles, a four-tiered marble basin, always overflowing, standing on winged beasts, could at dusk be a giantess weeping.

He enjoyed lingering as statues at the far ends of avenues slowly vanished with the sun. People vanished more quickly, reappeared less cautiously. He loved to follow people, discover their destinations, imagine their purposes, watch their behaviour, like a Prussian spy. Last week, as though someone had nudged him, he had pushed on a half-open door: stairs led through levels of silence to an attic almost roofless, as if for climbing into the sky or, more exciting, to await some descent.

Today he kept to narrow lanes, like an American deerstalker. Sounds could be weird in these short, winter afternoons, with hospital noises, the sky drooping, mist beginning, trumpets blaring far off like warnings from the Bible. Near the Jardin des Plantes you could sometimes be startled by the snarl of a panther. Once, out of the mist, a giant loomed, a Chang Wu Po, two heads stuck on muffled hugeness, but it quickly dwindled to a sailor with a child on his shoulders.

He had no particular friend with whom to share his private Paris. This he seldom regretted, though at times wondering whether a stranger might come, from the sea, a woodcutter's hut, or even from a picture, for pictures were windows, usually shuttered but which were known to open. Meanwhile, he clasped secret knowledge, won from streets, from books and dreams, from colours, for these were messages, very seldom understood. Watching Maman and Papa, he realized that adults, despite their powers, left many things too late to be understood.

Public walls were open pages and picture galleries, scrawled with threats, incomprehensible rhymes, caricatures of the Emperor as parrot. On a clammy, rusted *pissoir* was chalked 'Plunder the Plunderers', 'Vive Baudin', 'Shit on the Spanish Woman'. At school, rhymes were sung, which Henriette would enjoy but Papa and Maman would not.

> Hark to the sound of falling glass
> Madame Eugénie has broken her arse.

In the word 'Spanish' was mothy darkness, desolate heaths, mountains scraped bare, horns gleaming, witches crouching above bones.

Dodging a fiacre, wincing at a curse, then avoiding a vegetable wagon, he halted at a broken warehouse. Daubed on the planking, almost obliterated, a threadbare vaudeville clown was weeping above 'I invested Millions in Mexico'. On another, 'Destiny Cancels All'. More messages from beyond the air, perhaps from those Papa angrily called the Dark Ones.

Strewn for himself alone were signs from a Paris often hidden, but sometimes glimpsed, like when you awake from a dream already fading like breath on glass. Last year, with Maman, on one of her hasty charity visits to Belleville, visits in which the streets shed all glamour, were merely dirty, untidy as Henriette's blacking parlour, they had to avoid packs of men shouting, waving fists like knobs. Why?

'Darling, they don't believe in the Empire.'

How so? He kept silent, but the Empire was *there*, all about them, in police, soldiers, postmen and the horse-troughs, the horses themselves, M. Havet's cough. They had heard a shout: 'Vive le Vieux', which made Maman hurry.

'The Old One' was another password from Dark People, still unexplained but not inexplicable. Like 'Female Complaints' which made older boys shake with a laughter which never sounded very happy. Papa had once mentioned 'The Old One', then threw away his newspaper, frowning, the air becoming stiff.

Out here, under walls, arches, statues, he could understand that much was haunted by *Why?* A word disliked by parents, teachers, Father Jules, Father Alphonse, perhaps by the Emperor.

A new graffito signalled, words surmounted by a familiar face:

Wanted for Murder, December 4th, 1851, Louis Napoleon Bonaparte, Corsican Bandit, last seen posing as an Emperor. Places of Residence, the Tuileries, Fontainebleau, Compiègne, Saint-Cloud, Properties Stolen from the People. Associates include Foreign Woman and an undersized Male Child.

He stared, uncertain, gripped by *Why?* Maman loved the Emperor as she did God, leaving both of them vague, to be accepted like tap-water or toilet-paper. Papa said little, though occasionally joking about M. Moustachu. M. Havet had been overheard calling the Emperor a dancing-master trying to persuade cripples that they could lead the dance. That answered nothing.

The Emperor. Old Hairy Face. A tusked swollen head, a huge dome higher than the Column, the great N gathering the curses and *vives* of the city. That drawing passed from hand to hand in the play-pen, of a face whiskered, bearded: reverse it and, behold, a donkey's head!

More normally, the Emperor was a gentleman, top hatted, yellow as a Chinaman but who, like Maman, sometimes wore red paint, in a carriage escorted by the silver and blue Guards, or riding on horse-back, almost alone, holding Loulou, the boy prince, or arriving at a theatre with the Empress, fairytale Queen Crinoline. Chasseurs d'Afrique lining the streets and the people cheering.

Papa had been talking of the New Year Ball at the Tuileries. In glassy palaces, watched by the rich, by wigged servants in gold and green jackets and yellow breeches, standing as if carved, boys and girls danced naked, pretending to be Greeks.

> Old Nap
> Snipper Snap,
> Odd as God
> Or Marbles.

Emile hummed. Looked about him, saw a slim man with eyes like hooks, turned away. Soon he must return, yet drifted forward, sensing a quest, that he was being led, perhaps to the friend from the sea or a strange sister. At last he tugged himself free, set course for home and supper. People jostled him, hurrying from offices and barracks, once, in momentary panic, he felt lost, abandoned to wildness, but almost at once was touched back into the familiar. Yes, in that scrub of garden a live hen had been buried up to its neck, screeching like sawn wood as kids hurled stones at it. In that filthy yard, blurred, as if through lace, several figures stood in white, silent, like snowmen or monks. A stench blew up from Les Halles, another gift from old Nap, piled with fruit, meat, vegetables. On the corner, alone on a derelict site, shaking his head as if to recover a dream, was the man in a soiled, braided hotel overcoat, always motioning as if opening a door and inviting you to enter.

Papa had once said something very interesting: that hundreds of people vanished every year, as if drowned. After that, he sometimes detoured to inspect the Seine to discern any obvious rise; this sometimes occurred, especially in January, when food was short and beggars multiplied.

Adults might go out for bread and meet a Troppmann, children accept poisoned chocolate from a stranger or be gobbled by the Dark Ones. Once, everyone on the pavement went silent, while a huge black coach, unadorned, blinds down, had gone by, convincing him that inside, bent double in near darkness, was Death.

M. Havet, they said, didn't believe in God, yet he might explain that carriage. He could actually be interesting, when, during a dull lesson, he began talking of something else. Did you know that in English 'ghost' comes from the same word as the German for 'breath'? That was probable, for the dying, Maman said, breathed away their souls, and in the park a breeze would stir up leaves into human shape. In the twilit graveyard of Saint-Jacques au Cœur you held your breath and then saw cowled shapes squatting on the stones.

Half past four, the streets were darkening, the lamps not yet lit. All was in tumbling disarray, feet seemed larger, heads smaller, horses unfinished. Maman was waiting, Papa leaving the Department. But he lingered, at a shop window, edge of a world, saw his own face, nondescript, colourless, small eyes and pointed chin, then slowly repeated his litany. 'I am the only one in the world on this spot, on January 20th, in the year 1870, seeing a green hat, then rows of black shoes, a twisted scarf.'

He added, without knowing why, 'It's going to happen.'

SEVEN

IN the ding-dong the newly proclaimed Liberal Empire had won
first trick, reinforced by the opportune death of Marshal Saint-
Jean d'Augely, no longer useful save as a Bonaparte veteran, from
atrocious Moscow to triumphant Solferino. The funeral provided a
well-publicized State funeral, a reassuring panorama of military
authority, conduit for national pride, very passionate, very expensive.

Nevertheless, the laws of equilibrium or the whims of mischief
decreed restoration of balance. The government's concessions and
pledges were not everywhere deemed sufficient. Miracles had ceased
to be commonplaces: prices still rose, a few more spectacular bankruptcies were inauspicious, troops were combating strikers at the
powerful Le Creusot steelworks, owned by the President of the
Assembly, a successor to the illustrious Morny and, like him, a
backer of the '51 *coup*. The Emperor was ill again, and in a learned
journal a Sorbonne professor published a description, obliquely contemporary, of kings sacrificed to earth and sun when their vigour
dwindled.

Stentor, Gambetta of the mighty voice, had little interest in
anthropology. That voice had become famous, denouncing the
Empire in court after Baudin riots, then silencing a hostile Assembly
by orating that the regime had left itself no more blunders to commit
and was only a rickety bridge between the Republic of '48, criminally
betrayed by a perjurer and assassin, and the revolution.

In *Marseillaise*, Rochefort continued his fusillades of libel, invective, exposure of Court scandal, accompanied by further cartoons of the Emperor. His Gracious Majesty was Proteus; yesterday a ramshackle pretender dodging his creditors, today a beggar trapped in Napoleonic hat and greatcoat too big for him. Another, a plucked, woebegone eagle, had been confiscated by Pietri's police.

In February, a frolic card, like a gift from boulevardier Hermes, was dropped for the Left Opposition, which should surely scotch the Empire's risking a Plebiscite.

In rue d'Auteuil, pensioned by the Court but no part of it, dwelt one Prince Pierre Bonaparte, son of Lucien, independent-minded brother of Hercules, the greater N. Carbonaro, adventurer, conspirator, poet, expert duellist, Prince Pierre, coarse and ruffianly, was no comfort to his cousin, the Man of Order in the Tuileries. Known as the Wild Boar of Corsica, he had survived South American turmoils, had freebooted in the Empire's new conquest, Indo-China, had been a brutal republican but, steering by the wind in '51, defiantly bawled for the Empire, though forbidden its palaces. His many, often fatal duels, his rages, swagger, drunkenness, made him both feared and ridiculed.

Yesterday, in a fit of rage at an article in *Marseillaise* insulting the Emperor, he had sent challenges both to the journalist and the editor, Rochefort.

Tacitus, amidst buzz at the Madrid, chuckled. To have Rochefort plugged or spitted would well suit him. Gifted, under-estimated fellows were due for favour. Rochefort's derision had often tempted him towards a challenge of his own.

Now, imagine the *Marseillaise* office, weighty with cigar smoke. Several seasoned journalists and hangers-on lounge over wine and croissants, listening indifferently to Victor Noir, inky young hopeful, outlining some political skit. Abruptly, he halts in mid-sentence; the others at last look up as commotion erupts outside. A shot, 'Take cover', the joke is ignored, but the door is at once kicked open and the Wild Boar stands before them, black-bearded, black-browed, two black lines stiffening in parallel down his swarthy, enraged face.

'Where are they? Where's that traitor and master liar, Rochefort?'

A sub-editor timidly emerged from beneath a table. A shaky attempt to appease, even ingratiate. 'Your Highness . . . Sir . . . the Assembly is sitting. You must know that M. Rochefort is a Deputy . . .'

The intruder spits, with indirect aim. 'He's a common cheapjack scoundrel representing filth.'

The office revives, protests begin, fists clench, someone half rises. Prince Pierre's face goes mottled, splits open, shouts incoherently; a scuffle starts, heard two floors below. In uproar, confusion, flurry of papers, an overturned table, a pistol shot cracks out, the copy-editor, Ulrich de Fonvielle dodges, the bullet slams into a panel. But a second follows, Victor Noir yelps, his eyes are startled, then, incredulous, he drags himself to the door, stumbles, lurches down stairs, blood spurting like urine. He reaches the street, gestures feebly, arms uncontrolled, falls dead, Hermes watching with considerable approval.

Overnight, before newspapers surged from the grey hour with screeching headlines and lurid details, hidden fingers had blistered Paris with white, staring capitals, QTLZ. At first scarcely noticed, through a day of tumult and violence, the letters took root, settling like an itch. They were cryptic, indeed sinister. People stood arguing, venturing interpretations. Here must be a cipher, for seditious call to action, mystic key to salvation, a sally from some prankster. Some maintained that it portended a hurricane, others a hieroglyphic extracted from the Suez excavations, with fateful significance for France. A devotee of Gambetta jested that it represented a marmoset's fart, thus a fitting epitaph for the Empire. *Vengeur* reported that it was a cryptogram for the private parts of a Spanish lady. A wag suggested that it was the work of Chang Wu Po, signifying either his attempt to write French or a Chinese proverb, picturesque, laconic and untruthful.

Swiftly QTLZ was overtaken by fresh agitations. Another graffito gave toxic licence for those bursting with opinions and eager to make history. 'We Deny . . .', the blank space an invitation for any-one to complete. 'We Deny . . .' that M. Ollivier, though an Hon-ourable Man, is a Man of Honour, that Count von Bismarck devours only raw flesh, that Loulou has a foreskin, that God is only four feet high.

Insignificant in life, Victor Noir, like Baudin, was now invaluable as martyr, sacrificial victim, with Prince Pierre arrested for murder and Rochefort, leading the chorus, further infuriating Tacitus by using the words of Napoleon III against himself, culling from that stodgy *Life of Caesar* the conviction that, in crisis, the People may see more clearly than a parliament often preoccupied with factional or personal interests, events soon proving them right – a trick that Tacitus should have patented. People's Tribune, Rochefort, waved the red flag, summoning memories of '89 and '48.

'I was sufficiently idiotic to believe that a Bonaparte could not be a personal murderer. I presumed to imagine that amongst this clan, whose tradition and daily behaviour has always been that of brutal-ity and killing, there might perhaps be one with whom a duel could be fought with honour and chivalry. But we are now mourning the loss of our dear comrade Victor Noir, assassinated by that brigand Pierre Napoleon Bonaparte. It is now eighteen years since France was seized by the blood-drenched claws of these highwaymen. People of France, have you not, at last, had enough of them?'

Agitators pounded street corners, police were invisible, workers dropped tools, the poorer schools were ill-attended. Prince and

Princess von Metternich, outside their embassy, were assailed by hoots and yells: 'Free Poland', 'Free Ireland', recharged by 'Free France'. Thousands of red rosettes, inscribed 'We Don't Like *Her* Either', were sold within an hour of delivery.

The Right was, at last, cowed and irresolute, with Dark Ones emerging into the light, with secret orders from the International, the Marxist Red Star, the anarchist Councils of Action, from the Old One himself. Fourierists, Proudhonists, Syndicalists, Mutuellists for once joined hands in republican dance. Behind them loomed those whom *Moniteur* castigated as bohemian scum of atelier and dram-shop: scullions, porters, night-soil carriers, brothel bouncers, dismissed valets and concierges, students, the declassed, hashish peddlers, Algerian riff-raff, pimps, male whores, jobless clerks and hired claques. A final battlefield was decreed, the funeral of Victor Noir.

Humanity would triumph over Order at Neuilly drawing thither working men and women from north-eastern Paris, from la Chapelle, Saint-Antoine, Belleville.

Too valuable to risk himself in a mass demonstration, Tacitus ceased his wanderings. Anyone could march, the sensible man remains at work, writing, writing, praising that foolish toad, Noir, allowing a twitch of recognition even to Rochefort and Rigault, to promote the great day, unforgettable holiday which would out-measure even the Baudin riots. How good to be alive! He was delighted by a phrase drawn uninvited from his bronze inkwell, deep as genius, gateway to Fame: 'The parched earth awaits the return of poppies', poetry and politics intermingling, as they always should. Double-edged scimitar. He wrote on: 'Bullets of the soul', then shook his head; the soul was invention of priestcraft, exploited by State conformism. Then smiled, in his superior way, at the thought of Victor Noir's soul whizzing into heaven, alarmed angels scuttling aside. 'The acclamations of Earth are the haloes of Reputation.'

Perhaps, after all, he would retain the earlier phrase, with slightly different slant. 'Bullets of the Soul.' Good. By no means bad. Mere politicians, Camille Desmoulins, Rochefort's lamented pet, and Robespierre were ruined by words having severed their roots. Poets knew better, survived longer. Ah: 'Dull and gnawing as poverty.' He added his name to manifestos, letters of protest. More images of revolution and the People's virtues burst in red blossoms from that depthless inkwell. He issued, and signed, a leaflet that would both counter Rochefort and add tribute, *pragmatic* tribute, to Victor Noir. To be hawked at two sous a copy, it contained a single sentence: '"Permanent good can never come from dirty hands." Napoleon III, 1866.'

The funeral could be the day of reckoning. Processions, bombs, orations at the martyr's grave at Neuilly, then turnabout, one last heave, the victorious March on Paris, into the Tuileries.

The night was very cold and uneasy. After dawn, low, rainy clouds swung over Paris, strewn by dark wind from the north. In suburbs, the People, obedient to commands of Dark Ones, had already massed in dense, irregular formations, supervised by truculent, mysteriously appointed officers with red armbands, not manufactured but torn from shawls, curtains, stolen uniforms, bandages filched from hospitals and morgues. Chatter was incessant. Gambetta, Rochefort, Flourens Delescluze were to speak, Blanqui, *Blanqui*, was to appear, the Republic was as good as proclaimed. Men built like locomotive-tanks were singing obscene words to hymn tunes, also the proscribed *Marseillaise*. Police and National Guard had not dared be seen, though a few deserters were hoisted on high, applauded for devotion to the People. The red rosettes were everywhere, tiny lanterns shining in grey wastes. How many had gathered? Ten thousand, fifty thousand? A million? Students, builders' mates, bakers' skivvies, Halles porters, colliers, ostlers and those sprung ready-armed from basements, cells, sewers.

Tramp. The march began, women arm in arm with men or in their own cohorts, carrying staves, brooms, kitchen knives. Men had cudgels and sporting guns. Ahead, in a flower-decked cart, Victor Noir was being trundled, the coffin draped with scarlet. Banners, red tongues of liberty, streamed on all sides, incitements to vengeance and death, woven with sacred Revolutionary mottoes. Proudhon's 'Property Is Theft', Saint-Just's 'What Constitutes a Republic Is the Total Destruction of Whatever Opposes It.' Much fancied was a novelty: 'Strikes Are Dreams, We Must All Dream.' Periodic shouts rose in unison, for Committees of Public Safety, for the Commune.

Strangers swiftly became brothers and sisters, confiding their life stories, exchanging small gifts, making history in ways to delight Hermes, himself by no means absent. The Man of Order, he said over his shoulder to the Graces, had ample opportunity to keep order.

'Poor Victor Noir . . . they say he was only eighteen years old . . . Those monsters! Wicked men!'

'Did you know, he was actually Baudin's son. His mother . . . a seamstress, found dead, starved, cardboard in her throat.'

'I believe she was really a plough girl. But . . .'

'Politics. The conversation of sharks . . .'

'Have you heard . . . Last night, the university fellows clambered up the Arc de Triomphe, singing our songs.'

'Those brave lads . . . Perhaps they'll hang that vermin, Pierre . . .'

Many watching from balconies, windows, roofs would earlier have recognized the ogreish Rochefort, hair like black flames, sharing an open carriage with Gustav Flourens, bald, red-bearded, constantly risking everything for Freedom: Polish Freedom, Cretan Freedom, Mexican Freedom, Chinese Freedom. Everyone remembered his cut-glass smile in court, on being acquitted for treason, and his rather shrill outburst: 'Today, you have the power. Use it. But when I have it . . . seek shelter.'

Tramp. The wind stung with cold, but none flinched. The horizon promised glory. Rochefort would speak, of course, Flourens orate, perhaps M. Thiers.

Behind them, Hermes could observe another scene, quiet, almost uncanny, regular troops almost soundlessly ranked on the Champs-Elysées, at the unfinished Opéra, at all bridges. The Emperor himself, about his duty, in general's uniform, was at the Police Department, conferring with Pietri. More troops were strung round the Tuileries, Louvre, Hôtel de Ville, Notre-Dame, Invalides, round deputies at the Palais Bourbon, senators at the Luxembourg. Artillery, in best Napoleonic tradition, aimed down the long, straight, uncobbled boulevards of the New Paris, nerve-lines of the State. Atop his Column, Hercules was unmoved, N was serene.

There were crowds here too, sober, reassured, with shuddering memories of Terror.

Approaching Neuilly, all factions were now one, irresistible, with rising, tidal momentum, marching in disorderly fashion but disciplined by shouts, continuous, double-syllabled, of 'Rochefort', 'Gambetta', 'Flourens', 'Blanqui'.

Tramp. Ragged battalions sensed themselves following Victor Noir to immortality. That the day itself could end was inconceivable, each instant was an anthem, an oriflamme, a vision of glory. Now, as wind whipped up rain, the march was ending, the thousands clustering about a commonplace cemetery, the leaders, Rochefort and Flourens, certainly amongst them, above toppling mounds of humble wreaths and bouquets, wet and gleaming against the background of derelict trees, sooty roofs and walls.

Ovations, born on a gust of wind, yells for fraternity, victory, eternity, for all the Baudins and Noirs oppressed since '51. Martyrs of needless squalor and slavery. History was accusation.

Speeches were being made, but anonymously. Rochefort sat hunched silent and wet, Flourens seemed about to be strangled by his own beard, swamped by wind. Little could be heard, but, good-humoured, expectant, the concourse awaited the command, the turnabout, the march on Paris.

The vision was eternal, not of Offenbach frivolity but of rich on their knees and sent empty away, the mighty fallen from high seats, the hungry fed, the meek rewarded, after troops had hurled away weapons and rushed to embrace their brothers, priests ripping off cassocks, evil books stacked for the flames, saints like the Beloved, alone in his garret, at last receiving their due.

Not so. By no means. Powerful orators did not orate, Gambetta seemed not to have come, Rochefort, lover of humanity, hated crowds, like Robespierre, shrinking from embraces and, a glittering writer who nevertheless spoke badly in public, only sat scowling, saying nothing. Against all odds, the day of reckoning evaporated as the rain became a deluge, then a hail storm. Rumours, quick as Hermes, who may have scattered them, reached the sodden, now bewildered crowd, of a cavalry charge, actually imaginary, clearing place de la Concorde with atrocious blades.

None knew better than Rochefort that crowds are fickle as weather, hailing a god the moment after sacking his temple, ready to blame their heroes for this angry sky, accuse the Jews, the Prussians, even the Suez Canal for their disappointments. Exasperated, goaded by Flourens, shivering, he did finally attempt to address his worshippers but feeling their restlessness, that of an audience confronted by a cherished actor floundering in an awkward part. 'Citizens . . .' he coughed, began again, his hat dripping, his voice faint, 'Friends . . .' But the rest, very little, was unheard. He had mumbled that bloodshed was useless, that aims had been achieved, Victor Noir honoured, but his words trailed away; he shrugged, shook hands with Flourens, almost invisible within an immense raincoat and shako-like hat, appeared briefly to argue, remembered to bow to the stricken mob, then pulled himself down to a waiting cab, wild man suddenly tamed, unobtrusively driven off down a side street, leaving behind a silence fragmented by confusion, uncertainty, the storming rain and wind, a sudden need for warmth and drink. A few might have remembered Rochefort's prophecy, a few years back, that the majority of the People would one day raise the Republic, without violence. With Flourens too already gone, no one was prepared to harangue a multitude of deflated backs, to declare that only the fervid minority ever deserved support.

Hearing of the fiasco, Tacitus, snug, busy, almost shouted satisfaction. He himself, with, of course, that fleabody the ex-President, had won the day. Rochefort, dessicated sensationalist, fire-raiser, with Paris open before him, had turned tail, at best hankering for a revolution of guillotines without blades, courtrooms without judges, barricades littered with flowers. From various accounts he concocted amusing descriptions of the Fête Noir; Rochefort, sham fire-raiser, at his great moment, had lost the matches, having furiously accused the virtuous Flourens of being a government agent. Rigault had ineffectively screamed for the march on Paris, if necessary against the entire army, bombs enshrining the blessed memory of Victor Noir.

Predictably, editors refused this little masterpiece. He quivered with frustration, seeing the future slip away, filched by trashy papers, crazed demagogues, repelling the genuine, the heartfelt, or cynically deceiving them, like a husband's promise or the signature on a treaty.

The failure of the Noir demonstration simultaneously dismayed and relieved him. Blood speaks, he thought, though in truth he, Tacitus, People's avenger, man of blood, had almost fainted at sight of his daughter's nosebleed. Worse followed. Though his 'Fête Noir' was printed only in *Fiery Cross*, an obscure daily of wretched subscription, it nevertheless reached its target, Rochefort, who, in his next column, made a vile gibe:

'Our little friend Massonier, Charles-Luc de Massonier, *Monsieur* Charles-Luc de Massonier, lacks the imagination to venture a lie, though incapable of telling the truth, were he ever to know it.'

EIGHT

THE New Paris of slum clearance, property speculation, steamship and insurance combines, Bourse aristocrats and ennobled bankers, of wide-eyed tourists, of plate-glass and electricity, was not, as *Moniteur* put it, for sale to raggle-taggle terrorists, suburban arsonists, Saint-Antoine rat holes, Dantons without the stuffing and babes in prams drooling 'Equality'. In compliment to the Emperor's classical scholarship, the leader-writer added that Imperial Rome had likewise proved invulnerable to Catilinian nihilism.

Reverberations, however, only slowly subsided throughout March. Defending some feeble demonstrator for damaging State property, Léon Gambetta regathered forces of the Left, daring to inveigh against the December '51 affair. 'That foul date shall never be forgotten. We will never cease to celebrate it. But as a crime.'

Only a few weary courtroom hacks might recall the Emperor's gentle admonition to an inexperienced minister: '*Never*, my dear fellow, is a word we should always avoid in politics.'

Gambetta won more laurels but, as March ended, N still rode high, the eagles flew unperturbed above clouds. At bottom, the mood was quiescent, Prince Pierre was in prison awaiting public trial, and so – indeed, such was the Ollivier government's self-confidence – was Rochefort. He had been arrested while lecturing on Voltaire, charged with provoking disorder, his parliamentary privileges ignored. He had been sent to Saint-Pélagie gaol for six months.

Several riots had been easily suppressed, two of them staged by Pietri's police. At another, Flourens, waving sword and pistol, beard flaring like a red bannerette, attempted to raise the Seine malcontents, in hallowed Revolutionary language:

'Citizens, I summon you to take arms in defence of the laws and suffrage, violated by the seizure of our Deputy . . .'

His troupe had promptly pillaged the nearest theatre, rushing out in bizarre uniforms, with stage guns and spears, though within half an hour it had dwindled to one boy weeping for home. Paris sniggered, though for the first time in years, barricades rose and at the Temple a policeman was wounded but, though flamboyant and raucous, the defenders gave small resistance.

More important, far more important, most declared, after bitter weeks, spring was dropping its hints, customary but never stale. Chestnuts in the Jardin du Luxembourg were already guaranteeing moist splendours of green and white, the air was tinged with green under a warm sun. Colours linger awhile in the breeze, Tacitus wrote, in happy phrase. Already, children were bowling hoops, ladies and gentlemen exquisitely parading outside the Louvre, respectfully watched by lower orders. No Baudin or Noir disturbed the equanimity of the great, strolling in place des Vosges arcades, driving to the Bois, to the Opéra, at salons politely bargaining of the pick of *grandes horizontales*, dining well at Magny's, Maxim's, Maison d'Or.

Hermes is sojourning in Nice, a region acquired by the Emperor as *pourboire* for his efforts in the Italian war. As always, with little effort, he makes his presence felt. He is sensed in a horse-bus by an aroma fragrant but indefinable, is seen by children as sudden brilliance in a garden or park and, at times, is actually encountered on a sidewalk, at gaming-table, night-time bar or, straw-hatted, contemplating the shining rim of the sea. Periodically, in a deserted street, reluctant to forgo his own joke, he writes on wall or pavement: QTLZ.

His arrival is followed by minor incidents, gratifying his concern for oddity and disruption. A landlady stood on a barrel outside the mayoralty and recited a Hugo poem, backwards: a butcher caused a stampede by producing a snake from his overall: a child screamed in terror at a blank patch of air, his dog cowering and sweating: on the beach two donkeys brayed in unison with the first notes of a popular ditty beginning, 'Madame, my word is Love.'

His uniform unnecessary, the Emperor in formal frock-coat addressed Deputies and foreign diplomats. Unwell but resolute, he spoke briefly about very little, though editorials speedily praised his eloquence. He was, Tacitus dipped again into that miraculous inkwell, a muddy confluence of histories, a shop-soiled conspirator, ageing juggler throwing up shining globes, catching a few, spilling more, failures inadequately disguised by clumsy sleights of hand. Nevertheless, he conceded, that low voice, uttering platitudes, could be heard throughout the world. A very poor state of affairs.

Two days later, His Majesty spoke again, to such effect that Hermes at once returns to Paris. Listen.

'In sharing responsibility with the great bodies of State, I feel more assured of overcoming the difficulties of the future. When, after a long journey, a traveller drops some of his heavy luggage, he does not thereby weaken himself. He renews his energy to resume his journey.'

Action followed wisdom. Posted throughout France, under the laurelled N, was proclamation, ostensibly a request from the Senate to which the ruler was graciously obedient, inviting national approval of the Liberal Empire.

By balloting your assent, you will install both Order and Liberty on a solid basis, and render easier the passing of the Crown to my son. Eighteen years ago, almost unanimously, you conferred upon myself the most extraordinary powers. Today, be as numerous in supporting this transformation of the Empire. A great nation cannot perfect its development without relying on institutions guaranteeing both stability and progress. I ask you to confirm the reforms achieved over the last ten years, and to answer Yes. As for myself, faithful to my origin, I shall imbue myself with your thoughts, strengthen myself in your will and, trusting in God, will not cease to labour incessantly for the prosperity and grandeur of France.

The clericals hastened to ordain Yes. The Opposition engendered a new journal, *Eye*. Its title? Remember, during the Great Revolution, a huge painted eye, staring from wall, monument, turret, had symbolized the never-sleeping State, the supervision safeguarding Liberty and, like the sun, penetrating dark corners. Stamped on the front page, the eye was unblinking, inescapable as the concierge at your door. Its unsigned editorial had something of the style of the absent Rochefort, concluding, 'Unfortunately, we are forced to confirm the rumour that the Emperor is still alive.' Agitating No, to what it called the fraudulent prospectus of the Ministry of Pollution, it otherwise proferred the usual *ragoût* of ministerial and ecclesiastical delinquencies, mishaps amongst boudoirs, dressing-rooms, misappropriations within war-bond bureaux and colonial investment offices.

The Emperor himself was said to have found a copy under his pillow, read it with his accustomed patience, then remarked that its substance was spoilt by an overblown prose style.

Back from lounging by the wilful sea and tempted by further opportunities for amusement, Hermes decides to prolong his time in fair France. In the language of storytellers, a vivacious game is afoot. A stumpy-legged Agamemnon with comic-opera moustaches, self-styled socialist defusing socialism by supple appeals to the tribe, champion of family life with a regiment of mistresses, free-thinker whose bayonets protected the august High Priest in Rome, from the

Kingdom of Italy he himself had decreed. Can such a chameleon rely on an axiomatic Yes?

Languidly accepting *Courier*, Hermes notes that, even facing battle, Paris cannot be denied its joke. Madame Eugénie has lately presented her lord with a pet monkey, and wagsters are repeating that the first suggestion of the *Appel à Peuple* had come from that bossy animal.

Hermes, signalling a waiter, for he dislikes drinking more than once from the same glass, scrutinizes the exact wording of the Emperor's invitation. It is worthy of Hermes' own skills. 'The People approve the liberal reforms effected in the Constitution since 1860 by the Emperor assisted by Senate and Assembly, by representatives of religion and law, and ratify the Senatus Consultum.'

Clever. It will reinforce the moderates, divide the Left, for to utter No will denigrate reform, strengthen the Right, even excuse return to dictatorship. No space is allowed for qualification, analysis, query. Shrewd, cunning, the hermetic play of nice distinctions. Has man's creation of alphabets, he wonders, done him more harm than good, at best giving him a forked tongue?

Smaller print announced the resignation of two Ollivier ministers, suspicious of the either/or pragmatic sanction, but amidst the hubbub no one appeared to notice.

Tacitus, however, had noticed, and was further contented. Things were still on the move. For once, he breakfasted with his wife, then patted the girls as they left for school, promised to dine at home. In her bed, Adelaine stirred feebly, grateful for such attention.

He departed, smiling, Hamlet without the skull. Those messianic show-offs, Rochefort and Flourens, had failed their chance, were clowns ceasing to get laughs. They had flinched from a few bullets and a rainstorm. He himself had won through and, yesterday, achieved master-stroke, by a composition actually printed in prominent type in *Charivari*, a real breakthrough. Another pillage of the ex-President's slack-voiced, footnote-tasselled *Caesar*, marvellously appropriate to Plebiscite and trickery:

> The sale of consciences had so installed itself in public morals, that the several instruments of electoral corruption had functions and titles more or less official. Vote buyers were 'divores'; go-betweens, 'interpretes'; and the depositees of purchase money, 'sequestres'. Many secret cabals were formed, trading in electoral rights, and most of the election depended on them.

Exactly. Straight from the stable. Tacitus' pudgy face went knowing, as he meditated the Plebiscite. It allowed fascinating alternatives. The last, desperate throw of a ruined gambler: the panache of a rootless adventurer: another well-timed *coup*, perfected through the years by a conjurer with well-oiled hands.

His *Charivari* success was by no means all. From a crumpled, yellowing journal he had chanced upon lovely fuel for *Lame Pegasus*, a review of M. Flaubert's overrated *Madame Bovary*, prosecuted by the State not for its banality but for its lewdness, very trivial, written, or at least signed, by a newcomer, Mme Pauline Limayrac. 'How can anyone allow himself to write in so ignoble a style, when the throne is occupied by the greatest master of the French language, the Emperor?' There! How provident was life, how bountiful Paris, City of Light! Rochefort removed, that heap of manure, novelette terrorist Rigault, in hiding, fattening on boys and absinthe, politics brimming with possibilities.

The Plebiscite's wording, mendacious as a salesman's special offer, could well qualify for entry into *Lame Pegasus*.

Politics was exploitation of short memories, the adding of theory to prejudice. Understanding, possessed by so few, was vulnerable only to accident. In his next piece he would demolish for all time these Bonapartist 'democratic consultations'.

'Democracy' was an all-purpose trick, like 'World Opinion' and 'Constitution'. Probably none save himself remembered a liberal Grand Duke, Constantine, and barbaric Russian hordes cheering for 'Constantine and Constitution', imagining them man and wife.

Forgetting that promise of domestic dinner he descended on the Madrid, in an Odyssean Day of Return. As usual, each drinker was jabbering, not with but at his companions, sending telegrams to himself. However, Tacitus was greeted with even more acclaim than he had expected: his *Charivari* article had made a mark, notable absentees permitted him a seat of honour. An elderly bookseller, several times prosecuted, wrapped in an immense greatcoat, resembling a mangy bear, grasped his elbow. 'Well done! My congratulations!' though at once spoiling it by digressing: 'Our Goncourt friends have produced an appetizer which pleases me. They describe Robespierre and Jacques-Louis David as two icy geniuses in a volcano.'

Tacitus could afford to flick away Goncourts and their appetizers. 'Robespierre! He was the essence of tedium, uttered in the tone of a castrated camel.' A phrase to be stored for further use. 'A buffoon, licensed by the committees, on very short lease.'

Satisfied, he saw approval from nearby tables, nods from the old, heard chuckles from the young. At ease with the smoke, the fumes, the glimpses of heroic Revolutionary postures, long-departed saviours and tragic victims, he could afford magnanimity.

'The Goncourts I have never considered utterly despicable, any more than I have Hugo, despite his verbosity. I am inclined to agree with their diagnosis of history. That two currents are in perpetual conflict: sheer nastiness which manufactures conservatives and envy which creates revolutionaries.'

Protests were perfunctory; he was of course joking, what could a Rigault, a Gambetta, envy? He grinned, leaving the field for the novices, attending to his wine, looking about for a desirable girl.

Foiled, he did not much care, settled down to listen to the callow exchanges.

'This Plebiscite . . . a question of questions.'

'Well put, Anatole. Meanwhile, they say the Spaniard has fever. I don't blame her. The soul of France is rotting.'

'Her husband can always send for the vet. As for the Plebiscite, our blessed Empire has its follies, its graveyards . . . it's scarcely a matter of yawns.'

'I'm reading *Eye* . . .'

'You're wise to hurry. It'll be out of business in a month.'

'Some specialized language there . . . But, do you know, I've always felt that song preceded language. To this day, music penetrates the heart the more directly, the more immediately, where words must always fail. What we say, and perhaps someone has already said it, is a false echo of what we really think. No one, I suppose, would dispute that. The language, wordless yet intense, between man and animals. The language also, I suppose, of that fellow, God. I may be something of a pioneer. We'll be needing more mordant tunes . . . cascades of mere words can smother animal impulses!

'I'm not certain of that . . . indeed, I dispute it. Language does not clog my own impulses. Words throw off aura. Bright lights on Parnassus . . . despite those tiresome Muses intoxicating us with lack of meaning, overcoming the stink of victories with a Hugo lyric, Glory, I heard Louis Blanc say, is the sum of the dead.'

Tacitus looked up, regretting he had not intervened. He could have uttered all this, uttered it indeed rather more pointedly. He listened with considerable irritation, hoping for a chance to bring in *Charivari*.

'Last week I wanted a simile for "ugly". I tried "like a trull from a fetid ditch", but it didn't fit. Then what I liked to call my exultant spirit came along: "Ugly as Germaine Jacquier." But my conscience, very tactlessly, held me up, and I wondered whether Germaine is really so very ugly. After all, MacBryde stuck with her for three weeks. Anyway, I decided to find out. It was the day of the Victor Noir business. I rushed through that monstrous rain to her house. The concierge, Squinty Moll, said she was out. A word with as many petals as a rose. And because of an incident in time past, the hag wouldn't let me wait inside. So I waited under a tree, soaked, chilly as, let's say, Arcturus, until she deigned to turn up. With a man, of course, a drab-faced porker, like an unprepossessing head waiter, you know the type, probably discharged for theft or insolence. And, after all that, Germaine isn't ugly at all. She's . . .'

'Beautiful as drowsy July rain.'

'No, nothing like that. She's got a face unusual but not impossible. Like being a Chinese Jew.'

'My good fellow, you'll end up with just that sort of girl, with an eye on her jewels. Like that smell of bad garlic. Persigny.'

'Do you now what our estimable Empress calls him? A boiler, always blowing up.'

'Not bad. Like all Spaniards, she likes a certain sort of truth, priggish, selfish, humourless though she certainly is. There's undeniably something boilerish about His Grace, Duke Persigny. Especially in his ceremonials, strewn with cutlery.

Tacitus was bored. The mating arrangements of the ex-President did not concern him. He took out his notebook, sniffing importantly, safe from the sniggers of the absentees. He thought, he considered, had second thoughts, ruffled his thin, rather dingy hair, then, aware of respectful glances, wrote with elaborate slowness: 'In myself is the origin of the world, rose of dawning, both the full guts of existence and the twilight of the gods.'

Grandly, he refused another bottle. Tired air and second-rate liquor thickened the brain. 'The generous spirit gladly awaits the gifts of the day.' No, cancel the adverb, enemy of precision.

Becalmed amongst drunken idiocies, unwritten manifestos, incoherent mumbles, he was grateful for his own imperious perceptions, his glacial insights. Baudelaire, enemy of good taste, would have been grateful for his championship: he had been a genuine artist, for had he not defined the dandy as an unemployed Hercules?

This damned Plebiscite, a prize awarded by the ex-President to the Crown. Unless . . .

NINE

Aᴘʀɪʟ, as could be hymned, though weakly, was softly joining hands with May. Normandy was sprayed white and pink, Breton seas had lost fury, Alpine rivers leapt and sparkled, suns blazed over Provence. Magnolias flowered alongside chestnuts in the Luxembourg, warm air was cut by the swallows, sunlight tutored young leaf and fresh grass. Children wove daisies, poachers drank well under Hunter's Moon. From a dream of foaming waves, Aphrodite rose again, the world's darling.

All then was surely primed for untroubled, fancy-free summer. But wait, remember that May was month of the Plebiscite, festival of decision, perhaps of blood.

In the Assembly Jules Favre, leading the Opposition, had proposed the permanent abolition of plebiscites but mustered only forty-three votes against 227. Addressing the nation, over the Deputies' heads, M. Ollivier appealed to the steadfast and patriotic to, as he put it with lawyer's fluency, crown the edifice with a massive Yes.

He was listened to by Hermes, of whom Offenbach had made Orpheus sing that, lord of eloquence, he was father of lawyers. Thus also of swindlers, thieves and enigmatic crossroads.

Prince Pierre had been arraigned in the High Court, the atmosphere braced with the nervy animation of a circus. In the dock he had fought and shouted in his best animal manner, growling admission that he had fired a pistol. 'No man of courage or honour . . . I see none here . . . could do otherwise.'

Under tumult in the public galleries, the jury, presumably hand-picked by interested parties, acquitted him of murder but ordered him to pay twenty-five thousand francs to Victor Noir's parents.

A new poster promptly agitated the capital, displaying Prince Pierre's face, snouted, bristled, tusked, glaring, thickly fanged, dripping blood and, beneath, in letters red as Judas, the words 'And the Other?' Undisturbed by human questions, the bells rang as usual on Sunday morning: from Notre-Dame, Saint-Sulpice, Saint-Germain, Trinité tower and a score of others, dispensing a certain reassuring cohesion, like grammar. Children, moreover, knew that they expelled devils.

In the Sixth Arrondissement, Etienne attended Mass only at Easter and on such official occasions as the Emperor's fête. Amélie and Emile more often, though not today: Etienne advised against it, the Plebiscite was approaching, popular moods were uncertain, and Amélie gladly assented, nervous not of devils but of corner meetings, shouts from omnibuses and reports of 'red dogs'.

'The Emperor's a clever man.' Etienne crossed his legs comfortably. He knew things, was, in a manner, controlling them. His minister was renowned for informed sagacity.

Amélie, on the sofa, Emile beside her reading or seeming to, sighed. 'Yet, one hears . . people out there, in the jungle . . .'

'All will be well, my dearest. France can be trusted.'

That was ambiguous, but it contented her. Emile ostentatiously turned a page. The Plebiscite was a monster, looming and terrific. Etienne leant back, model father, public servant, citizen, voter. Also, cultured. For Countess Lisa he must be not only courtly, *insouciant*, but well versed, able to refer to masterpieces of Louvre and Academy. Dearest Amélie must be admiring his new volumes of Hugo, Gautier, Lamartine and, more riskily, the heavy edition of Thiers' *History of the First Empire*. Also of stacked numbers of the *Gazette des*

Beaux Arts, lying alongside Amélie's magazines filled with illustrations of Court personages and latest fashions.

'Emile, precious . . . you look tired. Do you feel well?'

'Yes, Maman.'

'You've attended to your studies, Son?'

'Yes, Papa.'

On his departure upstairs, Amélie's fair, rounded face looked up for support. 'Sometimes . . . I'm not sure. I worry about him. . .'

'But, my love, good parents are always worried. Someone has said, or should have said, that we worry continually about what has never occurred. Indeed, will never occur.'

Yes, she bowed to his unfailing wisdom, yet misgivings were not wholly stilled. 'He has secrets. He can look . . . strange.'

'What child hasn't got secrets? Only a freak, and an undesirable one. And every child looks strange. Often uncanny. You must surely remember . . .'

Husbands too, even if looking far from uncanny, have secrets. Devoted to their wives, they are nagged by dreams of countesses and those courtesans adrift in the empyrium, *les ogresses*, whom a Lisa can, of course, dissolve at a glance. Their rare perfumes envelop all Paris, their names are swapped daily like playing cards by fellows in the club, office, department store, lodging house. Coral Pearl, Léonide Leblanc, 'Madame Maximum', Céleste Mogador, once, like Marguerite Bellanger, the Emperor's playfellow, a circus performer, picked up in the Bois. Creatures wholly at odds with homely comforts, the sedate photographs and approved books, the fashionable journals, plump cushions, cabinets of bric-à-brac.

'My darling Amélie . . . you're adorable!'

Etienne fancied, against evidence, that deep in the air was a sound, not quite a cough, scarcely a chuckle, very faint, already gone, perhaps nothing. He looked up, but seeing only a loyal, tender face and loving eyes wondered whether Henriette was at the door.

TEN

HERMES wonders at nothing. He knows secrets of palace and temple, kraal and hostel, watch-tower and pyramid, of diplomatic bags, dental records and confidential memoranda. He absorbs the leagues of human effort cased in libraries, archives, the locked cabinets of rulers and in their lovers' baggage. All that occurs in this transient world spices his curiosity. To a taproom stranger he confides that one of the wealthiest women in Europe has been found chloroformed in a shabby fiacre left untended outside a disused railway siding in Budapest. He can mention the disappearance of the Duchess of Tourneville's black poodle and Lord Clarendon swallowing a fishbone, could list the contents of Count Bismarck's waste-paper basket and the Marie Corelli novel being enjoyed by Queen Victoria. Ahead of all others, he knows of the performance of *Othello* by Australian convicts; he has smiled at the laying of another electric cable between England and America, the birth of twins on a counter of a Toulouse branch of Crédit Mobilier. For himself, the impact of all, is uniform: terrestrial existence is no forest but a single structure shivering with universal connections, from a molecule secreted in the collar of an Academician to the movements of a squid, from the brain of Professor Renan who waved away notions of gods, to the orbit of a planet not yet discovered by humans.

Unhurried, incapable of fatigue, savouring paradox, grandiloquent nonsense, fake prophecy, he is the gourmet, adding a drop, a flake, a gloss to quicken the over-familiar. He is the quizzical gossip, gently tilting conversation askew by innuendo, a teasing query, an incredulous pout at some indisputable assertion, disconcerting status and rank, reducing everyone to groundlings.

This puny head-counting, numbering of the tribes, is a respite from ennui inescapable on earthly visits, for, to him, all seasons are the same: colourless, neither hot nor cold, mere blinks of time. For a while he watches, he overhears and, by doing little, accomplishes much. For such as he, very little history exists. Continually, the pack reassembles, to flap, crow, grunt, hiss, yelp; to drape itself with feathers, striped skins, claws, craving to embrace, then devour whatever it worships, hunts or invents. Humanity is uncertain whether Fate is inexorable or can dither, whether choice is allowable.

For Paris, however, history is again on the make. Despite shrugging it aside, Hermes can please himself with the latest sally, issued from infernal prison depths by Rochefort, irrepressible as a rubber ball, inscribed No. 'When Cortés, one of a hundred conquerors of Mexico, more recently emulated by French brigands, stretched Guatmozin's favourite on a white-hot gridiron, he doubtless complained of the wretched Aztec's protests as systematic opposition to himself.'

The Tuileries Monday Reception was ill-attended. The Empress had fits of premonition, praying more frequently, alone, apt to laugh unaccountably, berate her maids without reason.

Taking mood from her, the Prince Imperial, Child of Hope, was listless, still bruised by last year's rebuff when, awarding prizes at an official ceremony, he was bayed at by students, and the son of an old republican opponent of the father refused to accept his award from the hand of the son.

He was not singular in being distressed, not only by street cat-calls, by broadsides from Gambetta and his like, by squibs from

Rochefort, but by legends of the demonic Old One, Citizen Blanqui, though so few had ever seen him. Lonely bedrooms were haunted by the sewer-apparition of green hair and skin, leprous mouth, odours of rot. Blanquists terrorized by invisible manoeuvres were said to kidnap, blackmail, knife, for a one-word programme deadlier than No. The word? *Smash.*

Twiddling with events as he might with a humming-top, Hermes smiles. History, however evanescent, is not made by a Blanqui, a spectre of fleeting nightmare, initiating naught, exploiting the efforts of others, risking nothing at all. Gathering in attics, cellars, woodland huts, preparing to spike Yes, the Blanquists, in awe and fear, repeated the old story, that even in prison Blanqui kept a pile of locked boxes. What did they contain? Formulae for bombs more destructive than those with which Orsini had failed to kill the Emperor and Empress? Secret testimonies of Marat, Babeuf, Robespierre? The names of Blanquists suspected of treachery and pricked to die?

Hermes, of course, knows better. The boxes are empty, are props for the performance that will never occur.

In the higher reaches, the Emperor remained impassive. In the rarefied, vaulted Salle des Maréchaux, within the congress of the mighty dead, beyond reach of mortal ears, he attempts to ease the Empress's anxieties.

'My friend, I have often told you that my lifelong occupation is in finding solutions for the insoluble.'

He was, of course, smoking, pleasant but detached. Eugénie, slightly the taller, most beautiful of all empresses outside Vienna, was no friend of reforms, plebiscites, liberalism and certainly not of the insoluble. In anger or fear, her voice would hoarsen, a frown spoil her clear, superb skin and blue, faintly slanted eyes. 'To risk the Crown. Loulou's inheritance . . . to votes! It's madness.'

She glanced at the embalmed Napoleonic war gods nervously, as if seeking approval. Napoleon, never revealing anger or fear, smiled even more pleasantly, though his voice too minutely changed, more gutteral than usual. 'There is no question of risk. I am comfortable enough where I am. Madness is not an option. The succession . . .' He waved his cigarette in vague parabola, the beard, whiskers, half-closed eyes making the illusion of some genius of the theatre capable of vanishing at will, reappearing in guise totally different. The smile on the heavy, tallowy face, all folds and pouches, the expression in the eyes which at times seemed dead, at others drugged or battling against sleep, were as neutral as the wavy smoke.

He resumed, very patient, a portly gentleman in repose. 'The custodians of the Opposition, whose intelligence cannot be doubted, if not wholly respected, are reminders of the fable of the ageing lion. They begin by cutting his claws, then they remove his teeth; they leave only his name and believe themselves victorious. They are, once again, mistaken.'

He continued, in his stubborn, interior way, gently amused. 'We have the Name, a substantial one. And those who imagine themselves immortalized by cutting claws and removing teeth find themselves very inefficient, over-confident . . . and poorly rewarded.'

The faces, rigid, severe, judgemental, of Ney, Prince of the Moskowa, bravest of the brave, of Murat, King of Naples, appeared to confirm this. The marbled Hercules, N to the life, might have nodded.

Eugénie, standing beneath them, silken gown rustling, did not reply, though within she was not silenced. The unseen interloper knew her thoughts. That men, ugly or handsome, shrewd or imbecile, are subject to Fate. In France, at the start, a great lady, richer even than Baron Rothschild at Ferrières, is permitted all freedom but eventually is powerless even to walk down the common street.

Suppressing anger, more beautiful in her glowing temper than she had been an hour before, her eyes bluer, her stance more resolute, she had never quite relinquished a girlhood of courage, even recklessness. Mérimée had delighted in that youthful fieriness of spirit, elfin lightness of foot, her passion for matadors, bulls, perilous mountains and for headstrong riding. He had heard young Doña Eugenia declare that she was not destined to knit stockings.

At this juncture, May 1870, she had questioned her future. Grit was in the air, tormenting the nerves. Ten days, then the crucial Yes or No. Customary accusations abounded, Prefects would be pressurizing, bribing, promising, gerrymandering, menacing. Eminent savants looked solemn but committed themselves to nothing. Ancient Citizen Lambert in his eyrie cackled over reminiscences of the National Convention, by majority vote, permitting the existence of God. Conservative papers touched up photographs of the Empress braving cholera-ridden tenements, children's fever hospitals, pauper asylums in Cairo, cynosure of the world élite, at Fontainebleau, hand in hand with the Child of Hope.

In Paris, far outnumbering the sober Yes, posters appeared on walls, trees, statues, fountains, urging No in large red lettering. As Rochefort foretold, Pietri, resourceful though unimaginative, disclosed a plot to murder the Emperor, enabling him to arrest several hundred suspects, their examination delayed until after the Plebiscite. Left Bank protests joined those of Thiers and Gambetta, without avail. One morning, in more opulent Sections, long black poles were found, placed during darkness, unheard, surreptitiously, and now firmly protruding from kerbs and street corners, their purpose unknown but teeming with suggestion. Wagers at once began. They were electrically wired to paralyse rioters, were an Imperial notion for heating pavements, were to be hung with banners of Yes. Already, children were daring each other to touch them. No official announcement was made, and two days later they vanished as soundlessly as they had come, leaving behind further unease. They long remained evil portents in dreams and became ascribed to a Parisian fable, 'The Slant Grin of Hermes'.

The Plebiscite was polarizing debate. Utopianists and radical priests repeated to increased congregations that the first would be last, the poor, first, though concern for poverty was seldom pure. Beggars, slumped under arch and bridge and on the steps of Saint-Roche and the Madeleine, were being pulled up and escorted by individuals badly disguised as workmen, eager to explain the gulf between Yes and No.

Someone warned that when neighbours became the People good citizens should beware trouble. Up at Montmartre, Clemenceau, physician and mayor, tartly joked that only Chinese knew the difference between Yes and No, and they preferred neither. Young zealots, heads dyed red, in smart black coats, white trousers, red ties, marched from the Bastille to Père Lachaise, intoning such slogans as 'Spring Is Destruction, So Don't Vote', 'Remain Different', 'Madness Is Life, Reach Yourself', watched by crowds curious but unconvinced. A tumult occurred at a meeting under an immense placard. 'Love France, Therefore No.' Parisian wits, by now somehow aware of Hermes' ruminations, were now repeating a joke: 'How will His Majesty vote?'

In clubs and salons, conversationalists agreed that a low-pitched, Imperial Yes, inelegantly pronounced, would be charged with ambiguity, might favour ever more rapid reforms, a drastic reversal or, such was the Emperor's health, abdication. Thus the regency of the Empress. Unthinkable! Though . . .

At his most courteous with a minister whose dismissal he had already signed, at his least emphatic when planning a war, and whose silence might be indifferent assent or soft negative, Louis Napoleon, Napoleon the Little, Man of December, the False Louis, Master Badinguet, remained inscrutable. If, against all bets, No won the day, he might dissolve the Empire with an amiable pleasantry, then, as if in afterthought, yet always the sensationalist, offer himself to the People yet again and re-emerge as President of the Third Republic.

A step forward, a step backward, several steps sideways, periodically a leap, less drastic than it was made to seem, all are essential to govern those as volatile as the French.

On the eve of the vote, a hush descended on the French Empire, though with different levels of intensity in Departments, Sections, even single streets: the stillness might be that felt when a surgeon lowers his scalpel, in prison on a morning of execution, in an astrologer's parlour, at the Comédie, following the three warning knocks. Nowhere, apparently, was the peace of a fisherman, or of a monk, reading.

Children building sandcastles within the shadow of the Invalides, or rolling balls down the slope of rue Monsieur-le-Prince, exchanged bets on Yes or No, imponderables vague as the Emperor's cigarette smoke, took cover from adults furiously quarrelling, expected to see two moons glaring at each other in a firelit sky. In the green leather armchairs of the Philosophical Club in rue Martineau, grave gentlemen sat over wine, fingering *Journal des Débats*, *Revue des Deux Mondes*, listened to their oracle, a finely bearded essayist, renowned exponent of the adjective.

'I have often thought, gentlemen, that political adventurers, despots, extravagant speculators, have an effective time-span of some two decades, usually less. Then, the Mandate of Heaven is withdrawn. Energy, enthusiasm, the dynamic, to put it so, run out. The fellows may linger on but exhausted. Whether or not it was worth doing, their work is done. Necessarily in a hurry, never daring to relax, they drain themselves dry but must continue to provide novelties, invent fantasies . . . a Mexican Empire, an Exhibition, a Plebiscite . . to entertain, distract or bemuse what Shakespeare calls the general gender, at the expense of the established culture necessary for civilization. The ancient dynasties can sit back and do nothing, seldom, in fact, do anything else, itself natural, conforming to expectations, like a widow's tears. Well, esteemed colleagues, we too can sit back and await events with equanimity. Life, like a dog, every so often shakes itself, a new era begins or at least puts on the appearance of doing so.' He sighed, looking at roseate, comfortable faces, hands folded on paunches, legs outstretched, everyone ready for a doze. 'When I gaze at birds, gentlemen, I ask myself whether they have moods.'

ELEVEN

Paris waited. The outcome was like a gaudy kite still inert in its box. Caricatures watched, mute but expressive ghouls: two large circles around pin-point eyes and midget legs sufficed for Thiers, the eyes sometimes adorned with tears, for he could weep at will, effective in the political theatre. A black mouth open wide as a whale's was readily understood as Gambetta, an ingratiating smile stretched between tall hat and legal scroll was Ollivier. Particularly enjoyed was the Emperor as frock-coated pig, tail ajar from his falling trousers as he searched the night sky for his star, though onlookers usually preserved wary silence. On numerous respectable dining-tables maids placed a bird, silver, bronze, wooden, or indeed chocolate or marzipan, symbol of domestic disputes harmonized.

Rochefort's gibes were revived, fresh as pools blue after rain, ammunition for No. Ollivier he had designated as the Colonel Without a Regiment.

At Saint-Antoine, for voting day, the Beloved had hired a small pavilion in which, old and arthritic, he proposed to read from certain texts regarding tolerance and reconciliation, though as he had neglected mention of refreshments no one came. He was undismayed, paid his fee and returned home. 'One day, they will listen. They will remember how to play', contenting himself with a slattern's coffee and a hunk of bread.

The Honourable Gentlemen departed home, the Opposition dispersed, rancorous with each other. Thiers sat in his fine mansion, book in hand, pen and paper beside him, Gambetta, more secretive, lay with Mlle Léonie but with an ear cocked for news and, as voters swarmed past, hearing news-vendors' shouts, doubtless spurious, 'republican gains'.

Sailors swaggered, drunken, with tarpaulin rancidities. Respectable families kept children at home, but elsewhere, allowed holiday, urchins trooped to play, waving flags red as storks' legs, and fought with those bearing crucifixes, cardboard eagles, violets.

'Alex', impulsive editor of *L'Inviolate*, well funded by no one knew who, had commissioned a set-piece from the Tacitus of our times. Excellence was given its due, and, delighted, inspired, he had hastily rushed it off and, at this moment, it was being distributed, sometimes indeed purchased, on the boulevards, outsmarting Rochefort, turning Rigault puce, dissecting the Plebiscite as the most swindling manifesto since the Sermon on the Mount. The Saviour of Mankind, he continued, had expected the imminent end of the world, so does our self-styled Saviour of Society. And, in a way, he is absolutely correct.

Tacitus' satisfaction was exorbitant, overflowing. He was turning a page into the future, had all history, all knowledge, at his command. Listen, ye masses. Had not even Robespierre understood that, in his own words, all is permitted to Liberty in order to conquer Vice? Error must be corrected by dynamic anger which demolishes feeble scruples? Our authority for this? Why, our ex-President, in December '51. Violence assists ethical health, the torpor subduing people corrupted by cunning State hand-outs and political conjuring: it is the coarse, reckless sea sweeping away foulness, rot, atrophy, peasant caution and urban greed.

He inserted a quotation from a German whose name he misspelt but of whom none in France but himself would have heard: that war and courage achieve more greatness than charity.

The Empire lacked depth; hatred, bile, corruption spreading across it like ice. 'I hear the sough of worms turning. Grasp, then, your salvation. It consists of but one word. Proclaim it.'

By next afternoon, results were being telegraphed to Paris, those from the great cities arriving first, with startling majorities. Marseilles, No. Lyon, No. Toulouse, Rouen, Rheims, Bordeaux, No. In Paris itself, No from the suburban Red Belt, La Chapelle, La Villette, Belleville, Saint-Antoine, Montmartre.

Public Opinion, featured in *Orfée aux enfers*, had descended from stage to street, Imperial triumphs were being squashed like horseturds under your feet. In Left Bank cafés 'The Republic' was already a delirious anthem, in others a threatening slogan, in yet others a wistful lyric strengthened by repetition. At an Orleanist dining club hilarity rose when an unknown guest, dapper even foppish, neither young nor old, silver-haired, silver-tongued but otherwise indescribable, his demeanour politely insolent until you looked again and found it indeterminate, harmless, with sharp smiles running in and out of his face like, someone thought later, mercury, recalled the last plebiscite, when thousands, supporting the elevation of Prince-President Louis Napoleon to the throne, imagined that they were voting for the resurrected Martyr of St Helena.

At roseate sundown, clouds burning above Column, Dome, Twin Towers, newspapers fluttered like doves, political clubs were improvised, the capital a universal forum, loud with bucket-shop Ciceros and vengeful Antonys.

'The Empire was only a matter of bayonets . . . and bayonets are liable to rust.'

'Monsieur Bonaparte had a good heart. He may not have always known where to put it . . .'

'Emperors, dictators . . . I call them the exaggerations of history and am inclined to agree with the late de Tocqueville that Louis

Napoleon employed not ministers but conspirators. He had lived on his wits, a Mississippi gambler, with France as his saloon.'

'France and Monarchy, dear friends, are a union condemned in Heaven. Nevertheless, current medical opinion has it that most illness is self-induced. Suffering is the patient's own fault. Therefore . . .'

Darkness drifted up river, park gates closed, but the men, having voted, lingered on the streets, awaiting news, collecting around the brilliantly, defiantly illuminated Tuileries, the Imperial standard aloft under golden N, and outside that hotbed of revolution, the Hôtel de Ville, Commune of Paris.

Of the disposition within the Barracks, and amongst the National Guard, few claimed to know.

In the Sixth Arrondissement, Emile had retired upstairs, escaping Maman and Papa, so serious, so dull, in their talk of the day's happenings, though, of course, in his presence they so often used a code, maybe not worth decoding. More interesting was last night's dream, a dangerous one, on the edge, where he saw heads made of leaves and had awoken, drenched with cold sweat.

At school, everyone had giggled over a black and yellow leaflet which M. Havet had left on his desk as if he wished it to be seen and which must have been his own way of saying No.

Our Father, who art in France, dishonoured be Thy Name: Thy Kingdom is absent, Thy Will is undone on Earth as it is in Heaven. Give us back our Daily Bread, forgive us not our sins, as we forgive not the gangsters who betray us for lucre. Let us not be lead by the witch into Temptation, deliver us from the Devil.

Sudden clamour outside, bruised voices, jerked him from bed. He ran to the window. Gas-lit pavements were filling, faces were weirdly yellow, and, on the street, soldiers were marching. No banners, no music, but stiff kepis and red trousers, rifles. They must be going to defend Stumpy's palace. Had they been allowed to vote? He did not much care. Plebiscites were not monsters but only adult palaver, needing no urgent investigation.

People did not disperse after the platoon had gone and, elbows on the window-sill, in his night shirt, he heard unexpected laughter. Like a fountain, from wide grinning mouths, embraces, flourishes, stamps.

Street laughter was different from that in the houses he knew, where it was only from the throat, brief, boneless, feeble. Papa might laugh over his newspaper but with the dry wood sarcasm of M. Havet, Maman at some story of Henriette's, but the sound was only another caress. Henriette herself, in her common way, was livelier, laughing with all her body, harsh, too loud but jolly, washing around you like summer river. At school, laughter was subterranean, suspect, virtually forbidden, at best the artificial titter at a master's joke. In shops, cafés, in a *pissoir*, market or fair, it was more interesting: people suddenly laughed without explanation, at a cabbage, cat, mug of coffee, at nothing in particular, and others would join in, no one explaining. So what was there? He did not yet know.

Had they laughed at Troppmann's bloody head or at the bits and pieces of the slaughtered family?

The laughter below was a farmyard medley, but cheerful, apparently purposeless, from men and women, badly shaped, as if rising from jagged stones and earth.

Above them, he felt a Magellan, master of tides and men, a Man of Order. Maman had once read him a story of a flower, like the soul, unfolding into perfection. Boring, yet this tossing, flaring night was stem and colour, starting to unfold.

His hand strayed beneath the night-gown, on to what Maman called his region. Should he? Not yet. Certain delights, queer pains, were enjoyable even in advance, almost best when delayed.

He murmured, marvellously in love with himself, 'I can hear the laughter of Paris.'

TWELVE

WHATEVER its own vote, unevenly distributed, Paris was *en fête*, besnared by the magic of numbers. Dark Ones, desperadoes, irreconcilables, had crept back to their holes, fire-raisers contemplated only their sodden matches.

Pasted on Voltaire's statue was a large drawing of the Emperor, in shepherd's smock and cap, his crook pointing the contented flock towards paradisaical gates. Jockey Club grandees, high folk, foreign notables were back from safeguarded châteaux and Swiss or Belgian properties, sauntering through place des Vosges arcades, rue de la Paix fashion stations, ladies, in late afternoon, the modish hour, drove down avenue de l'Impératrice in elegant equipages, luxuriating in popular attention and, in their wake, fluffy gulls following the plough, the languorous courtesans were escorted by the pick of the *flâneurs*, buccaneers and brash experts of the Second Empire.

The Council of State, ministers, senators and deputies, and such privileged though superannuated fixtures as Persigny and Rouher, even the irascible, blood and thunder Plon-Plon, in all finery attended the Emperor at Saint-Cloud to watch the official presentation of the votes. Symbolically, they lay in two ornate caskets, one large, one small, the tongues of masculine France. Some eight million, Yes; under two million, No. Virtually identical with those that had inaugurated the Empire years ago. Rural villages and townships, 'the steady, unhurried heart of France', had routed the bulging cities whose temperament was incoherent and whose love was poisoned.

The Emperor, standing between the unsmiling, rather haughty Empress and the solemn Prince Imperial, formally replied to the congratulations, laconic, with half-smiling composure, addressing less the sparkling company before him than the journalists congregating in a shadowy gallery.

'Invited to choose between the Empire and revolution, France has indeed made her choice. We must now, more than ever, look forward to the future. Who, indeed, if of goodwill, could really oppose the progressive stride forward of a dynasty founded upon a great people when in the midst of anarchy and today fortified by liberty?'

At once, to editorial fanfares from the Right, sulks from the Left, Gramont, duke and ambassador, succeeded as Minister of Foreign Affairs. A duke in charge of Europe reassured those to whom domestic reforms and plebiscites were an intolerable stutter of nerves. Most, even its implacable enemies, agreed that the Empire had been rejuvenated by contact with broad, earthy loyalties. Earth, Family, Religion, the priests reiterated, from Paris to Algiers.

Left Bank cafés, disconsolate, too disillusioned for impassioned anger, tried to argue that Prefects and official agents had rigged the votes, bemused the peasantry with inordinate promises, that verbal inflation had fatally confused the issue, but feelings dribbled away to silence, explanations collapsed in mid-sentence. Gambetta told Léonie, 'We're wiped out.' Thiers continued to read his book, nothing was heard from Rochefort. Jules Favre, encountering Dr Clemenceau, remarked that politics had now come to an end. Clemenceau, still impetuous and aggressive as a Jacobin, laughed cheerfully. 'Nonsense, my dear chap. Just wait and see. Meanwhile, my patients await my attentions. Bloody-minded rascals. They took a bit of my money to vote No. They took rather more to make their dirty mark on you know where! Good fellows, all the same.'

Café Madrid still lacked its great men, and even Tacitus, now regarded as the most promising of the not so young, was absent. Voices meandered dismally above dirty glasses and unfinished plates of bread, onions, cheese, apples, the strident Revolutionary pictures around them now ironic or contemptuous. Even the waiters, lounging at the bar, scarcely bothered to look round when summoned.

'Well, we should have taken more risks. As it is, Loulou will soon be breaking out of the serpent's egg. He may be cretinous, but if he were a two-headed castrato he'd still be worth ten million votes. Give women their say, and he'll have fifteen million more.'

'Votes! They sicken every honest man.'

'Napoleon IV! Four too many. Unreason will choke this sentimental nation. People only vote for the past, and most of that is imaginary. The most powerful influences almost always come from those who never existed or are remembered only in fantasy. Don Juan, Jesus, that bore Hamlet. At Loulou's coronation, if he ducks a few right-minded bombs, the deaf, the dumb and the blind will convince themselves that his glance has miraculously cured them, even though their condition is unchanged.'

Reddened eyes, famished spirits were prowling for consolation, from a likely girl, a free drink, a telegram, 'You've won.' Unease flickered at an unfamiliar face. Government agents were about, Furies of the regime, demanding retribution for No.

'Do you remember, Marcel, that Louis Napoleon, already a blight, once refused an offer to become President of Ecuador, a country wholly without promise? One can only regret his refusal.'

'Better still if he'd become President of Mexico!'

'All the same . . . there remains one thing in our favour.'

'I hope you'll do us all the favour of revealing it.'

'It's not generally known.' The sallow face smudged with two days' growth under a messy cap of hair peered round for any Pietri spy. 'There's a primitive Russian word, *krasny*, which not only means "excellent", "beautiful", but also "red". Wouldn't you say that's a hopeful omen?'

'I would say it's absolutely futile. Utter shit. But I can tell you something far better than that.' Again, the cautious glance, the lowered voice. 'The Censorship works overtime . . . but it's more or less official. In the army . . . fifty thousand voted No.'

THIRTEEN

TACITUS was suffering more than dejection, perplexity now nagged like toothache. He had departed very grandly to cast his No. He did so, and at once, astonished, dismayed, realized that he had voted Yes.

In his opulent study, so far in fittings and aura from the Madrid, he stared so deep into himself that he felt helplessly muddled.

Much had been inexplicably enveloping him during these last hectic days. Taut lines of verse floated into him unbidden only to vanish in mockery before he could grab a pen.

There was more. His article, witty, allusive, irrefutable, in *L'Inviolate*, had found its way into Saint-Pélagie where Rochefort languished in some form of state and where, by another stupid misapplication of justice, he was permitted to issue remarks for publication. In the last issue of *Marseillaise*, he had repeated his gibe about the poet with nothing to say, jeering at a certain simile which, brutally wrenched from its context, undeniably appeared less appropriate. 'Bullets of the Soul,' Rochefort had written. 'M. Tacitus has exactly defined his own malady. Self-inflicted wounds, burial alive of whatever gifts he might have picked up or, more likely, stolen for plagiarism is his sole distinction. He is thus a suicide, the poet with nothing to say. Whether he rests in peace is immaterial, but, for all our sakes, let him rest.'

Intolerable. Rochefort should, must, receive the due aborted by

Prince Pierre's matador folly. Urged by unwonted compulsion, against all previous inclinations and convictions, Tacitus the humane, who so shrank from blood, nerved himself to stand upright against diabolic, jesting Rochefort, purveyor of malice, and who was daring him to submit to public indignity with the dumb patience of a lily.

As though some presence, unseen but ineffable, guided his hand, he had dispatched Rochefort a formal challenge. Tomorrow he would publicize it at the Madrid, by noon it would have reached *Marseillaise*'s front page. All Paris would resound with it. A gesture, powerful yet – and here was the keen twist of it – safe, with his opponent caged in Saint-Pélagie.

Excellent. Well managed. Couldn't be better. Yes, but that perplexity continued to nag, undeterred by the simplicities of intelligence, aye, genius.

Lately, during his rounds of Paris, he had begun to feel oddly uncertain, less of himself than of the world around him, in which the familiar appeared as an arcane travesty of itself. The vilified Emperor wins a massive, unassailable victory; the upright man, who is naturally pledged to No, unaccountably votes Yes. One could envy the late Morny, who would have greeted even the second coming of Christ with the courteous mingling of amused incredulity and ironic irritation he displayed when losing a fortune at Deauville or Longchamp. Lacking such sang-froid, Tacitus was convinced that, as if plagued by some small, unidentified malady, he had strayed into atmosphere in which he arrived at places he had not intended, made unplanned detours as if responding to nudges he had not actually felt. Perhaps the approach to death resembled this: unfinished thoughts, incompleted plans, a sort of awakening in strange places, a confusion of dreams and daylight. Such an unpleasant illusion, if it were illusion, was crystallized by a new acquaintance.

Some weeks previously, at dusk, appearing soundlessly as if from a crack in the pavement, as in a nursery fable, a man had accosted him, familiarly, as if they were fellow officers, clubmen, even friends, though the devil alone knew where they had met. The fellow, slipping a hand under his arm, had led him to a bar table, where he found himself, in uncanny almost hypnotized compulsion, ordering an expensive bottle of a wine he particularly disliked.

Thereafter, the stranger, *raffiné*, Tacitus considered, rejoicing in his cleverness, had repeatedly intruded, deftly slipping out from a porch, a latrine, from behind a tree or pillar. He had never divulged his name, for of course he assumed that his involuntary companion knew it, but he was known vaguely on the Left Bank as M. Que-Voulez-Vous?, often with several girls traipsing after him or lurking within call, mute as phantoms and scarcely of what could only be called *ton*.

M. Que-Voulez-Vous? was slender, youngish, with skin abnormally clean, slightly raffish in long chequered coat, broad, tilted hat, carrying a ram's-headed cane with sham-classical decoration, his hands finely cut and trimmed, imaginable as continuously stroking a cat, his gait unhurried and oddly smooth, almost a glide. His eyes were unblinking, disconcerting in that they either observed everything or were avoiding seeing anything. With his cane and fancy waistcoat he was something of a dandy, arousing some curiosity but, understandably, no affection. His talk, respectful even flattering, apt to include a quotation from one's own article or verse – or indeed from any writer you cared to mention – with unnerving accuracy: he was well informed, fluent, interesting, yet not wholly trustworthy, like that of a well-spoken tout, vaudeville agent, successful commercial traveller. He appeared to dislike sunlight and open skies, usually, like a footpad, to be seen in unlit passages, tipping his hat at some tart, under an arch, talking with Seine bargees beneath an oil lamp or with morose landlords and gamblers in an unfashionable tavern. A fly-by-night bat. On his finger a signet ring, two gold wings on dark blue, suggested the agile, the fleeting. He displayed certain skills, scarcely significant yet oddly memorable: exquisitely carving ham, telling queer anecdotes usually involving luck, coincidence, accident, whistling tunes from Salieri, Meyerbeer, Auber, and often hinting at important secrets, his manner suggesting that he himself was the most precious secret of all.

His expression was never entirely ascertainable. To show any response, only the corners of his mouth might quiver, his grey-blue eyes minutely quicken. His livelihood was unknown and, though his purse always bulged, it was seldom opened, people indeed grumbling that, on departing, he was always more affluent than he had been on arrival. Once, the music critic 'Big Jim' won a thousand francs from him: M. Que-Voulez-Vous? paid immediately with a money order that Big Jim placed in his pocket-book, which, when opened next morning, contained no such note. Someone joked that the newcomer could slip through keyholes.

'He has, how shall I put it, an oblique way of settling his debts.'

'There was a dispute . . . after a card game. Outside, on the pavement. Some of us were angry with him, yet, I can't explain why, were getting the worst of the argument. It was like being in court facing a Gambetta, Favre or Mâitre Ollivier but very quiet, very courteous. Feline. It was getting ugly, I was afraid of a real rough-up. I scarcely wanted to be entangled in a scene. So, do you know what? I prayed for rain and almost at once it occurred. A real downpour. And I was alone. Perfectly safe.'

M. Que-Voulez-Vous? could procure you tickets, for an opera box, an exclusive charity ball or for the Ballet Rose, proscribed by the police, in which youths in classical costume, or no costume, prance, pirouette, pose, their eyes, their hips making improper signals. Once, a white bird had alighted on his shoulder, as if reclaiming rights of territory.

Rochefort had called him an entertaining Professor of Sharp Practice. His talk, never fully serious but very fluent, in a French a trifle formal, even archaic, suggesting much reading and extensive travels. Nobody knew where he lodged, probably some hotel, small but expensive, if slightly dubious.

More often than was comfortable he waylaid Tacitus, deflecting him from carefully prepared plans. It was after their first meeting that Tacitus began finding certain days jolted askew. Resolved to forage in a church at Saint-Geneviève where a priest was suspected of, some reporter claimed, toning it down a little, unspeakable iniquity, he found himself in no church but in a tiny bar occupied only by the *patron* and M. Que-Voulez-Vous? It was as though he were being victimized by tricks not of minor circumstance but of tentacles of a dehumanized Rochefort, if granted that the ugly fellow was entirely human. Last week, on a clear, humid night, he was returning alone to that private attic when, without warning, his legs sagged and he was abruptly swaddled in mist so that, almost touching his own door, he lost all direction. The mist, like a deceiver's grin, vanished as swiftly as it had come, and his story was everywhere ridiculed, even by his concierge whose narrow, unsleeping eye missed nothing. No mist, too much liquor, the dirty tongues clacked. 'Peevish verbiage', Rigault spat out between gulps, 'can bemuse the senses, even of those who lack sense.'

Rigault was more dangerous than Rochefort, who desired no power save that of sarcasm, raillery, malice, the reduction of the topical to absurdity. Rigault wrote little and without effect, but with his errand-boy spies, his proscription lists, his hatred, he awaited the opportunities that revolution would have delivered him. A degenerate, a shrinking of life, he saw himself as a one-man Committee of Public Safety. Behind thick spectacles, the eyes were alert for enemies, the thin, chipped mouth primed to give orders. The little creature was a machine perpetually weighing different degrees of calculation. In '89, he would have been the first to reach power and the first to be overthrown, repelling even his own associates.

Rigault and Rochefort, preposterous couple! But for the moment Tacitus was thinking more of a stealthy, smiling M. Que-Voulez-Vous?, whom he now saw at Café d'Olympe, reading a book. Always, on finishing a page, he tore it off, crumpled it, then dropped it as if shedding leaves.

Intent on reaching an appointment in rue des Beaux-Arts, wishing to avoid him, nevertheless he was at once seated, fumbling for his wad of notes, feeling that well-appointed hand on his arm, hearing that dry, good-humoured voice, its clarity, its drop of condescension. 'My good friend . . .' The heavy-lidded eyes were never surprised, as though they had seen all manner of human folly, perhaps too much for their owner's good.

Tacitus, compiler of *Lame Pegasus*, a Villemessant in the making, a successor to Rochefort, master of his fate, laughed nervously, wishing he had stopped at Brébants or merely scuttled round the corner.

'You laugh, sir . . . well, yes.' The other's smile was faint, sidelong, not hostile but with only shallow friendliness, his pressure on Tacitus' arm deepening.

'An excellent article of yours in *L'Inviolate*. "The sough of worms turning." Just so. Highly effective. Congratulations are due and indeed to hand. But I was speaking of a laugh, more generally, of laughter. It is not part of the armoury requisite for animal warfare. Ah, many thanks, so generous, your good health, a toast to your future as an author celebrated and influential. The power and, how does it go, the glory. But laughter. As a poet, thus a perceptive observer, you will have noted the jocularity of transitory existence, the fine irony of the universe. The starveling beggar squatting on a hillock, unaware of the gold buried beneath him. The grand aristo, a Diomedes, a Buckingham, a Morny, dallying over his choice of new hunting boots, unaware that he will die before midnight. You are doubtless preparing to say, and indeed, my friend, as a recognized man of letters you may already have said it, more than once . . .'

Tacitus, at once suspicious, felt outmanoeuvred, forced to listen as to a prison governor, while street lamps now shone, carriages passed, strollers greeted each other and, around him, waiters bent, straightened, gentlemen in coloured cravats preened themselves, ladies spoke in low tones.

The other's voice, quiet, not obviously foreign, not quite French, flowed as if on rollers, while, though unordered, a cigar, 'House Best', was obsequiously offered, which he lit as if by a flick of the fingers.

'I have seen resplendent princes ascending the scaffold, the crowds almost helpless with mirth. There is the thin laughter of the dead, the giggling yelp of a child before beating, the inane mirth of lovers, not always identical. Beautiful girls laugh when they desire something, men when they have nothing to give. A poet, he could have been yourself, esteemed charioteer of expression, sang of the laughter of the sea. One must, as you teach us, approach words with delicacy, with restraint, with appreciation of nuance. Even the most celebrated writers can be deceived. "Laughter-loving Aphrodite." Ah, but Aphrodite, in her silken pavilion and hospitable bed, never loved a joke. She could tease and allure but no more than Doña Eugenia did she utter an authentic laugh. Your remarkable Emperor knows how to laugh, though you of course will have discerned that, if he ever does, it is insufficient to be heard. His hidden laughter, if misleading, may be his most crucial asset.'

He was incapable of relinquishing this not very interesting, perhaps spiteful topic, though his tone, persuasive, melodious, possessed undeniable charm – despite charm being a quality from which one kept a certain distance, like a garden bird, however well tamed, before the hand throwing it crumbs.

'Yes, you will concur that laughter, like glory, is a colour in life's mirage. One indulges in it at the sight of fashionable opera lovers sleeping deep during the second act. At talkative art critics at the Salon who hate paintings almost as much as they envy painters. At

Don Juans, incapable of love. I myself am gratified when atheists flee to a temple for sanctuary. I have heard, perhaps from yourself, such being your knowledge of men and affairs, that Helmuth von Moltke, estimable tribal leader from across the river and of whom we may hear more anon, has only laughed twice in his life. When his mother-in-law died and when he was informed that the defences of Metz were impregnable. He himself is, of course, of the type that, by grace of M. Jacques Offenbach, Parisians find so much to chuckle at. Well, I must not fatigue you by continuing.'

He puffed, he sipped, smiled abstractedly, then continued. 'Laughter at a cripple, at a sovereign, can be the same. Philosophic mockery or an upstart quiver of glands. Though I remember that whenever Nero laughed senators and knights held their breath and great ladies fainted.'

Tacitus was more than ever uneasy. The talk, too one-sided, had taken a displeasing turn. Furthermore, with no conscious decision, he had paid for a second bottle and 'House Best' was almost ready for replacement. Though aggrieved, and unaccountably drowsy, he yet felt himself lifting his glass as if for a libation, though disquiet was by no means assuaged by hearing that pleasant voice murmur, with elaborate unconcern:

'We must drink to the Promethean, the daring act. That is, of course, to your Promethean contest. That duel of yours . . . it's attracting wagers everywhere . . .'

FOURTEEN

CELEBRATING the Plebiscite, the faithful voice of France, Café Valentino Bal Mobile was charged with movement, chatter, easy tunes. More music lapped from Café Morel, Château des Fleurs, Les Ambassadeurs, was echoed in Galant Jardinier, Château Rouge, blared from public gardens, wailed or pulsed, from a solitary violin or guitar at moonlit street banquets, some of them covertly financed by local political agents.

At Fiacre Fou, palm trees in gilded tubs were festooned like arch-dukes, glowing with tiny green and scarlet lights while, aloft, gleamed Chinese lanterns sprayed with yellow butterflies spotted with red, hovering above pink lakes and mauve islands, the lanterns, on transparent ribbons, with the illusion of dangling freely in space. Dancers swapped smiles like banknotes, many glistening with cos-tumier's jewels from Passage des Panoramas. A mechanical piano, smaller replica of that at Compiègne, ground out popular melodies, a soubrette warbling from *La Belle Hélène*, dancers and diners hum-ming the refrain of Offenbach's *aubade* parody.

Yes, it's a dream,
Yes, a sweet dream of love.
Night lends her Mystery,
It must end at dawn.
Let's taste its brief delight,

Only a sweet dream of love,
No more than a sweet dream of love.

Etienne held Amélie close, scarcely moving, swaying placidly to the flimsy, innocuous music. Once again he realized that, full-faced, she was docile, tentative, soft, but, in profile, unexpectedly resolute, withstanding any affliction aimed at himself and Emile, also hinting at another, more sensitive personality that he should not overlook, should indeed welcome. Insipidity, not infidelity, destroys marriage; something should always be left on the plate.

Politics, business, plans were tonight demolished by insidious perfumes, wine, harmonies tinny but toxic, by anticipations roused by bare shoulders, glistening backs, risky *décolletage*.

Quiet as a mouse, Amélie's hand slipped back into his own. She too was roused, eyes unusually bright, her breath quicker. They were Adam and Eve under trees, they were – imagination dimmed with the notes – cloud and earth, sky and sea. Later, in their private term, they would garden.

Garden deep, Etienne thought, lips on her powdered cheek, on her neat mound of hair, though the limitless exorbitance of nakedness, its curves and ravines, knolls and copses, streaks of the unseen but thrilling, suffused him with vision of Amélie and Lisa naked, side by side, awaiting him. His dread was that, needing every bit of them simultaneously, he might, when mounting Amélie, gasp out 'Lisa!' *Only a sweet dream of love.*

They pressed, fondled, advanced, retreated in the pellucid rhythms, shuffling, together. She was immersed in the instant, the music, physical union, prolonged embrace, perfected by his murmurs, his skin upon hers, their being. She would never know that, within his caresses, the ardour on his pale, bearded, dignified face, a starry-eyed, jewel-haired phantom, with swinging stride and highborn style, would be extending hands to admirers amidst the lustrous porcelain and green silk of Duchess de Morny's Chinese drawing-room.

Very tenderly, husband led wife through the tables into the darkened rose-garden, to the wooden seat beneath trellised roses. Wine for him, sherbet for her. They sat hand in hand, thoughts rhyming with the piano, in the half-lights that transformed others to characters in Masquerade. Both were silent. As always, she was composed, grateful, he was bound to her, she was mother of Emile, provident as an estate. Lisa, both in and out of the Masquerade, was lady of fancy, of a year and a day, darting like a Rachel into capricious changes of mood, demanding extremes, flights of impossibility. She was Helen, Mellusine, hard as a rocky coastline, perilous as a Breton sea, imperious as Eugénie, yet famed for tempestuous surrenders. She had been at a Rossini concert sporting a golden bandeau. At the Empress's picnic she had worn a huge, floppy hat white as her hands. She had re-covered her bedroom chairs with crimson damask. Should there come another war, he would, as a reservist, achieve some gallantry of which she would read with admiration, perhaps a sigh of desire.

He rose, bowed to Amélie with teasing formality and led her back to the dance. They were happy, not, at this choice moment, thinking of Emile.

Henriette had winked in complicity as Emile took a key from the kitchen drawer and hurried outside, King of the Streets. This too was a fête; he had never before been out alone after nightfall. Lamplight was more exciting than stars, each street was a gallery of caricature. Gingerbread stalls, cat-skinners' sheds, booths, arches, omnibuses, drays, distant trains, were distorted; sharpened, illuminated more fiercely by the play of light on black, the infinite resources of Paris night.

In unusual bravado, he imagined himself riding with cavalry, nearing a frontier. Far-off sounds could be waves.

He had never gone to the sea and, thinking it nearer than it actually was, beyond Mont Valérian, of course, and Saint-Cloud but not much further than Meudon, would envisage a giant wave curling towards the city in winter gales. More immediate, though, was Papa's talk of the red wolf of Saint-Antoine, quite close. He must keep his eyes open. The Dark Ones!

Jean-Michel, in Class IV when he first saw the sea, thought it an animal and wanted to stroke it.

He himself, taking colour from sights around him, felt entranced, the air, now sparkling, now glimmering, filling with doors to be opened. This perhaps was the mood from which angels appeared. M. Havet had said that angels were Persian inventions, though admitted he had seen one on a Normandy beach. Eagerly questioned he could only make some unfunny joke about it being neither Man nor Woman, clothed but with nothing on. You wanted to ask if it possessed a 'region' but of course could not.

Though keeping to safe paths, he saw everything in the spirit of Jean-Michel's sea, M. Havet's angel, a many-armed god throned in a shop window was a spinner of night itself: scraps of music had dents and growls unheard in daylight. A patch of darkness between ancient gas jets transformed clothes on a washing line to a white horse.

He turned into a square, hitherto drab but now lit by a row of garish lights proclaiming what by day he had never noticed, the Cavern of Wonders, its entrance crowded and from which filtered novel sounds: pipe music, winding into the start of a tune, straying jerkily, always about to regain it, never doing so, blocked at times by an ugly drum.

Ticket holders were streaming on both sides of him into the Cavern. A well-dressed man, bare-headed, in black and white checked top-coat, seemed waiting for him. He was vaguely familiar, even though Emile could not recollect ever having seen him. Lured forward, with some qualms, he soon saw that the stranger, though unsmiling, was friendly and somehow, in the night's mysterious gift, appropriate.

Seen closer, the eyes under the full light were of nameless colour, the face narrow and what Maman called sallow. Without speaking, he gave a little bow and was already being led towards scarlet and white stairs. Sour smells were struck away by scents, huge bunches of flowers in hanging bowls. The stairs, filled with people in ordinary clothes, smoking, chattering, laughing, curved up to a gilded balcony lined with mirrors. He stared into one and saw nothing, into another and met himself, a dwarf with a mouth too wide for his face, into a third and saw a cracked oblong in schoolboy jacket, with sloping shoulders but no head. In this topsy-turvy land, outcome of that riotous Plebiscite, camels might reign, pelicans eat dictionaries, trees grow with roots in the air and, as if for drunken people, rules were suspended.

His companion, without touching, led him through an arch clustered with glass fruits, very bright, and they seated themselves in a crescent-shaped room, with several rows of velvety chairs facing a stage, empty save for a table, very black against blue curtains.

Cigars, cigarettes waved a transparent blur, voices were incessant, faces gazed forward expectantly. He sat back, easy, awaiting whatever might come. Then, a tall girl, thin and painted like a Sioux pole, handed him a glass. It looked empty but, moving clumsily, he found his sleeve wet, then he drank and at once felt dizzy but happy, nothing any longer strange.

All seats were occupied, a gong stilled the hum. After a long, trembling minute a tall white-bearded man in a dark cloak marched on to the stage. People clapped, he smiled, though as if to himself, he lifted a hand and the air around it yellowed, then solidified into a melon which he caught, then passed to a pretty girl in the front row, in green trousers, gauzy tunic, to pass round for inspection. Hesitating to touch it, then encouraged by several friendly faces, Emile found it unexpectedly heavy. Receiving it back, the magician cut it in two by a quick, almost invisible motion of hands and made each half dense with blood-red feathers. These he negligently emptied, and at once red doves were flying above their heads before vanishing. Bowing again, as if in afterthought he threw up the melon halves, in mid-air they puffed themselves into blue flame from which fell a large chocolate box which, deftly snatching, he upheld so that all saw a picture of the Empress surrounded by inquisitive elves. Everyone clapped; again he inclined but still as if thinking of something else.

Emile, unsteady, was scarcely aware of his new friend, so motionless that quite possibly he was, by some further trick, quite empty, his heart stolen or lent to the unsmiling performer of marvels. The magician, seemingly wafted from the stage by some invisible process, was moving between the rows. All were agog, almost breathless. Pausing, he smoothly extracted a wallet from a gentleman's inside pocket, shook it free of banknotes, then, shrugging, bored, he stooped, retrieved them, tore them into small pieces, which he sprinkled over heads and shoulders, then exhibiting the empty wallet, leaving its owner nervous, perspiring, resumed the stage. He motioned the gentleman to explore his pocket, he did so, found the wallet, once again stuffed with notes. A rapid succession of such feats left Emile spellbound, within renewed dizziness. He saw the multiple faces, hands, exits and entrances, dazzling sheets of colour. 'Something old,' the performer confided gravely, in foreign accent, pouring a shower of rainbow handkerchiefs from a tiny glass cube. 'Something new,' and they reassembled as a vase of coloured fish. He spun a hoop which quickly melted into an upright eight, then collapsed, undulating into the wings.

FIFTEEN

VIOLENCE, by corroding social torpor, assists moral health and political vigour. Reforms promoted by an unjust State, corrupt, by strengthening its source, are no more than window-dressing. Society needs a gale, a coarse restless sea, to batter against peasant caution and urban greed.

So argued the Irreconcilables, the Dark People, but, in early June calm, no one was listening. N sailed above the turbulent capital, erstwhile HQ of No, pearly heat seeming to detach it from its stem in miraculous exhalation, wedding of almighty sky and vernal earth.

Seething industrial slums were quiescent, not a whine, not a quiver from Bercy, Belleville, La Chapelle, Les Battignolles, Charonne, Vaughin, even Saint-Antoine. The gaunt voice of the Old One was silent, perhaps strangled. *Enragés* lamented: sunshine and fountains, polished leaves and shining pools, the docile apparatus of summer were never a question of votes, fake miracles, the platitudes of Honourable Men. The public trod its stupid treadmill, exerting itself towards nowhere, summer folk, concerned only with the trivial, the absurd, the languid and sensual. Buttock and wink in Montmartre and on Boul' Mich'. Gossip held court throughout Europe. A duke had paid a dancer, La Rigolbroche, five thousand francs to walk naked across boulevard des Italiens, in the theatrical quarter often styled the Clitoris. With mirth and much artificial indignation, readers of Left papers with little else to enrage them learnt that attentions for La Walewska's new water pipe was costing taxpayers four million, attracting much lewd interpretation. The dispatches declared that Mr Worth, English couturier, remained unquestioned, even the Empress having to await his pleasure. The new palaces, Le Printemps, La Samaritaine, au Bon Marché, rivalling the stupendous magnitude of the latest railway stations, offered unprecedented selections: ready-made, collapsible seaside cottages, novel kitchen and bathroom devices, refulgent satins, exotic Cambodian carpets, astounding haberdashery and millinery, outbursts of frills and creases, tints and gadgetry, the latest glassware, exquisite stationery embossed and crested, radiant umbrellas and patriotic scarves, lighting inventions that could transform a room into a grotto, a Bedouin tent, a turret retreat. Humble locks, handles, knobs, hinges were carved to resemble minarets, helmets, trees, waves.

'Everything for the body, a trifle less for the soul,' Monsignor Bauer, Imperial Almoner, commented in his smiling way.

It was the season of young housewives, assignments in conservatory and summer-house, the purchase of thin lingerie and unusual houseplants. Children were craving summer holidays. M. Havet, who disliked both children and holidays, rapped his desk. 'Not "Everyday Speech" but "Demotic Parlance". Write it down.' Obeying, Emile was not thinking of holidays but of rediscovering the Cavern of Wonders, which was more difficult than he had anticipated. Other boys were doubtless dreaming of cut-throat voyages under noisy top-gallants, girls yearning for robber-barons on hillsides, beneath Northern Lights, older youths planned helter-skelter raids on girls' beds and of climbing forbidden towers of love.

In keeping with the universal good cheer, *Temps* and *Moniteur* announced that the War Department was reducing its intake of conscripts by ten thousand.

No discord sounded at a smaller paragraph announcing the death of the Queen of Spain. One queen was much like another.

Only France and Austria had beautiful, exceptional ladies up top. The Crimean hero, Canrobert, had compared Her Britannic Majesty to an untidy cabbage.

Sunlight was unremitting, sentries at Tuileries and Invalides sweated under bearskins. Much verse was being written, salads for *Lame Pegasus*, and in which doves glimmered behind foliage intricate as Athene's thoughts, swallows swooped over love-trysts in arbours, lily and marigold were constantly invoked, archaic music filtered through the mysterious heart of the earth. Blue the sky and Seine, pens scribbled elegiacally, passionately, often sincerely, green green the Bois, crimson and white the Luxembourg roses.

Tourists at Versailles gaped at the vast canvas, *The Glories of France*, where Louis the Magnificent stood in pomp, though it was also a reminder of the Universal Exhibition, realm of Chang Wu Po, in which France came of age, together with tiresome England supervising the industrial era.

Politics was not quite in abeyance. *Marseillaise* flaunted a tall headline, 'Excellent News', explaining that the Emperor was unwell again, recuperating at the lakes and forests of Compiègne. All the world knew that the exalted kidneys were in poor shape, the bladder was obstructed by the stone and elsewhere was impaired by, well, yes, pursuit of women. 'No worse than my old man,' reflected sundry housewives. An anonymous article in *Figaro* related the sickness to His Majesty's incessant guardianship of peace and stability, reiterating his championship of a permanent international assembly, as protection against war, commercial antagonisms, Asiatic laziness. 'Our good Emperor,' upholders of Yes sighed. Others, tavern wiseacres, unemployed agitators, officers of unions licensed by the Liberal Empire, reflected that illness had further implications. Following the setbacks of Mexico and the Prussian advance after Sadowa, the Empress was in the ascent and her husband's maladies must further reinforce the pernicious woman.

Suddenly, as if to dispel confusions, a rumour sped through Paris. 'They're coming.' Repeated in parks and barbers' shops, sedate waiting-rooms and incendiaries' basements, in art galleries, hospitals, cafés, at the Grand Almoner's reception and in ministerial anterooms, 'They're coming.'

They? The Emperor, in whatever state, and the Empress, not from the therapeutics of Compiègne but the delights of Saint-Cloud. Ill-wishers maintained that they had already returned, stealing back by night like felons or absconding *sous-préfects*. But most, citizens and foreigners alike, were expectant and, stalked by that jungaloid metropolitan No and old gibes of Badinguet, wondered about the reception awaiting the Imperial couple. Embers of the Victor Noir upheaval might be raked, perhaps the Emperor's Salon des Refusés might be his final refuge.

'They're coming . . .' The cry could have been on a racecourse, near the finish of the prize event. The summer folk, shoppers and tourists, promenaders, midinettes, peddlers, salesmen, croupiers, dentists' assistants, coal-heavers, bully-boys from Les Halles, sportsmen from outlying villages, knew so well what to expect. The lavishly accoutred outriders on glossy mounts, the helmets and cocked hats, lances and swords, the lilt of court equipages, the theatrical cavalry and armed police, plain-clothes allies amongst the crowds, a detachment of infantry at the rear, all fashioning the image of Olympian power, harnessed to beat down convulsive Titans, any hoots of 'Republic', 'December', 'Vive Gambetta', while, in the high central carriage, huddled behind curtains, Badinguet and his Spanish tart breathed in terror of bombs.

By no means. In noonday heat the populace lined boulevards as they had done for the victorious return of the army from Italy, the state panoply for Victoria and Albert, the Imperial escape from Orsini's bombs, the crowned visitations to the Universal Exhibition, and today, behold, riding through them, unguarded, quite alone, in a small open coupé, no soldier or police in sight, Napoleon and Eugénie, opposite each other, the Prince beside his mother, passing at a leisurely trot to the Tuileries. The Emperor, holding reins with one hand, was raising his tall hat with the other, to continuous cheers, at this distance only a Hermes discerning the dyed hair, rouged cheeks, tobacco-stained teeth. The Empress, under a creamy hat topped with an ostrich feather, waved and smiled, with a shyness perhaps cultivated but which redoubled the acclaim and, delighting all, her son, upright, in Guards' uniform, looked simply what he was, very young, very appreciative, grateful for the operatic chorus of welcome, the fledgeling eagle, Child of Hope.

SIXTEEN

For the wide-awake at Saint-Germain-en-Laye, the night had been a foretaste of Hades, stricken by Rochefort's distorted face, that bubbled forehead, hair like a ravaged thicket, his very toenails claw-like, out of control, his humour distorted. Behind him, the noxious stare of Rigault.

For once, M. Charles-Luc de Massonier, gentleman, who buys flowers for his wife, rich sweetmeats for his children, would have gladly opened the door to M. Que-Voulez-Vous?, whose dexterity could surely succour him from the abomination he had laid for himself.

Two days ago, while he was congratulating his genius on headway made against crass editors and envious, vicious authors, two personages, formally attired but with ruffian faces, had ceremoniously called, not in his vagabond attic but here in the grand mansion he had thought so successfully concealed. With courtesies well groomed but mocking, they had the honour of informing him that, though personally unavailable, M. Rochefort accepted his invitation, his, ah, challenge, and was permitting himself to allow M. Fréderick Gronoy to act in his stead and the esteemed combatants to forgo protocol and decide between them the choice of weapons, bearing in mind the known weakness of the individual who had elected to name himself Tacitus.

Unofficially, the speaker advised pistols, for M. Gronoy was generally acknowledged the most proficient swordsman in France. The venturesome challenger shuddered. He who could stitch time into a metaphor, untie the universe with a subjunctive, summarize God with a laboratory formula and shake the Empire with a couplet, had never held sword nor pistol, only a sporting gun with which he had as yet hit neither game nor rabbit.

He knew about Gronoy. The mighty fighter was also a dramatist and theatrical producer whose tragedy *On the Bridge at Night* Tacitus had savaged without having attended it. He had read later that the work, too advanced for vulgar appreciation, had been praised by Saint-Beuve, Flaubert, Taine and indeed Rochefort and in which the vulgar were bemused by Louis XV asking Cleopatra the time: glancing at her watch she replied, 'Ten thirty, Monsieur.' If this is advanced, Tacitus had expostulated, then philosophy must scrap itself and start again. By now he regretted this.

In Gronoy's production of *King Lear* at the Calypso, most characters were silent, being reduced to huge blocks of wood representing storm, blindness, betrayal, existing only in Lear's maniac head as he gestured on a temple slab, a hovering, stork-like figure, masked, beaked, periodically emitting some indescribable noise, something between a caw and a hoot. Ludicrous trash, Tacitus had judged, posing as metaphysics, the servility of the inferior to the abnormal. Superior criticism, of course, but it would not ingratiate him with his opponent. Malice rises in proportion to one's lack of station. No magnanimity was due from Gronoy, who had protested that critics were boils unjustified by performance, without creditable reasons for existence and in need of extinction.

Furthermore, Tacitus, great critic, was convinced that horror of blood would paralyse his nerve. Fatally.

Now he must rise before ghastly dawn, having told his family of a summons to consultations of considerable importance. They were admiring, envisaging Court presentation, judicial conference, even the military seeking advice. Fortunately, Adelaine had a mind like a bag of feathers into which he could slip anything he chose.

Knock. The carriage had already arrived. In top hat and long, sombre cloak, he was on cue for an absurd melodrama, and most melodramas ended in blood and screams.

In the hallway his younger daughter, still sleepy, in dressing-gown, bare-footed, had loyally awaited him and, finger to her mouth, pressed a posy into his hand. She whispered, 'For Her, For Her Majesty.' It could be his funeral wreath.

Rochefort also had a daughter, Lucille, named in homage to the wife of that eloquent, rather silly Jacobin Camille Desmoulins, who had also perished through too free use of words.

Tacitus shrugged off Desmoulins but was already being driven towards the infernal, alongside his seconds whose names he fumbled to remember. Two Madrid regulars, they had been bribed into this ritualistic farce under strict conditions of silence.

He sensed claws dangling before him: the colours outside were barely awake. No one spoke. The carriage had the confined gloom of a coffin. The pace was funereal, the seconds sat like mutes, faces shuttered, demeanour inauspicious, their suits dingy, visitants from a region black as tongues at the Palais de Justice, the Bourse, the Central Morgue.

His stomach was empty yet filled with pain, as if something of soul was flapping in agony to escape. Visions crowded like sharp ravens: daughters fatherless, wife abandoned, helpless, servants pillaging the house, his attic existence exposed to the hilarity of nobodies, his career extinguished at the instant of taking wing.

Despite the slowness, the Bois was reached too quickly. Alighting, numbed, he soon shivered, seeing a skinny-eyed individual holding a medical bag which looked suggestively heavy. Rigault had arrived, early sunlight glinting on spectacles that guarded hell-cat eyes. Beside him was Raphael Brodie, *môme, mignon*, teacher's violet, misbegotten muddle of gender, pimp of nature. Further away, statu-esque on a slight rising backed by trees, a broad, slit-eyed apparition must be Gronoy, several strangers scattered around him.

All, like himself, were automatons, bowing, hand-clasping, rais-ing hats, mouthing formulae. Despite clear, fresh light he saw only blotches: bushes, clumps of grass, matted trees, furtive sunlight. A superb phrase passed into him, 'the crinkled skein of time', but use-less, wasted, as he trembled by the abyss of timelessness.

He blindly accepted a cold, metallic lump which thoughts shied at naming. His hand could scarcely grasp it, he could not remember the correct position. Around his heart, skin prickled, as if from droplets of chill dew.

On a boulder like a swollen peach-stone a bird, unnaturally dig-nified, was regarding him, beaked with evil interest.

He blinked, suddenly incredulous. He, Charles-Luc de Mas-sonier, the Tacitus of our day, had been abducted from an admiring family, from streets, cafés, salons, from the authority of words and luxury of print, and was being trussed for ignoble execution, under a sky bloodshot and unconcerned from which no intervention was possible. Police would not come and Gronoy was horribly close, surely too close, directly opposite, his posture negligent yet vilely professional, weighing his pistol, balancing it, until satisfied, giving a self-assured nod.

Shocked, Tacitus, renowned atheist, who had risked prosecution by calling the Virgin the most unconvincing female in world fiction, tried to mumble a prayer for deliverance but could then only remem-ber that Pushkin, likewise plugged in a duel, suffered in the hours before death and dreamed of clambering over tall bookcases. Pushkin, fellow poet. No consolation.

Prayer concluded, the deliverance followed. He was standing, pistol raised. Before the bark of command was uttered, Gronoy turned aside to speak to his seconds, leaving his back exposed. At

138

once, involuntarily, as if his arm had been jolted, Tacitus was startled by a shot, his own: his weapon still quivered as Gronoy's outraged face swung back, exclamations and expletives buzzing as such violation of murderous etiquette. To shoot without permission, bad; to fire when the other had his back to you, unheard of, outside even criminal annals. Already Gronoy and his troupe were departing through ferns and saplings, tight with disgust, and after them stalked his own seconds, towards the carriage from which he was inexorably barred.

He was safe, a live man, alone, deserted, amongst bird song, fresh green, the dewy delights of the Bois de Boulogne in summer, ingredients for a lyric not yet feasible.

SEVENTEEN

JOURNALS of all persuasions found impudent merriment in reporting the duel, themselves scarcely uniform. One had an account of a botched assassination, another wove a description of masterly, though unconventional, evasive tactics, a third, actually *Marseillaise*, had a predictable story, wholly spurious, of an attempt to gain publicity by a pedestrian writer, famed to be one whose works were rejected before they reached editorial offices.

No story, however amusing, disturbed June tranquillity. The long sequence of sunlit days was no more monotonous than the hourly progress of a marigold. All days were actually slightly different, fashioned by a master of indolent pleasures under an arc of ethereal calm.

Whoever struggles alone may forget to smile and Tacitus' face, never healthy, was barren, mouth as if tacked down at the corners, eyes often moist. Avoiding customary haunts, he did not risk leaving home, caring only to inform Adelaine that he was victim of slander, for which he would be instituting proceedings of the utmost rigour at his command, very, very considerable.

Later, he must, like Ulysses, retrieve his position. He had half completed a satirical mock-pastoral featuring a giant and a dwarf, rhyming the inadequacies of contemporary politics, subtly allegorical. Designed as invective against Ollivier and the Honourable Men, it could be diverted, though guardedly, against Rochefort and his toadies.

That must wait, while he grappled with ridicule and disappointment. The year had turned sour. The Plebiscite had gone awry, his scathing reportage, brilliant analogies, apposite revelations, had glanced off the State like hail upon iron. More than any Victor Hugo, protected on his island, he had braved assault on the Empire as rape, a *succès de scandale*, had trumpeted 'Moderation is Death', but the Empire was stronger than ever, the concierge's daydream, the stampede of grey clerks, and he was lying pierced, once again at the foot of the ladder.

The great man, while servants came and went with coffee and Adelaine lay reading love-stories, looked back on his life with the melancholy of one bowed by misfortune, by the mischief of rivals more pushing, more unscrupulous, and the throws of malignant but haphazard destiny.

He had often sensed an unlucky star, an intuition beginning perhaps at the lycée, when first jeered at as clumsy, impertinent and fat. Inset in his memory was, following a long, dreary classroom hour, everyone rushing out for a snow fight. Boys and masters released themselves into a whirling exultation, a blind *mêlée* of snowballs, fists, yells, flurries, downfalls. Status was revoked, then revised, teachers and pupils merged in the primitive, stripped to more candid identity as lovers and victims, rivals and abnormalities. Finally, as he stood helpless by the wall, not daring to join in, they had all rushed against him shouting 'Loony Luc, Loony Luc!', breathless, horrible, and after they had dragged him up, shoved him away, a master had laughed, then, dripping and shaking himself, queerly gratified, said to another, 'He'll be the first of them to look old.'

Deserted, in the freezing yard, bleeding, the fury long cooled, Charles-Luc still could not brace himself to move. In both shame and wonder he understood how different he was from anyone else, that nobody liked him.

Little ever changed, nothing was ever quite right. Balding, overweight, short of breath, he did look old. He touched gold and it darkened to lead. Mischances continually sought him: he had signed a very telling, though lengthy, poem, 'Tacitus', and Rochefort inquired how a M. Tacitus could in all honesty explode into such cascades of verbiage.

Smarting, close to tears, he remembered his unexpected invitation to luncheon from no less than the great Duke de Morny, Vice-Emperor, Croesus of racecourses, President of the Assembly, stage-manager of the Second Empire, suave *flâneur*, arbiter of taste, political manipulator, financial pace-setter, connoisseur of bodies, horses' and women's. An invitation from such height must be tribute to Tacitus' inspired dangerous radicalism or to his acute theatrical criticism, for Morny condescended to write slyly amusing vaudeville sketches, collaborating, it was said, with that Second Empire laureate Offenbach. Furthermore, he always maintained polite relations with the Press, even that of the Opposition. Seeing a bribe on offer, a decoration at hand, Charles-Luc had selected his finest suit and drove to Deauville in considerable grandeur. A marvellously panelled door opened before he could ring, footmen bowed almost double, a steward, ornate as a hussar, escorted him along intricate corridors past ancestral portraits: Mother Hortense, Princess Pauline, Princess Elise, Prince Lucien, frail but combative Madame Mère, leaning on a stick, earth-goddess of the Imperial stock, Hercules himself brooding on wonders, a malodorous crew, brewing the national payroll. Eventually he was stationed in a lofty apartment lined with red damask, all converging on a lengthy ovalled dining-table of many covers, a sheen of immaculate linen, glass, porcelain, silver, carnations in slender, gold-tinged vases, pyramids of fruit in coppery bowls.

At once he had the uneasy conviction that he had arrived too early.

In some torment, despite his contempt for the rich, he waited alone until the doors opened again, the farce of obeisant flunkeys was re-enacted and Morny was greeting him with purring delight, implying that he had passed the last decade in eager though civilized hopes of this delightful encounter.

Very bald, bearded in Imperial style, Morny was as fastidiously groomed as his own soapy retinue, in oak-leaf green velvet jacket, violet cravat, lilac waistcoat, his skin, pallid, supple, daintily scented. His eyes, indolent but shrewd, might suspect that the visitor's suit had been hired for the occasion, but his welcome was gracious: 'Now, my very dear fellow . . .'

Morny laid a hand on his arm, leading him to the mighty table prepared as if for a banquet of the gods or, rather, Tacitus was loyal to his principles, supper with the Devil.

Morny's voice seemed beseeching forgiveness. 'You must not be offended if I explain our small, foolish ways. All this cutlery, it looks, does it not, as if we're preparing to resist commotion from our kennels. But no. You must understand, comprehend, that some of us are greedy enough, fortunate enough, to expect a number of courses. Foolish, but there it is. Just watch your neighbours and follow their usages. These clusters of glasses . . . they do service to those of us sufficiently unwise to indulge in a selection of wines . . .'

The door, as if by unseen hands, allowed in a bulging fellow, red-faced, rough-haired, peasant-like, slouching in as if he had a mortgage on the place, a tinge of garlic trespassing on the ducal demesne.

Morny, carelessly graceful, shook hands, then turned back to Tacitus. 'My good man, allow me to present my friend, Count Luis d'Aragon, Marquis of Montmériel.'

So little conformed to its promise. That unexplained luncheon remained a humiliation worse than those inflicted by Rochefort, worse even than the duel lampooned in *Marseillaise* as the Flight of the Cuckoo.

On the last Sunday of June, though still unwilling to risk café sniggers, he did dare the streets, but soon, unexpectedly tired, already surfeited by unpleasant trippers and stinking horses, on what he assumed was a whim, took refuge in a low, pinkish building, near Pont de Carousel, M. de Talmonté's Grand Palace of Wax.

Also, perhaps by one of those coincidences approved by fate, Etienne and his son, street-loving Emile, were standing within part of a group surveying effigies of the Imperial Family, in an atmosphere respectful, indeed devout.

Etienne waited, tolerant, enjoying the boy's absorption. He himself could remember another family in this very vault, King Louis-Philippe and his much larger brood, and searched, though vainly, for some Latin tag to round off solemn reflections on change and decay.

Emile had many feelings. This was an offshoot of the Cavern of Wonders, which, despite several attempts, he had still been unable to find. Daylight paths seemed to lead to the familiar square: the repertoire of shops, market stalls, tiny gardens, decrepit sheds, railway arches, steps receding from stone pineapple-shaped urns, lamp-posts and horse-troughs were apparently unchanged, but, at the last, as though a prize had been snatched away, he was rebuffed. In the square, marvel, there was the arched porch, though unilluminated, drab. But he ran towards it, only to find that he had been fooled; the arch and door were an illusion, flat, painted very realistically on the wall.

It was like gazing up at gargoyles squatting on Notre-Dame: they looked solid, but, however often he counted them, the number was always different, mocking him.

Papa had been noticed by an acquaintance and the two had stepped aside to chat. Meanwhile, the effigies, on the dais behind scarlet ropes and gilded posts, were fully recognizable yet unreal, in dim atmosphere lit from concealed lights as though pursued by darkness. 'Old Nap' had one short leg stuck before him, as if advancing towards you. His big nose was bent, his small eyes foxy, the dull face was not quite yellow but like old marble stained by wet and branched with the famous waxed moustaches. He was smiling but, no, looking again, you doubted it. He was in a sort of uniform, like a waiter in officer's tunic, the gold blocks on his shoulders were like upside-down hairbrushes, jewelled stars, a broad, red, slanted sash were on his front. He was holding a horn cane mounted with a gold eagle. His top half did not exactly fit the lower, like an egg too large for its cup.

The Empress, carrying a small yellow bag, was taller, her blue eyes drooping above small mouth and several chains of pearls. She stood, the catalogue said, in coronation robes once worn by Empress Josephine: wide satin, long train like a waterfall, transparent veil, diamonds everywhere catching the light in all colours, a thin crown glimmered on her conker-brown hair. What tiny shoes! She was quite unlike Maman's photo of her, head thrown back in laughter as, Papa explained, she footed the Spanish fandango. At breakfast, Maman had said something about Spain. Oh yes, a dead queen.

Slight, in a bearskin, holding a sword like a pet, the Prince Imperial. Child of Hope, people said, did not look very hopeful, and, inspecting, Emile felt uneasy, without knowing why.

At night, when all was deserted, these rigid, unblinking figures, like gargoyles and statues, might become live, and he wanted to amuse Papa with a thought of the Empress dancing cancan with who else but blood-dripping Troppmann, but Papa was still talking, perhaps conferring.

An earlier gallery had exhibited the mass-murderer under the guillotine, very composed, clutching a nosegay. Did the gaolers supply it, or admirers, or the priest?

Imagining the Prince Imperial naked on a stool sprayed with sapphires and flushed with Assyrian scents, Emile simultaneously, in double-focus, saw the magician from the lost Cavern smartly transforming the family to a turtle, a cuttlefish and, of course, a red ibis.

He would like to have seen an effigy of Mme Gallifert, known to have one eye blue, the other brown.

Tacitus and Etienne, chosen favourites, had now converged on each other from opposite doors and, as if pulled by the invisible, were standing side by side. Emile only noticed without interest a puddingy lump of a man and again scrutinized the Empress. Tacitus was more interested. Pretty boy, very vulnerable . . . he had to batten down a teasing flake of desire. In the unjust world, he reflected, novice beauty, unconscious charm retain power. Detained by unusual interest, he lingered. Boyhood trespasses on the mysteries of adults, and *not knowing* gave generous scope for inventive fancy and sharp enlightenment, which, as *Lame Pegasus* so amply testified, few had stamina to pursue.

Both man and boy fancied sudden chill from behind, then a sceptical laugh, and both looked round as if at a forbidding touch on the shoulder, but no one was there and the pipes must have gurgled. Emile, recovering, smiled at the flabby gentleman, who did likewise. Each hesitated. Tacitus was about to speak, but Etienne was back and was already departing, hand on the child's arm. As for Emile, he suspected that some waxwork had made a sign.

Leaving the tedious exhibition, Tacitus felt lonely, aware of some missed chance and in need of a friendly face, even that of M. Que-Voulez-Vous? with its questionable in-and-out smile. He was walking with no purpose save fear of stopping, until, near the Pont Magenta, he had sudden premonition, like a half-slip on an icy pavement. Then, the shock was appalling, the apparition of Daniel Réger, a novelist long dead from suicide or malnutrition: Tacitus had considered his obituary too generous. Yet here he was, elderly, falling to bits, slow-moving but unmistakable, and one was helplessly walking towards him, the encounter unavoidable. Almost at once he stumbled on cobbles, jarring his foot, and he cursed the maladroit town planner.

Réger had been so everywhere acknowledged as a good man, honest fellow, that Tacitus had felt impelled to demolish a Réger novel. M. Réger, he insisted, had industry without talent, not promise but blight, demonstrating that literature was under siege from mediocrity, critical obscurantism, the indulgence of manufactured fashion. He had been proud of his final sentence, that most gifts soon wither on the bough, but M. Réger had not been granted even a twig. No other work followed and the man had died in obscurity. Hearing of this, Tacitus had mused that the genuine writers, Baudelaire, even the new comet from Uruguay, Ducasse, were usually unsavoury, jealous as ladies-in-waiting, untrustworthy as tipsters, mean as pawnbrokers, whereas the virtuous Réger mistook haphazard piles of words for literature.

What, at this crisis, was particularly worrying Tacitus was not the opinions he had vouchsafed, these were of course irrefutable, but that he had never actually seen the tiresome novel.

Already they were very close; it was almost worse than facing Gronoy, pistol aiming at his heart, throat strangled, eyes uncontrollable. He attempted to move aside, head averted, yet was unable to do so, was as if strapped. The creased, ageing face gave a smile, faint but friendly, and, tactfully not pausing, Réger bowed gently, raised his shabby hat, then was gone, as though he had never been, so that Tacitus, leaning against a bookseller's shed, managed to convince himself that the meeting had been wholly unreal, product of his own dejection and maltreatment.

Emile too was dejected, without knowing why, save that walking with Papa somehow took everything back to ordinary. Only a glint from the slim, golden traceries of Saint-Chapelle spire signalled from a special Paris now deserted by the grinning gingerbread mammy, Algerian jugglers, the one-eyed youth on red stilts. Instead, churchgoers, grim ladies with bags like dead seal cubs, undertaker husbands, horses stumbling through muck, no one bothering to notice the public letter-writer.

Did Papa think of girls hanging themselves from rafters? Or of stars falling into the sun? Did he stare at things long enough to make them something else? Henriette's wart could thus become a wide wood in which she could lose herself. Maman was a comforting tent, Papa kept his moods in a dark, narrow box. The obvious questions adults never appeared to ask. Does air have holes, what colour is God?

Papa was walking faster. Perhaps he too was beginning to think of dinner, losing himself not in Henriette's wart but in her best dish, Suet Oozing Apple.

EIGHTEEN

CHAMELEON Paris, prismatic City of Light, had the imperishable imprint of a colossus: Arc de Triomphe, Column, the Twin Towers, Dome, the superveillance of N. But there survived warrens of the poor and renegade, subterranean hovels, tenements condemned but still bulging with lives sullen, febrile, hopeless, scorned, demented – lowly entrails ignored by the New Paris. Also, strange sects, mystagogues, unfrocked priests and jobless prophets. Here, Gambetta had no place, Thiers no being, Persigny was unknown, revolutions, plebiscites, reform passed unnoticed. Here, ageing men sold elixirs of eternal youth, claimed descent from Pyramids, Delphi, the lost Jerusalem Temple. Far beneath the newest hospital, the latest hotel, the most gorgeous arcade, mall, esplanade, clustered phrenologists and alchemists strove to transform sand to gold and fashion magic bullets to shoot into Great Ones. Much was flitting, half seen, crepuscular. In small suburban outhouses and wastelands, by inhaling saffron you could see and talk to the dead, who were often too busy to respond. Somewhere, undisclosed, the wise men of the Grand Orient plot world dominion, people are shown their own ghosts and invited to purchase the future. Electricity has not dispersed wraiths seen by agonized savants huddled over cabbalistic texts and gnostic scrapings. In badly printed pamphlets, Napoleon III is reviled as Antichrist, the Prince Imperial as limb of Satan: Jesus is pronounced as born under Virgo, with pessimistic implications.

Newly translated by M. Le Pelletier and much publicized by Abbé Torné, formerly a Bordeaux curé, now a royalist opponent of the Empire, are the prophesies of Nostradamus, endlessly reinterpreted by crones in back rooms and failed professors of language, with cryptic forebodings about 'the Nephew of the Blood' who the prophet, three centuries previously, had discerned purloining the sceptre by processes distinctly shady. Also honoured in this limbo is the Reverend Baxter of Philadelphia, who, the year before Sadowa, had published a treatise identifying Louis Napoleon as the Fruit of Destiny, World Monarch, foreseen by the prophets of Israel and who will fix his seal to a covenant with the Chosen People in the Courtyard of the Millennium. Napoleon III will reign over Europe and America, savagely persecuting Christians, though witnessing the resurrection of the Wise Virgins. He will perish within seven years, fighting at Armageddon, preliminary to the Descent of Christ.

M. Flaubert had declared that when people cease to believe in the Immaculate Conception they will believe in table-turning, and, in heavily curtained rooms, where light and darkness met in tremulous indecision, tables gave messages, upsetting marriages and, from the Other World, disembodied voices revealed that at four o'clock yesterday somebody present had coveted a piece of string. Unseen hands twisted gentlemen's cravats, picked up bouquets, the dead tapped out warnings against plague, crusades, an eye operation; a gaseous outline of the Empress drifted through a locked door without touching ground and, at seances in different cities, a piloted balloon was seen flying from a mass of flames.

The Emperor notoriously followed his star, the pious Empress, with her talent for caricature, hankerings for bull-ring and horses, passion for wild Spanish mountains and Scottish lochs, was addicted to spiritualism. All knew that, in childhood, an elderly nun had assured her that should she enter a convent she would forfeit a throne. Latterly, at Court, an Anglo-American, Mr Home, had demonstrated levitation, conjured up spirits, made objects shiver without touching them, lengthened the head and arms of a medium.

Unlikely to be similarly welcomed was Le Grand Témoin, darkly robed, fierce-eyed, who had informed believers that the Prince Imperial would never be crowned.

The religious had been outraged by Professor Renan's *Life of Jesus*, which had far outsold the Emperor's *Caesar*. It had angered even the godless sovereign, who had fitfully supported him. Enjoyed like a novel, the book had demystified the Saviour, subjecting Virgin birth, miracles, resurrection to elegant but sceptical analysis, offering a Jesus recognizable to the nineteenth-century vogue for science, progress, scholarship. It was intellectual counterpoint to Offenbach, whose light satires translated gods from almighty Olympus to rapscallion Hades, modelled surely on the Tuileries, and mocked the Napoleonic heroes of Greece and Troy. In all, a Hermes décor, though its perspectives did not much intrigue him save as further instances of mortal folly, resentments, the intricate architecture of self-deception. Occasionally, however, he indulged himself by taking a hand.

In the Sixth Arrondissement, overlooking Parc de Jemappes, stood a smallish eighteenth-century hall, once an outhouse of a monastery destroyed during the revolution. It had recently been reborn as the Chapel of World Conference which Amélie had secretly begun attending.

When tribalism becomes civilization and splinters into millions of separate families, secrets start – not only those of adultery, treachery, minor theft, but of disturbing thoughts and vague longings. Loving wife and mother, respectful of convention and established authority, Amélie, in magazine stories, at Mass, in quiet gossip, sought refuge from her own secret, an unspectacular weight of guilt preserved even from her mother, her confessor, even from Etienne.

She had been close to her father, yet, at his death from cholera, had been astonished, then stricken, by feeling not sorrow but relief, an escape from the constant pressures of love. She had lit a candle and, weeping, wanted to dance. Now, years later, she was haunted by terror that, should Etienne or Emile die, she would behave likewise.

Etienne was highly educated, with a Sorbonne degree, no less; he would rise to the top, but he would not understand what she needed and would be harshly disapproving at her presence here. This was her third attendance, after several ventures to churches, discussion groups, ethical lectures, none of which had given real solace.

No lamps or candles were visible. The atmosphere, very warm, was etiolated, obscuring the size of the gathering, though it was observable as largely affluent, despite a few beggars sitting drowsily at the back, perhaps tempted by erroneous reports of free distribution of bread and wine, also of phials of blue ether which, when sniffed, apparently dissolved sky and earth, carpet and jug, into a single flat pattern like a tapestry. A faint smell of wood smoke, both sweet and acrid, hung from the low, raftered ceiling.

Fortunately, none here would recognize her. The well dressed were sitting absolutely silent; near her, even in poor light, knuckles had whitened, eyes were tilted, the breath of the man beside her, grey, distinguished-looking, perhaps a diplomat, had slightly hoarsened. It was, she thought, as though all clocks had stopped; no, as though clocks had not yet been invented. Ahead was a lectern, dully bronze, backed by a dark-blue curtain sprayed with zodiacal signs, together with a cheap-looking sun balanced by a half-moon, beneath a Gothically woven '72', and '18', which she did not understand. From somewhere was a very faint, monotonous hum, overlaid, despite the heavy air, by the twinkling notes of an outside barrel organ, playing a *chanson*, impish in vulgarity.

A murmur crossed the congregation and at the lectern was tall, bearded M. Coster, in cardinal-red gown and black beret, a Creole who liked to style himself 'the Pangs of the Messiah'.

He surveyed them, magisterial, in possession, face and hands gleaming as if from within.

'I wish you to imagine Nothing. Nothing at all. Empty your minds utterly.'

His deep voice tolled, very calm, not allowing much time to consider nothing or anything. Amélie frequently lost direction, oppressed by heat and wood smoke, hearing the words as if through tissues of variable quality.

'Let us be precise in our terms. In ancient Judea, for instance, "Son of Man" denoted not exclusive divine paternity but a generalized man of righteousness.' Austere as a cromlech, he looked down at them as though not unrelated to remarkable birthright.

'There is substance in beliefs even more ancient. That the visible world was created by angels, but angels destructive or at best inexpert, bored or wilful. Therein originated evil. Impatient, God, in his magnitude, resolved to destroy their handiwork, perhaps replace it with his own creation, which by definition would be sinless, perfect. Eventually, however, he was merciful and adopted Jesus to teach mankind better ways, expel the gods of impulse and will, create a new understanding. The Resurrection must be properly understood as not the end of Jesus' mortal existence but as his initiation into spiritual life, at baptism. There he acquired the higher awareness he signified as the Kingdom. But, listen well . . .' His severity caused an uneasy stir, Amélie's placid face looked older, strained, that of the woman she would become in old age, lonely. She heard new and disquieting words. 'Jesus, though by no means sinful, was nevertheless imperfect. A being of electrifying energy, he yet lost stamina in a disappointment which goaded his vanity to despair. Like God, he lacked patience and retired too soon. Evading execution by means still disputable and indeed disputed, he journeyed deep into Asia, practising as shaman or sorcerer, yet, at behest of conscience, often wishing his magic, his vital energy, to fail.

M. Coster, Pangs of the Messiah, paused, looked around, then was more conversational, even casual. 'This energy is symbolized by the colour green, visible only to initiates, the selfless believer, as a green flame. Unless he seeks it with total being, it is inert as a lamp before ignition. You, even the proudest amongst you, must seek, seek wholeheartedly, and find within yourselves force, powerful as electricity, to which it has elemental affinities. It has no knowledge of your name, no apprehension of your personality, occupation, superficial resources. It ignores earthly allegiances. To call it Father, Saviour, let alone Queen or Emperor, is diabolically misleading, servility towards imbroglios of self-delusion, purveyors of falsification, like rotten coinage.' The words rolled out, sibilant, oiled, with immaculate precision. 'Such elemental power can only await your prayers, your complete concentration of essence, the vibrations of selfhood which Plato named soul, and the Mysteries of Isis, Osiris, Apollo and Koré so well understood. Seek, and you will indeed find.' He smiled, as if he had made a joke, as perhaps he had.

They sighed with abstruse satisfaction though, unable to attempt complete concentration, Amélie only groped for her handbag, sat upright, attracting notice. A comely woman of some means, unescorted, must, for the first time, be realizing her true self. But listen.

'There are keys to understanding lying bright on the ground before you. Not all of you have stooped to pick them up. Remember, no one, nothing, hears you but your own self. All of you live alone, in the eye of truth. Far away are those who have perfected both understanding and energy. They transcend the false consciousness represented by the dynasties and badges, votes and manifestos, newspapers and slogans, the gross larder of Europe. I promise you this: one of us, before the sun has set, will meet one of the Perfect. A

hand will wave, a circle be traced on the air. You, or you, or you . . .'
he pointed, indiscriminately, 'will be invited to step into it. You will
enter enhanced clarity, free of time and space, you will be as gods.'
Amélie was failing to qualify; always, at serious moments, something small distracted her, like a picture hung just below eye level.
Were she a man, she would be thrilled to her limits at obeying an
order personally delivered by the Emperor. Her will was leading her
astray, back to her grandmother's stories which she had told little
Emile at bedtime as he lay, happy, seeing old kings lost in bat-ridden
but enchanted castles, the moo-cow dairy maid, the hare who spoke
riddles, Jeanne d'Arc and the witches of Domrémy. A little girl, she
herself had seen a wishing well in which she had dropped a stone and
heard nothing, then she dropped a flower and heard a soft tinkle.

Faces creamed, painted, in veils, fashionable hats, rich earrings,
were thrust forward, straining for the green flame, the silver keys.
The barrel organ had ceased, the underlying hum had quickened,
the voice continued, as though a cello at its deepest was sustaining a
single note, very occasionally pausing for a drum tap.

'When all is well, gold and silver are flowing, then, be assured,
ruin approaches. The Church, supported by the State, has befogged
the world by terrible, even criminal error. Consider, my dear friends,
the long generations of agony bred from Jesus' alleged threats of
Everlasting Punishment. Yet, and listen well, that *everlasting* originated in what very few of us have realized, the mistranslation of a
Greek word meaning "for a considerable time", and *punishment* is
more correctly rendered "the correction of error". So be not afraid.'
His hands approached each other slowly, effectively, parodying
ecclesiastical piety, his face hung with the sombre knowledge access-
ible to righteousness, or to a messenger of deceit, master of imper-
sonation who, to his own unobtrusive glee, makes a milk jug gleam
into a chalice, leads pilgrims towards a cliff, transforms paper to
doves. 'I tell you this, that gods, however powerful, require not

witless praise, flaccid adoration, but help, your help, my help, in thought, in deed, in resistance to primal germs of destruction.'

His smile must be of universal benefit, but Amélie needed home, its familiar contentments and possessions, old letters and nursery books in cupboards, a cracked Chinese cup of her father's, the routine of locking against thieves, disputing with M. Reinach the grocer, warming Etienne's slippers, worrying about Emile, his quiet ways and self-control.

Unexpectedly, she had a sensation of barely precedented horror, as if she were in the path of a roaring, firelit train, lurid, unstoppable, while she stood unable to move. She closed her eyes, M. Coster's voice scarcely reached her through a spasm of faintness, and she was convinced that if she risked seeking his face she would see only an open-mouthed skull.

NINETEEN

HERMES still lingers, detained by no vision, no expectation of novelty but by the small talk of existence. In his sojourns below, he is something less than a god while remaining more than a man. In his very laxity, his partial indifference, is his abiding strength, curiosity. Curiosity can nourish some feeling, toying with perishable specimens, even provoke hopes, seldom fulfilled. Fooling a puffball scribbler or dreamy schoolboy blows nothing into eternity, scarcely piles Pelion on Ossa.

That a god has no limits can be as restricting as mortality, by lacking challenge and grief, perplexity and intoxication. Bacchus had been a human impostor, an attempt to deify a debased notion of awareness, in which men treated women as buckets, women raved themselves into witlessness. Hermes is singular in loving the half seen, the barely apprehended, the gaps which he himself can fill. Particularly delightful are rims, horizons, parentheses, meltings, in their suggestive evanescence more substantial than world rangers and the Twelve Labours. Sharper than a sword, more powerful than a howitzer, are the confidential aside, artful hint, conspiratorial whisper and flattering *bonhomie*. He could teach restraint to fashion houses who, behind acres of glass, display too much, imply too little.

The deficiency of cavalcades and hecatombs, expeditions to Thrace or Suez, voyages that take the longest route to reach harbour, are too explicit, like flags. Heroes at their most vainglorious remain flickering, meandering: goldfish in a bowl. The past, in the eye of Hermes, is always the same, unalterable by historians and poets: the more the revolutions, the more glaring the façades, the less perceptible are the changes they promise. The heroes are identical. Ostracism, plebiscites, last charges are vain efforts to break the circle. Within the most feared satrap or famed senator hides the immemorial cowherd who slips on a turd.

Hermes' amusement, when discontented with serenity, is in observing the trivial outbidding the momentous, the momentous itself born of the insignificant or overlooked. A moody child gaping at commonplace magic is briefly Icarus, soaring aloft, the woman hired to cross naked a busy street achieves more than braided puppets, though, like them, she is enslaved to contingency. Through inhalings, sippings, sniffings, humans imagine themselves on Olympus, impervious, eternal, star-blessed.

Few mortals observe what is occurring, to others, to themselves. All is illusion. A haughty advocate strides into à l'Auberge Gratin and orders not his usual *fin* but champagne. He is handed a mug of water, smiles gratefully. 'Ah, just the right year. Altogether . . . what I required.'

Divinity, with powers over words it seldom bothers to wield, being most fully alive not in language or action but in music, is trapped neither in flesh nor consistency, though vulnerable to memory of Uranian Chaos, titanic collisions of matter, primal swirl without shape or language which gods can obliterate but which inexorably claws at mortals in what they call dreams, hallucinations banked down by light, thrusting up after dark, and wherein they see underworld monsters, fearful hybrids, gigantic waters.

Gods and mortals alike are offspring of Chaos, thus intertwined. Like athletes, many gods over-specialized, in war, adventure, sexuality, meditation, ultimately completing their obsessions and being left with the static, the boring, the purposeless, so that they dwindled to symbols and nuances. He himself specialized in nothing, thus enjoying delicacies of experiment, of dawdling, a half-master of many trades.

Certain gods became too dependent on human love and lost fine edge, like a Caesar posing as immortal, sniffing incense and falling flat on his face. Others, freed from preoccupation with Earth, still insidiously controlled lives, leaving men to whimper midway up a cliff, opening the wrong door, signing a fatal treaty. No human is free, being tied to dreams, mayfly authority, cardboard beauty. In rare initiation, a mortal has taught that whoever imagines that he acts from his own free will is dreaming with his eyes open.

Some have so developed as to realize that in total pointlessness is total freedom, the space which permits enjoyment of all sources of being. Freedom to gather meaning from ritual, then enlarge it to a story and move on, towards that divinity which has no belief, tradition, dogma. A true god is simply himself or, for some, itself. To conceal this truth, to hide from fears, people spoil life with incantations and sacrificial fumes, attempt to repulse fate with oaths, loyalties, drums, the sorcery of numbers. Through laughter, grotesque bravado and the irregularity that rejects paralysis of symmetry. From foreknowledge of unavoidable death, yet ever resisting it, mankind reaches its supreme achievement, Tragedy, beyond the scope even of gods, though to them it is alien, absurd, unbecoming. Cravings for colour, news, the extraordinary so evident in Paris, have the wonder, pathos, gullibility of childhood, in which children are nearest the gods, perceiving a chair grinning, a gun about to laugh, a frown on a waterfall. Few of their elders stand upright: when one brays the rest bray, the cripple yearns to lead the dance, fire allures. The tribes surge to lying oracles, to trophies and danger, they howl for the squaring of circles. Earth remains in love with stories. The hero dragging another through blood and dust outside a city, a sombre prince finding the universe within himself as he plots revenge. That golden

N topping a green dome is the deposit of infinite stories: of calculated killings and arresting gestures, of loss and possession, defeat, and exquisite days of return. Gods are themselves stories, distorted, travestied, transmuted.

Mankind invents its own story, wayward tribal memory is condensed to history and years. Blocked by death, it clasps memories as staging posts, survival tactics, to warn, encourage, unite. Inhabiting timelessness, a god requires no such tactics; he bothers to recall only a few salients, peaks shimmering ,answers given without questions, certain jokes. QTLZ. Smooth clouds may part, revealing a Carthage, a Paris.

Hermes sighs. His curiosity in the subspecies has limits. Railway accidents, sinking ships, a hospital in flames finally affect him less than the flight of an imaginary eagle. Success, guilt, ambition, like colour, are poor substitutes for dreamless, untroubled being. Lacking ambition, he needs no accomplice, is sufficient to himself, within what mortals dimly perceive a soul, what the clean but absurd Chinese term *tzo*. The soul, imagination, has intermittent hold on Earth, chiselling, through arts, sciences, language, towards Zeus the Light, syntax beyond alphabets, yet envisaging little more than sirens, singing rocks, stumbles towards brilliant gardens, saviours that had never been.

Hermes orders wine he will not drink. He surveys quiet citizens who, to be taken seriously, can reach for the knife. He is the trickster, quicksilver messenger who bears no tidings, an immortal of nothingness needing no favours from a Paris or Berlin, scornful of power, yet, by a nod, an ambiguous witticism, an indistinct murmur can twist history. After some farewell gift to fair France, a stylish irony, a smirk at correct procedures, one last but faultless trick, he must depart.

TWENTY

JULY. Caesar's month. Paris lowered its head in dreamy supinity, tranquil sea-visions. Holidays were at hand, rejuvenation of the Empire, of France, had been celebrated, contentment wafted smiles and fragrancy over cities, hitherto restless, under the protecting wings of the Plebiscite. Troops were to break the Le Creusot strike. By night a vast, parchment-hued moon hung above a metropolis almost satiate with pleasure, fantastic illuminations seeming a legacy of the Universal Exhibition. Even in the skeleton regions of the poor, the rags and blouses, shawls and skirts drying in sunlight could be mistaken for the flags of recently paid mercenaries. Politics scarcely intruded, though, within a weary debate on army affairs, during which the Opposition denounced the expense of unnecessary reforms, Hermes overheard M. Ollivier, joint-architect of the Liberal Empire, address history.

'The government has no uneasiness whatsoever. Wherever we look, we can discern not one disturbing question arising. At no time in human records has the maintenance of European peace been more absolutely guaranteed. European cabinets acknowledge respect for treaties. We ourselves have developed Liberty, to assure Peace, and the accord between Nation and Sovereign has, with overwhelming popular assent, established no less than a French Sadowa.'

From across the Channel, a senior British official added a codicil:

'I have never, during my long experience, known so profound a lull in foreign affairs.'

Tacitus, who had somewhat recovered, was forced to agree. The lesson to France from stodgy, roast-beef-and-sour-ale England was that exciting government is usually bad government. He himself disliked summer lull and political apathy and listened with impatience to a chanteuse in an almost deserted café, humming a trite Offenbach ditty:

> The only true bliss
> On Mount Olympus
> Is sleep.

Instead of belabouring the fraudulent Plebiscite, exposing the true state of the ex-President's health, newspapers were prodigal with inessentials which nobody bothered to read. Yesterday, *Temps* spread itself with information that in seventeenth-century Philadelphia Dr Benjamin Rush testified that leprosy had changed Africans from white to black, in Rheims an alabaster Virgin was bleeding and weeping, so that spoilsport cranks were announcing that in earlier times, particularly on the Mediterranean Littoral, such manifestations from a carved Isis or Mary Magdalen presaged danger.

God damn such arcane verbiage, which should provoke derision harsh as a flapping tent. People should be analysing the effect on armaments of the Creusot strike and the significance of the soldiers' No. Instead, nothing at all, mere slumber under a torrid sky.

Manfully, he kept to his post, newspapers accumulating around him. Only in Spain passions were still aswirl, keeping the throne empty. Paris, however, was disinclined to contemplate the ancient enemy; French appetite for glory was stifled by a summer simultaneously drowsy and vulgarly, raucously cheerful. Tuileries fountains were more jewelled, trees in Jardin d'Hiver more glistening, more generously outflung. Foreigners swarmed, for, with its exhibitions, shopping developments, parades, the Empire was substituting tourism for travel. Seine *bâteaux-mouches* were gay with pleasure-seekers in flimsy skirts, straw hats, flannels, girls exclamatory as geese, their pomaded escorts extravagant with petty cash, as they alighted for picnics in meadows, on shaded islets, for wine and pastry at bankside inns. People entrained for seasides, quiet villages, some to mountains, all suffused with what Tacitus had described, more than once, as loose flashes of spirit, disgusted though he was by this gushing overflow of amiability.

Reading further, he learnt without interest that numerous north German professors had been seen in France with large notebooks, some of them contemplating the Alps and complaining of their lack of symmetry.

The eye continually turned, not only to legendary peaks and immemorial rivers but to common toys. Loosed by inarticulate hopes, kites darted and wheeled, soared and pranced, scrawling infinite patterns, wild signatures on cloudless blue. Balloons floated above towns and hamlets, tinted dabs on honeycomb air, drifting above Norman sands and the rocks of La Rochelle, above white villas of Nice and the breakers of Biarritz. In Paris, one had lodged itself atop the Column, dangling from Hercules, supreme N, as though he too had snatched fruit of the season.

The hour was for the sailing of midget boats, the watching of puppets, the races on grass and shore. All girls were marigolds, all boys hussars. Adults lapsed into their childhoods, surrendering to never-never balm offered by park and avenue, woodland, sky, to statues of shy though undraped virgins and snobbish, elegant unicorns. Of satyrs, sly and grinning. Trees, awash with green flecked with gold, were arcadian: graceful parterres guarded the summer from winter spies. While children played, quarrelled or clamoured for Latinville's spectacular ice cream, Maman and Papa gossiped, absorbed tunes, recalled moonlit assignations, real or imagined, jaunts to golden fields and merry vineyards: demure First Communions, rose coronels on cooling brows, whispers at dewfall. As students they had disputed, fought, embraced in dram shops, promised themselves wonders, built superb bridges to the horizon. In every quarter were the pledges and nothings of lovers, the soundless explosions of dreams.

Official processions carried remnants of fairytale: the prince, the swan maiden, the enchanted trumpet, the cheeky irrepressible drummer boy who wins half the kingdom. Touched with exotic gleam, great yachts glided through shimmering Apollonian calm, slid across flat seas towards the ethereal, those realms glimpsed in Louvre sunset masterpieces, read in showy romances, where lovers lay naked on islands, sharp-eyed cupids lounged under urn and pillar, centaurs peered into sunset orchards. Actually available in this season of butterflies and lazy afternoons were tantalizing visions of bathing parties, indiscreet couplings, artists' ateliers with their unfinished landscapes and tortured saviours, their naked models.

The warm stillness underlying summer frolic was so delicately poised that it had odalisque languor which was yet so intense that the fall of a petal had the impact of a shot. Marvels of noon and dusk, twinkling paradises, old songs, distances mysterious, rapt, wistful, and, out of untroubled sunlight, the smiling promise, 'Tomorrow'.

In Paris, twiddling his cane like a Yankee, Hermes gave his wink to slutty Graces, tilted his hat at whatsoever and sidled back into invisibility.

TWENTY-ONE

THAT wink was sufficient. A cipher passed between Madrid and the Spanish Embassy, leaked or sold, appeared in the international Press with sensational impact. With formal approval of King Wilhelm of Prussia and the Spanish Cortes, Prince Leopold of Hohenzollern, son of Prince Karl Anton, cousin of Wilhelm, younger brother of the new King of Romania – a kingdom regarded as Napoleon III's creation – had been offered, had accepted, the throne of Spain.

The July idyll was splintered, as if by Olympian thunderbolt. Black headlines touched off uproar throughout France. The threat was brutally naked. To endure a Spanish Empress in France itself was bad enough; to have Prussians ruling on either side of you was intolerable, to be vetoed at whatever cost. In the Senate, the Duke de Gramont elicited unrestrained applause as he rose, attempting a stance Homeric in stark simplicity.

'The Hohenzollern candidature must be renounced. Otherwise, all of us know how to fulfil our duty, without weakness, without hesitation.' An unconfirmed report in *Figaro*, additional fuel, ascribed to Count von Bismarck the Prussian retort: 'Insolent and bumptious beyond anything we could expect.'

The French Senate's fervour was repeated in the Assembly. For the Opposition, Jules Favre began pleading for caution, for time to await official confirmations, but protests, then cat-calls silenced him with caustic reminders of his taunts at the Emperor's apparent inertia after Sadowa, the Left's unending denunciation of Niel's army reforms, the futile waste of energy by factional viciousness.

That afternoon, *Siècle* reported that the British minister in Berlin had already appealed to old Wilhelm's wise and distinguished magnanimity, so that he should refuse to sanction Leopold's claim.

Political tit for tat exposed rifts within the Opposition. A few republicans called for peace at any price, maintaining that working men owed no allegiance to dynasties or national states and were above patriotism. In contrast, Thiers, hitherto suspicious of all belligerent policies, demanded immediate cancellation of the Spanish offer and was backed by Felix Pyatt in *Vengeur* and Jules Wallès in *Cri des Peuples*.

The majority reiterated that the Honourable Men must cleave to necessity, France safeguard her interests, her mission, indeed her very existence. The Empress was said to have exclaimed in fury, 'We must finish it.'

Yet how serious was this? Could it be but a tonic for the lolling summer, a newspaper scare, a carnival scherzo, a frivolous galop or a trap designed not only by Prussia but by those strenuous Frenchmen who favoured 'certain moments'? While groups argued in cafés, on quays, in provincial communes, Gramont, descending to the Assembly, was offered his opportunity to decide history. Novice statesman, short-tempered, reputedly Eugénie's protégé, partial to Austria where he had been ambassador, he again spoke. At first nervous, stammering, he gained strength through exasperation at a taunt of cowardice.

'We have no intention of interfering in Spanish affairs, but do not believe that respect for a neighbour's rights obliges us to allow a Foreign Power to disturb the entire European balance by installing a prince of its own on the throne of Charles V, to our own disadvantage, endangering French concerns and . . .' he paused, not losing direction but for effect, 'and French Honour.'

Honour. Explosive word, epithet loaded with immemorial associations. Unease stirred amongst the most pacific, chill wind over a cornfield. While belligerents renewed their approval, none could have forgotten that at the Universal Exhibition a prize had been won by Herr Krupp's fifty-ton monster, the largest gun in the world.

Gramont, his effect successful, continued, not conversational but heated, finally declamatory, inspiring a dense crescent of beards, whiskers, startled eyes: faces perspiring, alarmed, angered, excited, a few thoughtful. Then the minister lowered his tone, slowed, adopted gravely statesmanlike demeanour.

'We nevertheless entertain hopes that none of these fearful expectations will occur, will indeed happen. To avert it we rely, we place reliance, on the wisdom of the entire German people and on the renowned good sense of our Spanish neighbour. But . . .' He fondled the small word, a word that could nevertheless demolish a continent, consign Great Powers to oblivion or, some must be thinking, to glory. 'But if the reverse should happen, with the support of yourselves and the whole French nation, we will without hesitation or weakness, recognize our . . .'

He was interrupted by a spontaneous shout, 'Duty.' Honour and Duty, brothers-in-arms. Gramont bowed, at the clatter of stamps and bravos, though he might have noted that Gambetta, very pale above his black beard, had remained seated, mute, fists clenching and unclenching. Favre, looking about him, seemed undecided. Thiers, grey coxcomb quiff uncombed, sat hunched and apart, light settling on his spectacles with a suggestion of blindness, concealing whatever calculations were struggling behind them.

Gramont departed to the Senate. In late afternoon, after a roll of declarations, infuriated, menacing, rhetorical, Emile Ollivier, meticulous in frock-coat and black cravat, at last marched to the tribune, dark-bearded, youngish in skin and profile, in speech and posture never quite shedding his dry, legalistic training.

'The government passionately desires Peace.' Of all those present, he was the least passionate, the man with the reins. 'But . . .' again that impish word, delivered without emphasis, 'but Peace with Honour.' An attempt to renew the cheers was stifled by a short gesture of impatience. 'If war becomes necessary, the government will take no action without your consent, for our regime is strictly parliamentary.'

The atmosphere at once cooled, the words disappointing, too political, touched with a suspicion of a shifting of responsibility within sentiments impeccably democratic. Also, another small word had at last been cast into the open. War. Ollivier said no more, was already disappearing, leaving behind a silence so unusual in this place that it was eerie, even Thiers unwilling to be first to shatter it.

With each hour now a gala performance, crowds were parading around the Tuileries, Luxembourg, Palais Bourbon, chattering good-humouredly, collecting newspapers, grabbing rumours that flitted everywhere, many perhaps invented by interested parties then printed as facts. 'Heard the latest?' With papers outspread, people walked into each other, knocked against barrows, prams, lampposts. The Emperor, enclosed in champagne brilliance at Saint-Cloud, was probably lying in dazed incomprehension, preferring pain-killing drugs to a major operation, the Empress had recovered her youth and had written a poem about storm-tossed seas, Count von Bismarck had removed his investments from Berlin to London, the Prince Imperial had been seen at a mirror flourishing a sword. A sword too heavy for him, unkind voices joked.

Most agreed that the Court was divided between war and peace, which, in the country, submerged, or should submerge, issues that confused the Left and enflamed the Right. The Sovereign's attitude remained opaque, doubtless stranded betwixt his mild nature and resounding name, the far-seeing and contingent, and the tortuous ramifications of N.

No ultimatum to withdraw the Prussian candidature had yet been dispatched. Another rumour asserted that troops were surrounding Bismarck's ministerial quarters, against indignant, peace-loving Berliners, though a special correspondent in *Jaune* wrote that the French Embassy had already been sacked.

In Paris, dragoons returning from customary exercises at Longchamp were cheered rather hysterically, as if on rebound from Austerlitz. In *Moniteur*, a retired general, hero of Crimean and Italian campaigns, decorated for gallantry in Algeria, Indo-China and in Mexico where, almost single-handed, he had unsuccessfully defended a barren hillside, diagnosed the prime factor in French invincibility: Prussia indeed vaunted its needle-gun, but, urged for years by the Emperor, himself, like his uncle, a master of gunnery – had he not provided the Swiss with an artillery manual composed by himself? – France, under his guidance, had now adopted the irresistible *mitrailleuse* for the artillery and the *chassepot* for the riflemen. Such a gun as Herr Krupp's monster was a grotesque museum piece, bulk without relevance, Neanderthal in immense uselessness, for Sadowa had proved that modern war was no longer a matter of prolonged sieges and long-range bombardment but short, swift battles designed by impudent genius, fought with panache – French qualities never in short supply.

If reassurance was needed, here it was, though, as dusk gently flopped into the parks and boulevards, people surreptitiously stole to priests, astrologers, backstairs oracles, learning further instances of the wayward affairs of gods and men: a flood had occurred on Mars, an earthquake on Saturn, a sunspot had convulsed the nervous system of the universe, unusual planetary conjunctions loomed with effects not yet quite ready to be divulged. Horoscopes of the notables were consulted, even sold, showing exactitudes of astral detail but inconclusive conclusions: churches welcomed more crowded confessionals.

In a quayside brothel a youth, undeniably French but with a German name, hitherto popular, was thrown through plate-glass by red-light Maries and bumboat Sylvies, for the slur on patriotic sensibilities.

From his attic, the Beloved, limping, stick-bound, mocked by ragged urchins as Uncle All Your Years, was begging subscriptions for animals likely to suffer, particularly horses. For once, he provoked irritation, many calling his activities ill-omened and were incensed when a horse, distracted by the hubbub, fatally kicked a child. Tension lifted only when a woman, the old fellow's assistant and an assiduous collector of mynah birds, embezzled his funds and vanished, leaving the birds to be sold as scrap.

Café Battur, Café Riche, Café Montpellier, Café Anglais, Café Graz, Closerie des Lilas all seethed with prophets, political soothsayers, amateur strategists alike wrangling over *chassepot* and needle-gun, enthusing over the Emperor's explosive rockets at Henvault, his new carbines and omnipotent ironclads.

'Rapid advance over the Rhine. South Germany will rush to us for protection against the Bismarck boys. Count them . . . Bavaria, Württemberg, Nassau. Unfortunate Hanover bristles with anger against Prussia. Austria will not have overlooked Sadowa. Watch and wait, as the Saviour enjoineth.'

At the Procope factions tore at each other as they had at the Plebiscite, each weighing its chances. French victory in the field would be republican defeat at home. At early reverses, the Empire would collapse.

Heads and shoulders, proletarian, *declassé*, or unclassifiable, pulled closer, as if over an extraordinary suit of cards. Routine toasts were gulped to Mégy and Beaury, nonentities imprisoned for the alleged Plebiscite plot against the Emperor's life, but thoughts were elsewhere, wondering what was really afoot, how great the chances, how real any danger. With vestigial childhood memories, atheists remembered archaic images. The Bridegroom cometh, Last Days are at hand.

Dr Clemenceau had looked in, scowled, accepted a *fin*, carefully forgot to return it, uttered an excruciating pun, then hurried away, beset by practical affairs.

Arguments continued. 'From Spain comes nothing good. Eugénie . . . interfering baggage!'

'Beauty ripe for a tumble, eh! Hunkered!'

'It's odd . . . I can never think of a Prussian in a latrine . . .'

'For my part, I never think of him anywhere else.'

'The generals . . . that oaf MacMahon. Only the back of his head suggests he was ever young. Bazaine scarcely dotted himself with glory in Mexico. Looks like a shifty collier, though I hear the ladies . . . as for Boubaki . . . almost worse than that madman Plon-Plon.'

Raoul Rigault, for once not at the Madrid, was listening carefully, dominating by saying little. Despite the humidity of packed, unfumigated bodies, his face was glacial. Neither liked nor trusted, he was nevertheless accepted, like weather, like news unpleasant but significant.

'When the tocsin sounds . . . well, spirit of folly, hold up your head!'

'You think there's real possibility of war?'

'Very unlikely. They'll not dare risk it. A bit of bluster, a few cunning bulletins. Nothing more. The Bourse won't allow it. But I do feel tempted to go down on my knees to Our Lady of Victories.'

'Prussian victories?'

'But of course.'

Greasy, shabby, Bohemian groups, together with a few

respectable foreigners or provincials drinking the best wine and imagining themselves heroes of Balzac and Dumas, were tempted to raise glasses to King Wilhelm and the opportune Prince Leopold, though none was willing to be the first. After an awkward pause, a wag recalled the Emperor's exclamation, while commanding at Magenta. 'A victory, is it? And I was about to order retreat!'

'That pox-filled old Machiavelli . . . that pike . . .'

'Robespierre once said . . .'

'Robespierre!' Rigault at last deigned a few words, 'His day was done almost before it began. His greatness consisted only in the size of the chances he missed.'

Dismissing the Incorruptible with a flea in his ear.

Next day's sky was even hotter, the sun at aching height. Water carriers continuously flushed the streets, ice cream and orangeade were quickly exhausted, in the fields peasants would be cursing, watching for rain. Everywhere, national flags were draped around N. News mingled truth and falsehood indiscriminately. Hanover, annexed by Prussia after Sadowa, infuriated by the imposition of conscription, was pleading for French assistance. At the Sorbonne professors were maintaining that the French Emperor, though an internationalist, nevertheless, as a preliminary, had always supported Polish and Italian independence and was now, against apparent evidence, secretly conniving with Bismarck for the single German Reich dominated by Prussia. Many pondered this, few believed it, while inhaling 'the latest' with insatiable appetite for barely coherent fantasy, for unreal sorts of fulfilment. Most clung to N and the eagles, to the Saviour of Society, both scared and fascinated by red dripping jowls not only of a Man of December but of Troppmann. In the outer suburbs, blue-bloused youth gangs were tramping the pavements, truculent, waving clubs, demanding money for 'volunteers'. Wagers were being laid on how far the *chassepot* would outrange the needle-gun.

On pavements, strangers accosted each other, sometimes embracing.

'They say . . . Algerians, real blacks, will be brought in.'

Swiftly, in the general flurry of excess – at times spiced by M. Que-Voulez-Vous? as he sauntered through taverns, public gardens, riverside greens – the drinkers were exclaiming that Algerians had actually been seen, massed in dusky splendours outside Gare de l'Est, preparing to entrain for the Rhine, savagely resolute to defend Empire and *la Patrie*.

Such stories thrilled yet were also unnerving, part of the repertoire of M. Que-Voulez-Vous?, whose lop-sided grin could be sensed in many sites simultaneously. Within knife-sharp atmosphere and imperturbable sunshine, mystagogues might have gazed at a simile in the ether, not genial but sardonic. In a leafy, artificial bower secluded behind place Saint-Jacques, robed purple as an Indian sun-bird, a celebrated healer, Magister Mundi, called for vengeance on Sodom, and the Chapel of World Conference swarmed with devotees, though Amélie was too agitated, too preoccupied with ironing Etienne's reservist uniform, to join them.

In many such places, star-spangled, zodiacal, toxic, anxious women, furtive men, bearded archangelic elders, transmuted arcane fables of capricious rulers emptying their own cities, expelling their subjects to death by thirst, claw, fang, of gods transforming beautiful boys to hyacinths. Hushed tones revived the tale of a caliph rolled in his most sumptuous carpet and beaten to death by Mongol fanatics. Much quoted was the Trojan Horse, evoking oppressive unease. A voice from the air announced to bowed heads that Jeanne d'Arc was deceased but not dead. Suddenly recollected, seldom mentioned but which had been unconsciously secreted in worry, even fear, was that cryptic QTLZ, hermetic signal, which agitated the thoughtful by implying that politics, institutions, patriotism, the very universe if not rubbish were at least nonsense.

Merging with war talk and hallucination were the customary apparitions of summer carnival. A whey-faced clown in yellow cloak and winged, crimson shoes, eyes like electric lamps and apparently lidless, capered at sundown between the massive ferns and coppices of the Bois, in and out of the last sun-slats, improvising lightning pirouettes, a frantic will-o'-the-wisp, now here, now there, leaping high, descending with unnatural slowness, his joy mirthless in striped, dwindling lights.

Such immoderation was unthinkable at the Philosophical Institute in rue des Archives where, undeterred by clamour and moist flesh, gentlemen in formal attire continued, somewhat manneredly, an inevitable discussion under pictures of Bossuet, Descartes, Voltaire, Condorcet, and busts, vague in the subdued lighting, of Plato, Epicetus, Aristotle, Marcus Aurelius. Waiters stole as usual between the settees, armchairs, little tables, distributing coffee and liqueurs. Fresh flowers and women would be a unlikely as porcupines and children an abomination.

The talk was punctilious in courtesy, exact in definitions, agreeable in exchanges.

'Jesus' doctrine of indiscriminate love I find, at this instant, unsatisfactory, indeed repellent. In a word more temperate, injudicious. It is discrimination that refines barbarism to civilization, brings culture to supreme pitch, virtually renders progress no longer necessary. Denied it, we wallow in intellectual mire. To enfondle at random muck-swillers and cattle-drovers, Prussian pork-butchers, sins against all prospects of global enlightenment and can be said to be part of what I have elsewhere termed the slow methodology of evil.'

'I can refrain from disputing that, any jot of it. But, to the more immediate . . . the howls and cravings we are being forced to hear, not far from these very windows, tempt me to wonder, no, to reconsider, those Spartans dooming themselves at Thermopylae. But for what? A vision at best frail? A gesture thrown into the annals? An effort to preserve Hellenic disunity and win a move against Athens, the jabber-pot of the classical world? Personally, I would have preferred Persian order, regularity, calm to the upheavals of Greek cities, each its own font of irresponsibility.'

'You exaggerate, my dear friend, as you always do. It is part of your charm. But, for my own part, I am no pronounced disciple of our reclusive Gustave Flaubert – how little are we inclined to address him as Gus – . Nevertheless,' the old man was speaking defensively, as if by mischance he had encountered a Greek, not monstrous but cunning, 'nevertheless, he has set his mind, indeed his intelligence, to something which has preoccupied what I venture to call my own mind, my unadulterated consciousness. You will wish to hear it.'

None of the wrinkled, placid faces showed such a wish, but, impervious to the shuffles and commotions without, they displayed the masterful detachment of the Stoic.

'He writes, I could say inscribes, his belief, his axiom, that people are devoted to falsehood. Falsehood throughout the day, falsehood at night in the wilful tides of dream. It is, in our parlance, a dedication, not far from the sacred. Such, our esteemed colleague pontificates, is human nature.'

Another gentleman unexpectedly stirred, as if rescued from the wilful tides of dream. 'Do I hear pronounced the name Flaubert? Now that you feel called upon to, so to speak, admit him to our presence, I must confess that I am at times convinced that he is endowed with but one eye. A sharp one, we must admit . . . not one that might be termed sottish.'

Faces, unseen for years, reappeared. In the salons was seen M. Baptiste, 'Count Know-all', once republican, formerly royalist, now Bonapartist, said to have murdered two mistresses and consistently anti-German. German barbarians had destroyed Rome, itself reincarnate in the Napoleonic Empires, and had been taught under-standing of true religion only by the fierce sword of Charlemagne. Prussia was notoriously Jew-ridden and diabolic.

At open-air tables in place du Palais Royal queer jokes circulated about 'the Second Reich', the first, descendent of Charlemagne, being the ramshackle Holy Roman Empire, which had collapsed, very aptly, under onslaught from the first Napoleon, the superb N. In the grimy yard of the Tavern of the Three Terns, a Saint-Antoine pot house, a red-headed spade-bearded bargee, scarred like a map, spiri-tual godson of Blanqui, muttered, as if over a favourite menu: 'Smash! A total and god-sent smash!'

Voices clattered on, with recollections of Bismarck at the Uni-versal Exhibition, contemplating Herr Krupp's masterpiece and per-haps observing more than he pretended.

'This life of ours . . . I'd call it little more than an ill-conceived notion . . . nevertheless . . .'

'Verily I say unto you . . .'

'There's a Greek saying, whoever gives quickly, gives twice.'

A chuckle followed, implying obscenity, in keeping with the frac-tious, quivering moment. From another table disputes had started.

'But you don't have to storm the castle, merely subtract the key.'

'To thrash the Prussians . . . well, it amounts to a quack remedy, but aren't all remedies no more than that?'

'The situation, crisis, if you prefer it, draws like a badly stuffed cigar.'

TWENTY-TWO

AMIDST the Promethean furnace of words, one voice was still silent. Late at night, Louis Napoleon was alone, in his study, Saint-Cloud hushed and dark, despite the dull clamour from across the park. The clock, a squat, gold masque of lions and gryphons topped by an eagle clasping the dial, was discharging July 1870 as it had July 1770. A single lamp on a buhl table, scarcely penetrating the reaches of the great room, left him in a small circle of light as, in faded and almost ragged smoking-jacket, he sat, sloping, in the deep chair, his waxy features indeterminate. Beneath shabby hair within thickening pouches the eyes were lustreless, almost obliterated. Some softness of expression and posture recalled Hortense's Creole heritage, now overlaid with weariness, even distress.

Here, where shadows made spaces vaster, unfinished, he looked small, dwarfed by the thickly columned rosewood cabinet, occasionally blood-red from a sharp splinter of light from windows uncurtained but still closed, despite the night's warmth. He enjoyed stuffy, overheated rooms: six years as a state prisoner had left him rheumatic, often chilled even on a hot day.

On the opposite wall, two dark blotches were maps: one of old Paris, a jumble of crooked lines, dangerous corners, red spots of cholera and unrest, the other of new Paris, his Paris, unfinished but crossed with black rays, the long airy boulevards, light and trees, safety. Future developments, unseen even by Haussmann, were hidden in the safe disguised as another cabinet, its outside shelves widened to hold cigarette boxes, unread memoranda, satirical journals, 'artistic' pictures unconcerned with art. The only art he allowed here was the marble head of his mother, beautiful and wilful, shrewd and impulsive, indolent, possessive, loving, devoted to himself and the Napoleonic Idea.

Other maps now lay on a stool beside him. He always enjoyed atlases, each line a possibility, a frontier or drama.

Stubbing out an unfinished cigarette he at once lit another, the little flame briefly illuminating the long rows of books, richly bound, embossed. Then they too lapsed into shadow and his head, too heavy, sank lower.

Emperor of the French, King of Algeria, he had had adventures with few parallels, dice throws at Fate, gleams of his star. Yet, of the Empire, who would be remembered? Morny, for his Grand Prix and amusing scandals, de Lesseps for the Canal, childish Bernadette of Lourdes, M. Charnier for that interminably expensive Opéra? M. Delibes, Mérimée, Flaubert? Just possibly, M. Offenbach. Well, history could do worse. More likely, Mr Worth, ladies' darling.

Again, he threw away the cigarette, half smoked, only to begin another, bluish fumes hanging about him like the clouds round Offenbach's Jupiter.

As for himself, Haussmann would take credit for the New Paris, MacMahon for Magenta and Solferino, Saint-Simon for the planned modernizing of France, Ollivier for the Liberal Empire, leaving him only minor pickings.

No French ruler had so encouraged credit and lowered the price of bread, but who was he? His face, twisted by more than physical pains, subsided further into the darkness beyond the little lamp, his body shrinking, as he traced himself as if on another map.

He was Louis, a name of charm, elegance, politeness; he was also Napoleon, Herculean saviour and challenger. Louis had dispensed opulence, theatre, good times; Napoleon had avenged disaster in Russia, displaced Waterloo, redesigned Italy, completed the Algerian business, shown ample generosity to Prussia.

That false cabinet concealed other verdicts. The Goncourt pair, serious beyond measure, had sneered that the Emperor resembled a circus manager sacked for drunkenness. A private face in a public place and the husband of his wife. Who had written that? Intelligent, razor-toothed Thiers? Rochefort? Never allowed to be forgotten was the street rhyme that had so disfigured his childhood reveries:

> Le Roi d'Hollande
> Fait la contrabande,
> Et sa femme
> Fait le faux Louis.

The false Louis. Had Offenbach supplied a tune, the Plebiscite might have been lost. France was ever susceptible to epigrams, innuendo, mischief. Ridicule, more powerful than Orsini's bombs, could perforate Caesars and Alexanders.

Yet, yet, he would outlast gibes and travesties. Human nature was older than good and evil, than right and wrong, a truism he had known at close quarters, in prisons, on battlefields, in gambling houses and amongst courtesans, in secret confabulations and public gatherings, in converse with d'Orsay, Disraeli, Prince Albert with his kilometres of advice. His experience outreached anything risked by Bismarck and Thiers, Mr Gladstone, Tsar Alexander, who scarcely dared leave his own palace, and that vulgar, ungrateful Victor Emmanuel who owed him his throne. Almost alone of them all, he saw far beyond the New Paris, which he had made the hub of European congresses, exhibitions, fashions, enterprise for the approaching century. He could outline a New Europe, his revision of the Idea,

179

offspring of revolution, virile, meritocratic, universal. He could repeat word perfect lines from his *Caesar*.

'When Providence elevates such men as Caesar, Charlemagne and Napoleon, it is to demonstrate to peoples the course they should pursue; to seal with their genius a new era, and to achieve in a few years the labours of many centuries.'

Momentarily the distant hubbub, the war cries, had subsided. His fine brow contracted, thoughts trudging back to streets and assemblies.

Gramont was insisting that Bismarck had secret understanding with Russia, who would attack Austria if Franz-Josef joined France in arms. There was also – another small burst of flame – an unfortunate paper on which, in discussion with Bismarck at Biarritz, before the Austro-Prussian war, was jotted the French suggestion that, if Prussia achieved victory, France, as reward for neutrality, should absorb Belgium, England's pet. Bismarck, bloodshot with his high voice, affability and gross appetite for Genoese sauce, had smiled, nodded, pocketed the document for further scrutiny and had carefully refrained from returning it. Should he now publish it, all European sympathies for France would be forfeited.

No gambler, however professional, always wins. Louis Napoleon had gambled on becoming benevolent arbiter after Austro-Prussian stalemate, he had gambled on Mexico. Now, Maximilian was dead, Carlotta had screamed at him for treachery, madly waving his signed pledge to protect Max in all seasons: Danes and Poles reproached him for passivity, Russia had not forgiven the Crimean business, the Pope, whom he still defended, had called him liar and cheat, Victor Emmanuel had acquired Venetia, but that owed little to France. England remained jealous and suspicious. He was hideously alone.

In their Triumphs Roman Emperors carried a slave behind them to whisper reminders that they were mortal, to avert jealousy of the gods. He needed no such slave. He had Rochefort and Gambetta, the dead of December '51. That cavernous safe held anonymous letters, open denunciations, the fulminations of Victor Hugo, which he knew as intimately as he had known Eleanor Vergeot's body:

'M. Bonaparte, in his Presidential Manifesto, pledged his word of honour to retire after four years. He swore his oath to the Republic. Later still, he massacred two thousand Frenchmen while forswearing his oath. People of France, have you forgotten?'

In prosperity, people forget their own birth but, when the barometer falls, they recall even a dead mouse. He could withstand Bismarck more easily than the December days and the quip of Talleyrand's, that crime is the last resort of the political imbecile.

White trees rustled in the park and the shouts were resuming, he perforce recited, though silently, more venom from the great poet:

'Though he has committed enormous crimes, he will remain paltry. He will never be anything else, the nocturnal strangler of liberty, the pygmy despot of a great people. There is a slight difference between conquering an Empire and stealing it. To the Horses of the Sun he has attached his *Cab*.'

An Emperor does not wince while the populace stares. Not so a quiet man in private, with a beautiful wife and a child of hope. He needs patronage from no Goncourts and Flauberts, these could be kept in check by old friends, Mérimée and clever, brusque Mathilde. Then his thoughts, as so often, too often, slid aside, deflected by Cousin Mathilde. If her father, old Uncle Jerome, had not dismissed his suit, as that of a penniless exile without a future, would their marriage have solidified his throne? No longer a beauty, never really a beauty, she had adamantine good sense. But instead, Eugénie, mother of Loulou, supreme mistress of ceremonies all Europe admired. She and Mathilde disliked each other, neither revered himself. Mathilde was devoted only to her intellectual salon, Eugénie reserved her love only for Loulou. His cousin despised his wife for cultural backwardness, Eugénie resented Mathilde's forthright independence and ungovernable clique. Cato's injunction forced a smile from his fatigue: 'Never kiss your wife unless it thunders.' Thunder was beginning, though for years she had been in no mood for kisses. In crisis, however, she would show pluck, the gracious unconcern of her lineage, as she did when confronted by sullen crowds, when visiting fever hospitals, as she had done when Orsini hurled the bombs. Inwardly fierce, she wore dignity in a manner beyond reach of Mr Worth, yet retained the impulses of girlhood: the fearless rider, swimmer, climber, bull-tamer, who had once stabbed her wrists to excite a supercilious Englishman.

He had his own courage, not of the theatrical sort. As a youth he had risked bullets in the Campagna for Italian freedom, French bullets at Boulogne when, as pretender, he had raised his flag against Louis-Philippe. Throughout the reign, within each public appearance, lurked an Orsini to once again bespatter him with blood. To drive defenceless through seething, dangerous Paris had never dismayed him. At Magenta and Solferino he had shrunk only at the carnage inflicted on others.

If his star was fading, Eugénie's was brightening, after her world triumph at Suez. Pietri had reported that flunkeys, bribed by journalists, had whispered that at first news of the Hohenzollern Candidature Gramont had sought audience not with the Emperor but with the Empress. Her fiery-spirited arguments, like those of so many women, were unanswerable but, as they had been over Mexico, often inaccurate.

For the moment, no woman was needful, however beautiful, resolute, brave. An Emperor needs a reliable intelligence service, unobtrusive police, prefectorial initiatives. Pietri was worth ten of Mathilde's intellectuals, who so despised the Court, especially if uninvited. One required not the simpers or rhetoric of poets but contacts with popular opinion. Pietri should have been employed in Mexico.

No smiles were possible over that. Mexico was not to be remembered without a shudder. Maximilian had once said that Napoleon III was less an emperor with a sceptre than a ring-master with a riding-crop. He, Eugénie, Rouher, even up-to-date, resourceful brother Morny had been gulled by persuasive hidalgos, scheming clerics, touting speculators.

Any thought of Morny led to women, and he involuntarily glanced through the shadows to a row of double-locked drawers, which contained the memories shared with those as indispensable as Pietri himself. Since boyhood, with Hortense, women had preoccupied him; their flesh, their secrets, their demands. Naked or over-dressed, they glistened through cigarette smoke as if from a stage cauldron. Eleanor Gordon, 'Singing Amazon', pistol-cracking on the boards and off them, so provident with money for the future Empire: Catherine Walters, delightful 'Skittles': Miss Howard, now Countess of Beauregard, another whose professional earnings had been so useful, and though her demands for titles and pensions were still tiresome she had raised his two sons, born by lusty Eleanor Vergeot, kindly laundress at Ham: then Rachel, greatest of actresses, with that flamboyant toss of the head: Virginie, Virginie de la Castiglioni, another sort of actress, white sheen on black sheets, one leg slightly raised: Emily Rowles, of green Chislehurst: Marguerite Bellanger, Venus of the Second Empire, who had once cavorted in circus rings: La Rigoleuse, acrobatic dancer, with her hoarse brogue and moony breasts: Marquise Belboef; Lady Douglas: grisettes from *bouffe* and cabaret supplied by Bacciochi. One girl, nameless, common as a biscuit, had been abashed by the size of his knobbed, barely controllable organ, which finally made her frantic, though a bracelet of diamonds set in black enamel eventually cooled her.

He had always needed women more than men, though only to Hortense had he been able to speak freely, and seldom even to her. Now, more distinct than anything at this hour, he could see images, broken, as if in cracked glass: Marguerite's careless wink, Harriet

Howard's smile, calculated according to the wealth and prospects of her suitors, Louise's delicate flanks. As for men . . .

He was feeling very old. He had, after all, once been at upheld at baptism at Fontainebleau by the great Napoleon, had known Lafayette and enrolled, under no less than Wellington, to protect London from rioters; he had chattered pleasantly with the futurist Proudhon and employed de Tocqueville. In this sleepless extremity he should ring for a hot drink, but, no, he was too weary to do so and reluctant to disturb the footman.

Few men had stayed the course with him. D'Orsay had gone, his mentor in dress and deportment, at those distant evenings at Lady Blessington's. Le Bas was dead, his tutor, high-principled, whom he had loved and whose father had died with Robespierre and Saint-Just, steadfast in the Revolutionary ideal. Stern, affectionate, noble, Le Bas had adopted Saint-Just's complaint that, in appalling mis-judgement, people confused happiness with pleasure. Loyal to the Republic, Le Bas had sadly forsaken him, on proclamation of the Empire. Walewski too was dead and brother Morny, now the most necessary of all. Also Niel, whose army reforms had been unremit-tingly opposed by those now baying for war.

Of the survivors, Conneau, loyal doctor who had shared captiv-ity at Ham, was politically naïve. Plon-Plon, always noisily, uselessly scheming, was scarcely able to address him without a sneer or Eugénie without insult. Rouher was administrator but no statesman. Persigny, a liability in any crisis demanding diplomatic finesse, was noise without substance, a clown without a public. Ollivier could be the trump card, his own choice, proof of his particular skills of adroit discrimination.

He blinked, slightly turning up the lamp so that recesses gained shape: books, chairs, maps, his mother's blind orbs. Oppressed by headaches and abdominal scourge, he was muddling all colours. The clock's emphatic tick was more stable, though his eyelids, refusing to respond, long refused him a sight of the slim, golden hands. Pressing back the pains he strove for clarity. Throughout, he had moved with the times, often ahead of them, pledged to the century ahead. If the Empire looked back to Jena, Austerlitz, the Revolution, it simultaneously promoted steam, electricity, oceanic cables, the new science of statistics, expanding the Idea in ways never considered at St Helena. Anchored in lessons from classical Rome, he used perspectives unavailable to most of his detractors. Present-day journalism was lifting political nihilism to a moral principle: in Augustan Rome, trust had been the guiding rule. The status of a guide, whether ruler or teacher, is in the trust he evokes, not in birth or university degrees. Like Caesar, he had been attacked for creating an aristocracy without nobility, democracy without people, but he could glory in rewarding merit from all classes. Republican Rome, Republican France shared two evils: patrician selfishness and plebeian turbulence. His had always been the middle course. No Thiers, Gambetta, certainly no Rochefort, could teach an industrious student of Rome and England that a caste, unless renewed from below, is condemned to extinction, that prolonged absolutism endangers whoever exerts it, that prophets of total freedom are the first to be destroyed by it. Le Bas had known that. A state is weakened by exaggeration of the very belief on which it rests. His own belief was in fluidity, adaptation, the graph between the dictatorship and the Liberal Empire. Revolution, heady, headstrong, finally headless and demanding a new one, rages at will but leaves a mess for N to clear up. In an aberration of time N must break pledges, obligations, contracts, defer to no currents of opinion, bow to no mediocrity, find no excuses to procrastinate. Thereby it saves society and may never be forgiven.

Corruption, faction, disorder had justified December as they had the Rubicon. When society hastens towards ruin, authority is vital for salvation. Again the night was silent, though he fancied he still heard the clamour for ultimatums, guarantees, war, the final decision which he alone in Europe could ordain, a thought from which, until morning, he could only flinch.

Of those who preached the downfall of the Empire, only Thiers and Gambetta had substance. He lacked their genius, but he knew how to build. The remainder, Blanqui, Flourens, Rochefort, a sorry crew, scanning the ends of the earth but unable to see the ends of their noses. Screeching for freedom, they would shackle even their own adherents.

Moreover, only in spontaneous, electrifying instants was anyone free: a Greek had written that Zeus alone possessed freedom. Efforts to prolong those instants, to wrest oneself from desires for martyrdom, annihilation in flesh, to destroy, could be catastrophic.

Napoleon stirred, attempted to straighten his woeful body. He must hold on, ride this perilous week. Always clinging to him – for Eugénie, admirable mother, was strict – was Loulou. Another three years and the boy would be eighteen and, youthful, irresistible, would inherit the crown, his parents retiring to Biarritz to contemplate the waves. Until then, persistence, caution, balance were essential. Ollivier could steer the Empire to safe haven and unspectacular liberties, disproving de Tocqueville's belief that an oppressive regime is most endangered when it initiates reform.

He felt better, pains were ebbing; he must have slept a little. Pale stars were vanishing as grey light touched the trees. Thought resumed. He had been rebuked for short-sightedness but, like acrobats and high-wire artistes, a statesman must live in the present. The long-sighted and philosophical lose themselves in abstractions, theories, nothingness. A Plato, allowed power, with his hand on the tiller, drifts, self-satisfied and talkative, for the rocks. Alexis de Tocqueville, whom he himself had appointed Foreign Secretary, had achieved nothing.

He too was a dreamer but governed by daily exigencies. When wine is offered, one drinks it. He had been despised as an adventurer, though few positions were superior.

War, without swift, overwhelming success, would endanger everything. Memory of his days as commander in Italy only exposed his limitations. Yet he was dogged by N, the heroic legacy, without which he would be pacing a Swiss townlet, Roman suburb, London square. Not genius, not philosophy, not even Harriet's cash, had swept him to power but a song, Béranger's; 'O the Old Days, the Old Deeds', the unfathomable human craving for the lost and the golden that politics could exploit but scarcely control.

Le Bas had taught him poems, Schiller, Hölderlin, during the Arenburg years, and lines could slip back, often inconveniently. Presenting a prize, receiving an ambassador, entertaining provincial and readily forgettable dignitaries, he might be interrupted by a verse from years ago.

> Ah, but where are the thrones, the temples, and where
>   are the cups,
> Where, for delight of the gods, flowing with nectar, is
>   song?
> Where, O where are they now, all the wide-ranging
>   oracles, flaming?

He had contrived to produce that for Prince Albert: it had been easy to play the respectful scholar to that solemn German. He himself read books, wrote books, because he wished to get somewhere.

Bismarck was less easy, but France was the more exacting, loving risky foreign policies as it did cavalry and uniforms. These he had bestowed with a touch light as Mozart's 'Petits Riens' that Hortense used to play to him and Le Bas. France was so unlike England, with its arts of compromise. He had thought much of England when designing the New Paris; of grandeur of London parks and of Lady Holland's gardens, the calm greenery of Virginia Water where he had rowed, and almost upset, the Disraelis. Then those evenings gambling at Harriet's and James Fitzroy's establishment in St John's Wood, those exhausting hours plotting in King Street with the devoted bloodhound Persigny.

Amongst documents strewn haphazardly on the desk were latest reports intercepted from London, one of which must be concealed from the Press: 'A new Germany is looming out like some huge iron-clad from which no sounds are heard but the tramp of men at drill, or the swinging upon their pivots of monster guns.'

Alone, he could pacifically manage Wilhelm and Bismarck, but the Revolution had bred a factor unprecedented and inescapable, public opinion, ignorant, irresponsible, inflammable, but sufficiently influential for Offenbach to allow it a part in *Orfée*.

Morny should be at his side. He had managed the Assembly as he might a favourite horse. Dying, he had murmured against any possibility of war. 'All's well that never begins,' he had said, summoning his vaudeville mood, then managing to repeat that the fate of the Empire depended upon peace. Le Bas, Prince Albert, Mathilde, had spoken likewise, and none knew better than himself how chancy, how incomplete, had been French victories in Russia, Italy, Algeria, Mexico; and that unfortunate sack of Peking with the English was everywhere deplored. In contrast, Prussia had crushed Denmark within days, Austria in a fortnight. He himself had written a pamphlet diagnosing and extolling her army. Prussia itself was only fulfilling his own intermediate doctrine of nationalities.

All regimes, whatever their form, secrete germs both of creation and dissolution. The balance between them was the motif of the Liberal Empire. In vital compulsion, he gazed before him to identify, in their bound and elaborate magnificence, the two volumes of his *Caesar*. He could repeat exactly yet another paragraph:

The kings are expelled from Rome. They vanish, because their mission is accomplished. We may say there exists, morally, physically, a governing rule which allows institutions and certain individuals alike a fated limit, marked by the extent of their usefulness. Until that limit, fixed by Providence, is reached, all opposition fails: conspiracies, revolts, all crumble against the irresistible force which supports what some wish to demolish; but if, on the contrary, a state of affairs, outwardly immovable, ceases to benefit human progress, neither the empyrium of traditions, nor courage, nor memories of past glories can delay by one single day the collapse decreed by Fate. Once the moment arrives, when the kings cease to be indispensable, they are toppled by the merest accident.

Closing his eyes, he yearned for the deliverance of sleep but was unable to risk it. Paris would soon be awaking, ministers and generals awaiting orders, *public opinion* finding voice or trumpets. But he must continue resting, then, later, again consult the maps.

N should acknowledge dependants but require no allies. At this instant, France possessed neither. Italy was only a jackal. Austria's ambassador, pleasant Richard von Metternich and his ugly but delightful Pauline, Eugénie's favourite, had assured him that Vienna would give no help until after the first French victories. Visiting the Exhibition, Franz Josef, whom he had worsted in Italy, had been friendly enough, Eugénie had handled him admirably, but his brother Max had been lured to a Mexican firing squad, and the world had pointed accusingly at the Emperor of the French.

England, with churchy platitudes, would be neutral but favouring Prussia, where Victoria's daughter was Crown Princess.

He was too tired even to reach for a cigarette; plans, facts, possibilities, stumbled in disarray. The body offered too many choices, concealed from ministers, unmentionable to journalists. He breathed more slowly, if indeed he was breathing. Dawn lights had diminished, the lamp was wounding his eyes; he relapsed into grey negations. Sometimes disaster can be relief from paradox and contradiction, the interminable ache of responsibility; death itself could be medicine from this goading, surreptitious pain which dragged down spirit.

To Eugénie, he never confessed this sickness; she dismissed most sickness as self-induced, and doctors resembled builders, always discovering new faults, new areas for profit, though to Conneau, faithful, discreet, he should confide more freely.

Unable to move, he could feel the ultimate temptation to leave all to fate and, like a Chinese sage, accomplish all by doing nothing. Whatever fate intended would occur. In the long, disheartening years of exile and mockery he had played the game of chance, opening at random a bible, a book of texts and maxims, a deck of cards, to discover what was offered by what, despite his irreligion, he so often called Providence.

His body, after several warnings, convulsed, the stabs almost making him cry aloud, before, retching, he lay back, waiting to be soothed by another cigarette. His face, grey as the wedges of sky before him, quivered, then relaxed.

The cigarette restored clarity. The Hohenzollern Candidature, less infamous than the mobs believed, must nevertheless be countered, in keeping with the legend of N, of Jeanne, Bayard and the knights at Roncevalles. In crisis, these would outbid Red Menace and boulevard jabber.

Gramont had his orders. French embassies were opening instructions, Leboeuf at the War Ministry was prepared. Military success was in accumulation of details; railway timetables, arms storage at key bases, generals' signatures on reception of clearly enunciated plans. Leboeuf had promised his overall supervision and had eagerly accepted his sovereign's personal insistence on the *chassepot*.

The half-smoked cigarette fell into a brass tray, a groan subsided into a sigh; again the Emperor slept. Through tight windows under pelmets now gold and green in early sun clamour was resuming like a biological imperative, Paris again on the move.

TWENTY-THREE

WITHOUT consulting the Palace – and, without knowing it, challenging Hermes – M. Ollivier, man of good sense and moderation, gave formal notice to the Assembly that the contretemps with Prussia was over, that worse had been averted.

Applause, though prolonged, was not unanimous. Some of the Right growled that insufficient had been demanded of the upstart Teutons; on the Left, Gambetta, powerful Stentor, for once was silent; Thiers hid behind his spectacles which suddenly appeared larger than himself. In public galleries, faces were mottled in strenuous satisfaction.

At once, throughout the West, newspapers shrilled that, under serious pressure from the French Imperial Government, certain foreign powers, and the familial influence of King Wilhelm, Prince Antoine von Hohenzollern had requested the Spanish ambassador to inform Madrid that his son's acceptance had been withdrawn.

Paris, followed by the great cities, at last recognized a French victory, the triumph of skills over clumsy muscle. Rising from torpor, the Emperor was back in the saddle, working behind the scenes in his customary way. He had regained initiative, and, after a brief ministerial conference at the Tuileries, drove back in some state through a delighted populace, which could discount all bankrupt notions of pusillanimity. Sadowa was avenged, Mexico clamped down in the rubbish bin.

Arriving home early, leaving the office still celebrating, Etienne was pleased to see his family obediently waiting. Henrietta took his hat and stick, grinning, as though he personally had managed the national fête; Amélie embraced him, her body, pressing against his own, had the light violet scent he preferred. Emile rose from his chair, though with his customary, far-away look. Did he too wander some forbidden path, an esquire following a lovelorn chevalier?

Seeing Amélie's unspoken request for further news, he slowly parked his portfolio, then turned back to her, man of affairs, of confidential information.

'Yes, I can substantiate everything. It is indeed all over. Berlin has, as they say, caved in.'

His rather narrow face was solemn, his demeanour of martial youth surrendering to the dignity of middle age. Husband and father, he was sincerely gratified by the Prussian's renunciation; as reservist, as the romantic lagging behind the important official, hankering for attention in celestial quarters, he was disappointed.

'I understand . . .' He sat down, man of consequence addressing an audience, 'that Her Majesty is dissatisfied, convinced the solution was too mild. I've been told . . . confidentially of course . . . that she complained that Prussia's in need of a trouncing. Her exact words. Not what I care to call diplomatic. But I have always found her lacking in restraint. She believes, I would say, that pacific overtures demean the honour of France, that the Empire's becoming an old woman.'

He paused, interlocking his fingers in the way his minister always did, his voice now ponderous. 'I gather, furthermore, that, at the Council, in the Emperor's presence, General Boubaki was so angry . . . incensed . . . that he banged his sword on the table, almost smashing both. He thinks that the very proposal of those Spanish gentry, and its acceptance, was an infamous insult to us and should be avenged.'

His smile was brisk, capable, and for a moment retrieved the boyishness that he had once captivated Demoiselle Amélie amidst the roses and lilies. 'As to that . . .' he shrugged, spread hands, glanced at Emile, hoping to rouse him to appreciate the giant significance of the official world, 'Well, at least it's robbed Plon-Plon and Persigny of their last chance of becoming Marshals!'

He repeated the old gibe about Lafayette as a statue in search of a pedestal. Amélie, who had been told it several times, smiled to order; Emile seemed not to have heard.

Summer dresses fluttered gaily on the boulevards, in fierce scribbles of light. At the *bouffes*, a clown joked about Bismarck wearing his trousers back to front, his smile upside down. People laid flowers before the bear-skinned Guards sweltering at the great gates of the Tuileries. The Prussian climb-down was the masterstroke of the Empire, exquisite as a Fabergé egg. At the Red Velvet Cabaret a new song satirized the Candidature as an addled egg laid by a cuckoo too large, *let us say*, for its own boots.

The long, shady day slowly wore itself out, twilight descending over a scarlet rash behind the Invalides dome. The mood, however, was perforated not by scarlet but by green, not the vernal gloss, woodland fancies, Arcadian meadows but of absinthe, wolves' eyes, Transylvanian blood, for the hermetic catalyst was still at work, having quickened urges not easily subdued, and Paris remained bellicose, unwilling to retire home for the quiet drink and need for love. A fresh tale sped through Paris as if on electric wires: on the Emperor's personal order, Duke de Gramont had summoned the Prussian minister and demanded that King Wilhelm should offer public contrition, an official apology. Almost at once, a new word was insidiously dropped into the fermenting brew of barely coherent passions, a word like the incantation of a conjurer. It was simple but combustible. *Guarantees*.

TWENTY-FOUR

THE age expected ever-swifter speed. During the Revolution messages had flashed across lands by semaphore, flags, balloons, carrier pigeons, breathless riders. Today, cables tied Europe to America, M. Reuter's telegrams reached everywhere within a quarter of an hour. Railways hurtled down tracks, steamships outpaced sail.

Such phenomena, however, are nevertheless nothing to a Hermes, for whom the passage from Rome to Babylon, Delphi to Peking is an instant, as is that between Paris to Berlin, Berlin to Ems, less than a blink. Such travel is a telegram of spirit. The spirit of this loud moment is decidedly playful, accompanied by a distinctive laugh, that of a comedian who can turn terrible. Listen.

Within a capacious room in a Varzin mansion, Berlin, inquisitive eyes saw three heavy figures at the dinner table, each set in his large shadow, breathing hard though slowly, as if at some ceremony, and saying nothing. The meal was perfunctory and unfinished, only the beer consumed with the same resolution. Everything was heavy: dark tables, consoles, mahogany chairs, the square, darkened portraits of bearded, armoured *Herrenvolk*. The air was marmoreal, clammy in sunless warmth. Papers and files were stacked on chests, stools, tables, the effect brooding, as though they were unpleasant warrants. Lamps were unlit so that cupboards loomed like barely seen headlands from an undergrowth of crevices and boulders. An atmosphere Bismarck, who flourished some literary style, considered was like the breath of a ruined governess.

Berliners joked that the Chief Minister loved trees more than his dog, his dog more than his wife, his wife more than anyone else. Neither dog nor wife was present, and in this overcast afternoon his broad face, streaky with reds and purples, seemed incapable of anything save despondence. Bald, his crown grey-fringed, thickly moustached, weighty like the furniture, His Excellency dominated the occasion by a fixity of gloom which, had they not known him for so long, the others would have found alarming.

His guests, General Count Albrecht von Roon and General Helmuth von Moltke, victor of Sadowa, had arrived early, at five, for dinner and found him reading the latest report from Ems, where the King was on holiday. Greeting them, before escorting them to the study, Herbert, the minister's son and confidant, had told them that the Berlin papers were still awaiting the final communiqué regarding the new French demand and which required his father's approval.

Finally, Bismarck, in silence, handed them the report, after a massive shrug of impatience. On a low table beside him lay the lengthy communiqué already drafted by his officials. This explained that the King had been walking in the public gardens when, surprisingly, against convention, the French Ambassador, Count Benedetti, had accosted him. After routine compliments, the old man had courteously congratulated the envoy on the successful outcome of the dispute, then, raising his hat, made as if to resume his stroll. Benedetti, however, detained him and conveyed the demand of his overlord, Gramont, for a royal guarantee that such a candidature should never be renewed. Steadfast in the manners of an earlier age, Wilhelm replied that such a guarantee was not within his prerogative. 'And Prince Leopold, my dear sir, has retired from all consideration. Sufficient, surely sufficient.' Avoiding expostulation or further talk, he again raised his hat and rejoined his aides.

Some hours later, Benedetti's request for a formal audience was, though in mellifluous diplomatic language, refused, presumably at royal command.

Bismarck studied the paper, brows contracting. Clearly, beneath his courtesy, the old gentleman had been irritated, not only by Corsican ill manners but by conviction, probably correct, that the demand for the guarantee had come from Napoleon himself. He had complained that the public exchange had been a *faux pas* unimaginable in polite circles, and indeed humiliating.

The two generals waited. Having examined the report, they too were disappointed by its lack of real drama. The King had defused behaviour undeniably tactless but no more. It scarcely helped provide effective response to the morning papers brimming with French cock crows, reeking with Gallic insults to Prussian honour, valour, arms.

Already, within hours, plans known to some of the Great General Staff but not to the King and Cabinet, precisely formulated but with very little transcribed to paper, had gone awry. Leopold should have been inserted on to the Spanish throne before anyone had time to squawk protests and assume boxer's stance. The damned cipher clerk had given the ersatz Napoleon a simple chance which, for once, he had not fumbled.

The three stared at the dishevelled table, untasted meats, the last of the beer. Bismarck's breathing was laborious, almost hoarse. Eyes and mouth, very tight, suggested very deliberate concentration which the generals were disinclined to interrupt. There remained that matter of the final communiqué.

The draft ended: 'His Majesty leaves it to His Excellency to decide whether M. Benedetti's new demands and His Majesty's response should be released to the Press and the Diplomatic Corps.'

This too was mild, colourless. The afternoon closed in, soundless and oppressive. The clink of von Roon's knife accidentally touching a metal tankard startled his companion, but Bismarck's features betrayed nothing.

His Excellency had scant respect for the Diplomatic Corps – of which, in Paris, in St Petersburg, he had once been a member – and even less for the Press. Now bowed over the report, in this gloom, he was a colossus stricken by malevolent dwarfs and unfriendly Fate. Then, the others were astounded by a laugh, surprisingly light from so bulky a frame, but candid, you could say, jovial.

Yet he still did not speak. Holding the paper, he gazed, first at one, then at the other. The damp mouth, beneath the moustache, was slack, the eyes less so, apt to stiffen into displeasure, anger, total disregard of others, at provocation not always easy to comprehend, though at present they were at rest, entertained by private thoughts.

As if tweaked by unseen fingers, or by the spirit of mischief, and with the crude, even urchin humour of a practical joker, the Chief Minister reached for a pencil almost as thick as a teacher's ferule, and, like a painter, with unexpected grace, that acquired from so many audiences, levees, balls, receptions, he began making small dabs, erasures, excisions, emendations, watched by the two, motionless on their hard chairs. After only a few moments, he had done, surveying the new document with another smile, compared by von Moltke to that of a victorious corps commander, a reminder of the charm he was so often ready to exploit, a further part of his weaponry.

The draft, under his ministrations, now scarred by black lines, retained only a few brief sentences, like a telegram. Before handing it to von Moltke, Bismarck at last spoke.

'The account of His Majesty's performance is perhaps too majestic, too magnanimous for our coarser purposes.' Like an actor delaying a *coup*, he was still unwilling to release his handiwork. 'We have no need, however, to add anything, to alter the essence. A slight modification of phraseology, yes, a few suppressions, ah, of the niceties of protocol . . . some trifling application of shears will save newsprint.'

At last von Moltke was allowed it. Roon crossed over, reading it over his colleague's shoulder, their leather-bound features creasing in satisfaction. The ponderous surroundings lightened; stags' heads on walls nosed out of obscurity, portraits resumed identity and as if well satisfied.

Von Roon stood, not at attention but as if ready to dance. 'It is the challenge. Just now, it was nothing. But Your Excellency has transformed it to a hunting call.'

Von Moltke also stood up. 'It is good. It is very good.'

Bismarck remained seated, thoroughly in command. He began another laugh, decided against it, instead said in mock gravity: 'Call it a red rag to the Gallic bull. No doubt, tomorrow we will hear French yelps for intervention from Europe. Well, gentlemen, I have always found the word *Europe* on the lips of those statesmen who desire something from others which they don't care to risk asking on behalf of their own country.'

He jangled a bell. Orderlies were at once setting down more bottles, the tankards, foaming with dark Westphalian beer. The Chief Minister, convivial as a trooper, pulled over a dish of cutlets, long cold, and began devouring them in greed long celebrated. Between gobbles, in which his tongue seemed rummaging amongst a stockpile, his utterance was thick but decipherable. 'I think we can rely on the gentlemen on the Paris streets to work on our behalf.' He wiped his lips with the back of his red, bristled hand. 'From a distance, the French Empire is a wonder. Approach closer and you see nothing at all.'

TWENTY-FIVE

DELIVERED to Paris editors, uproar at the 'Ems Telegram' was that of Titans mating, gratifying any sardonic god of messages. Left and Right headlines, editorials, commentaries were hysterical. For the first time in history newspapers were usurping direct authority, their alarms summoning back the hordes. Yells for *guarantees* rose again, then were submerged by those for arms.

Vouched for by Count von Bismarck himself, the Prussian communiqué was not designed to soothe, placate, show obeisance.

> This afternoon, King Wilhelm, walking with his adjutant, Count Lehndorf, in the Kindergarten, was waylaid by M. Benedetti, who had peremptorily thrust at him the French demand. The King had politely and constitutionally demurred, but, when the demand was repeated, requested Count Lehndorf to inform Benedetti that there was no further reply and that he could hear no more.

From Palais Bourbon to the thieves' coven slumped beneath Montmartre, from quai d'Orsay to the barges, the Ems Telegram laid a trail of fire. Without time for breakfast, Gramont hurried to Ollivier with the *Norddeutsche Allgemeine Zeitung*, flaring as he thrust the text at the astonished Premier. 'It's an insult to the French nation! They wish to force us into war!'

Calmed by brandy and biscuits, he reported on a further text, potentially catastrophic, to be denounced as forgery as speedily as possible. The London *Times*, moderate in its account of the Ems affair, had, in the English way of disguising vehement indictment in a show of sententious though measured prose, placed, more prominently, a résumé of French proposals in '66 to annex Belgium in return for neutrality in the Austro-Prussian conflict.

Ollivier gazed back at him, shock now penetrating his thoughtful, legalistic exterior, his plans, his achievements, his very position rocked by what he had not hitherto considered, the equivocal promises of war.

With all fuses exploding the carefully planted mines, Paris was holding a new Exhibition, advertising prodigalities of delirium, undisciplined music of senses, akin, a Conservative academic wrote, to the thunderous noise storming from Munich, where Wagner stood counterpoint to that Atlas in white uniform who had strolled so affably through the Universal Exhibition. Bismarck.

At cafés, under awnings striped gay as children's calls, Prussian absurdities were swapped like cards. Dreary Biedemeier households, porky folk with stately hymns and cringing hearts.

M. Que-Voulez-Vous? has not forgotten Tacitus. Yesterday, three young women, grubby of face and attire, impeccably proletarian, had approached him at the Madrid, waving his old pamphlet, *The Necessity of Fire Raising*, urging him to address a weekend public protest against the war preparations, to be staged at ample premises hired by the Society of Equals. Delighted, he at once began to work, his pen stuffed with tirades against Prussian and French deceivers. In the fevered mood around him he could not dare transmit open republican hopes of capitulation to Prussia, entailing, *guaranteeing* revolution, the barricades rising, red flags waving, the People, the People, honest men, honest talent, retrieving their own. Instead, he would contrive a witty allegory of Imperial Rome, that speciality of the ex-President. In gusts of inspiration he had already compared excited Paris to an overblown translation of Ovid's *Metamorphoses*. He delineated a city transforming to a zoo without bars, a dangerous medley of roarings, brayings, the soft pad of tigers in the streets. He had still to fix it closer to immediate events and the overall record of the Empire and then discovered what he did not recall writing:

Black echo
Of Mexico.

He could safely preserve that and meditated a peroration of anger and pathos, urging on a mass of rapt admirers a vision of Carlotta, young Empress of Mexico, going mad in the Vatican, raving of being poisoned by the Devil in French guise.

A choice victim of statecraft, Hermes considers, glimpsing her over fifty years later, hidden, old and crazed, in a Belgian castle, survivor of the greatest and most fateful of mortal wars, who, once a year, would leave her well-appointed but darkened tower, suddenly calm, and, descending to the moat, stand before a small boat, quietly announcing, 'Tomorrow we leave for Mexico.'

People were not bothering to glance at public clocks, they merely judged the enveloping chatter of news, now violent, now diminishing, as headlines toppled into each other like battlements under fire. Saint-Marceau journeymen were dropping tools to cheer, for the first time in years, none other than the Emperor, disowning their indignant union leader. From working-men's clubs at La Villette, the lazar-houses of Saint-Antoine, from sweat-shops and hotel kitchens, men and women marched in some order, to place de la Concorde, not with red flags and staves but under the patriotic tricolour. Girls from Folies-dramatique, costumed like infantry, paraded behind a festooned drum-major, imploring *La Patrie* to stand firm. High-born relics in Faubourg Saint-Germain, implacable in disdain for the Empire, paced salons and drawing-rooms, discussing the situation with convictions very slightly impaired. Let Bonaparte destroy himself, but French defeat . . . fine speech faltered, shrugs were uneasy, while valets hurried in with the gist of Ollivier's speech in the Assembly: 'We hold Peace in our hands, we will not let it escape. But . . .'

In the Senate, Rouher, former 'Vice-Emperor', 'the Man Who Said That All Is Well in Mexico', Rochefort's butt, was assuring sovereign and nation that war, should it come, was opportune, because, since Sadowa, despite financial and political opposition, the Army, the glorious Army of France, had been perfected.

Gramont's message was less direct, a drizzle of hints, suppositions, oblique calculations. Possible military understanding and latent alliance with Austria, initial negotiations with Italy, a contact with Bavaria not yet to be divulged; a sonorous repetition of *collateral*, potent as *guarantees*, indefinite but reassuring; a telling reference to Hanover, a mention, understressed but noticeable, to Danish anger at Prussian seizure of her provinces in '64.

Papers were selling by the thousand, with ever-enlarged supplements, experts and amateurs, inspired prophets and passing celebrities jostling for position. Anonymous eye-witnesses described Prussian brutality in Holstein, special correspondents remembered scores of foreigners, last year in Alsace, German-speaking, dressed as tourists, with maps and spy-glasses. There was more concerning that mystical 'Second Reich', no longer so amusing, and accompanied by graphs and statistics proving that Germans were breeding faster than Africans and Indians and disclosing that Bismarck was secretly permitting farmers to marry two wives to swell births of future conscripts. Lustful, primitive, arse-loving forest people, *Vengeur* considered, falling in line behind the roaring and outwardly patriotic.

A more sober front-page column in *Figaro* included photographs of King Wilhelm returning from Ems and apparently welcomed by hordes of Berliners, with flags, songs, flowers.

That afternoon, with only a few cries of dissent – and an accusation, swiftly crushed, that a Bourse clique was manipulating the arms market – war credits were voted, 'just in case'. London's offer of mediation was accepted by Berlin, on condition of Paris' assent, a proposition scorned by government and populace. There followed a bulletin, explaining the hostility of Court, Senate, Parliament and all patriots to Wilhelm's terse refusal of *guarantees*, essential for national dignity and security. In theatres, squares, churches, the 'Marseillaise', hitherto banned, was sung with impunity. Around the Luxembourg, Senators were met with crowds shouting, 'A bas le Prusse,' 'Vive la guerre,' 'Vive l'empereur.'

At the night sitting of the Assembly, Hermes was in place, unseen, following proceedings as if at an opera not wholly wrecked by impure singing, absurd acting, inappropriate stage design and a restless audience.

Left sceptics, following Gambetta, demanded the exact text of the original Prussian communiqué, said to be lengthier and more temperate than the published insult, but, stilling the hubbub, a junior minister declared this irrelevant, quickly adding – and gaining many cheers – that mobilization preliminaries had already started, 'just in case'. Ollivier appeared at the tribune to dispense a few technicalities regarding call-up of reserves, giving his small, considered smile, handling his brief with the assurances of a man still young, if scarcely youthful, who had already come a long way, anticipating an agreeable future, like some senior partner in a marriage of convenience.

'Had we delayed, we would have allowed a potentially hostile Power to complete vital preparations. For the rest, one fact alone will suffice to answer the gentlemen so anxious to proffer surrender, who rejoice in the timid, the abject, the disloyal. The Prussian authorities refused to receive our ambassador while negotiations were still in hand. If a French Assembly could be found to endure such treatment, I would leave office within five minutes.'

Few cared to contemplate bed, in this miraculous climax to summer, a gala of surmise, virtually transcendental.

In more sedate gatherings and quiet households, serious discussion was attempted, attempts to shut out rowdiness and threats and disentangle fact from rumour. Almost all agreed that a Bonaparte, bearer of N, could not haggle over terms like a fishmonger. He must dictate terms or trample them down.

'It looks like Bismarck has set us a trap. Our Badinguet may fall into it, if he lets himself get more or less strangled by misbegotten legends. I'd call them archaisms.'

'Let's hope that head of his may be better protected than his conscience. Otherwise, his young brat may be awarded an order. Order of dismissal.'

'Still, my friend, when all's said and done, though he may have shopkeeper's instincts, he has a good heart. The freedoms now available . . .'

'With all respect . . . at bottom I see no freedoms available. Blood, nerves, little cells dictate our destiny. Life, in fact, has no particular point, though I have to confess that I get plenty of pleasure in pretending that it has.'

With Rochefort imprisoned, Blanqui, as always, invisible, probably dead, crystallizing into myth, Rigault said to be in hiding, peering about for his chance, Flourens ill, the Opposition muffing its lines in Assembly, Tacitus was riding into his great day. Melodrama, he reflected, can be more truthful than the subtleties of Tragedy and the blazing storms and refinements of Herr Wagner's music of the future.

He was, as he put it, grasping with all hands his well-deserved, too-long-obstructed opportunity. The largesse of justice. While clamour outside was reaching crescendo, he was occupied in composing his speech. He would be addressing more than the Society of Equals and a flock of gosling Jacobins from the New Cordeliers Club, he would be encouraging History, giving it purpose and edge. Without time to leave his library, he was laying out paragraphs as though piling up bricks for a Parthenon, swept along by his insights, perceptions, consideration of realities too often overlooked by powerful mediocrities. The performance was for this very evening. His photograph was on posters; young ardents had assured him that all tickets were sold.

His pen rushed as if born by cavalry. The nonentities stuffed into *Lame Pegasus*, the ageing misfits who had sneered at him for so long – even Rochefort – would unfreeze, would admit that his acerbic levity was swinging into higher orbit. Envious smirks would be effaced, innuendoes numbed, whispers suppressed and spirit, imagination, the sheer gaiety of revolution given full due. Visions were spreading like blood under a microscope. He could distinguish an editorial chair, a ministry in the Third Republic, a collected edition.

'War', he had begun with clarion brio, 'was the scarlet acid to corrode plunder, corruption, hypocrisy, the customary occupations of Honourable Men and the apathy of those whom the Great Revolution had dismissed as passive citizens who were entitled to no rights.' Tacitus, an active citizen, paused for breath, head flashing with signals. Momentarily he was outraged by the spectacle of the People pouring themselves not into the flame, the ecstasy of creation, but into the clutches of the ex-President. *Clutches?* Too commonplace, but could be amended later. He must hurry forward. His problem was not of the niceties of vocabulary but to convey essential revolutionary message without violating the patriotism which, though archaic and absurd, could still enflame even the Left, like love or religion. Even Citizen Rochefort, latter-day Friend of the People, sniffed at Jews as at a bad smell. Furthermore, such an important speech would be delivered under the eyes of the police. While showing his devotion to France, he must simultaneously insinuate that French defeat in battle, ensuring the downfall of the Empire, the *gimcrack* Empire, would be victory for France. The People, ah, the People, could be released. By battle, no, by 'the packed violence of a jewel'. The first Prussian onslaught must ensure a genuine Empire, enlarging the frontiers of self, reconstituting elements of being, exploring the possibilities of soul.

'Common sense argues for a successful French passage over the Rhine, a blaring march on Berlin. But common sense was unknown to Homer, championed by Shakespeare only by his most ignoble characters and despised by Baudelaire. It creates no masterpiece . . .'

There, the correct balance between caution and daring. Homer and Shakespeare would confuse the police, prevent any chance of their intervention. Like a plebiscite promoter, he was able to see all sides of a word; he could not lose, had the Empire at his mercy, which would not be granted. Its Napoleonic heritage was its most vulnerable spot. What, in happy phrase, he called the modernization of death, the Army Reforms, had been stalled by the courageous valour of those like himself.

He resumed. 'Flattery is the midwife of crime and doom.' He was excelling his own gifts. *Categorical Imperative?* No, few would understand it, the police might suspect some illegal rallying cry. Was he indeed planting too many abstractions? A few anecdotes were needed, sops for hangers-on, flattery for the People. Personal tales. His sandy eyebrows lowered, his fattish cheeks crinkled. He pouted, ranged all history, then smiled. He, great hater, implacable enemy, champion of merit, was always moved by Mlle Eglée, young prostitute, condemned by the Revolutionary Tribunal and in prison rebuking a scared nobleman: 'Monseigneur, in this place those without a name get one: those with a name should live up to it.' His eyes moistened, or wanted to, then he commented: 'For years, whores and pimps are never in prison, they're in power.' Neat, terse, unanswerable. Or too strong meat? We will see. He could now return to prospects of war, with a reminder that the ex-President had indeed been gazetted an army officer – the Swiss Army! The humane and poetic must be further reinforced by the judicial, nay, the analytical.

'Since Switzerland is mentioned, we can reflect that republics differ from monarchies. Both must provide bread, but one despises glory and circus, and labours unceasingly for public benefit, the other exists only for the tawdry and exploitative.' *Monarchies* was clever, for the regime always denied it was a monarchy, a word applicable to the now forgotten reign of Louis-Philippe and the royalists.

Time for recapitulation, truths must be incessantly hammered home. War was necessary purgation, the proper use of night soil, transforming braided louts to useful citizens, the Glory of the Crown to the Glory of the People. Prussia was a transitory, substitute *brief*, aberration, national prestige a manufactured lunacy. A war could be chrysalis for pristine human relationships, a New Paris, not a sink of profiteers and overpriced marble but an edifice of wholesome travail, no, better *work*, of ideas, of literature.

Intoxicated with words, he was writing almost at random. 'Memory is rooted in Fear.' An astounding message. He saw a lively imp of truth darting around a mendacious giant.

A useless adverb must be erased. There. But, within an instant, a fleeting shadow across the window distracted him into an unwelcome thought of M. Que-Voulez-Vous?, sly intruder into this temple of correct feelings and accumulated knowledge, a mark of interrogation, elusive but always unobtrusively mocking, murmuring elegant apologies for being over-punctual for a meeting which had not been arranged.

At once he had an uncomfortable sensation that he was no

longer alone. Had Adelaine dared . . . ? He looked about him. But no, all was undisturbed; rows of books, stacks of newspapers, an emptied coffee pot, his box of pens, the view of the sun-swept, drooping garden.

He wrote another sentence, shifting history with a few blobs of ink, but was again arrested, not by adverb or shadow but by recollection of a patch of blood that had once appeared on the ceiling beneath Adelaine's bedroom, presenting him gratis with an idea for a story he had yet to complete.

Unaccountably – another adverb – in mid-peroration, he was pulling up in fatigue, eyelids battening down in drowsiness, pulses slowing, muzziness overwhelming him. He groped towards his couch and at once was asleep. Having commanded that he was not to be disturbed on any pretext, at any hour, he remained outstretched and dreamless, not waking until late the next morning.

The Emperor had driven from Saint-Cloud for the Council, painted and besashed as if in Roman triumph, his open carriage frequently delayed by crowds cheering but belligerent, shouting for instant reprisals on Berlin. On this heated July morning, *reprisals* were preferred to the finality of *war* or were perhaps an appetizing preliminary to the main and delicious course. He would have heard the 'Marseillaise', Revolutionary in associations but stalwartly patriotic.

No *guarantees*, apology, no response of any kind had arrived from Potsdam; the international Press was joining the French, fanning a wavering glow to conflagration. At Cherbourg the fleet was mobilizing for an attack, presumably on north German ports. The Empress had already been rapturously greeted, wholesale victory promised.

In the State Council Room an ornate clock, golden as Apollo, on ivory supports, showed half past four; the generals, statesmen, councillors and those ministers not facing the agitated Assembly or with Rouher in the Senate were already displaying signs of fatigue, even distress, propping themselves on elbows at the long table, its thick dark-green cloth littered with notepads, blotters, heavy silver inkwells. The Emperor, in his genial way, permitted others to join him in smoking, and cigar fumes curled and hovered above them, stubs messily piling up on square saucers of sham-Grecian design.

At the head of the table, Napoleon, in tail-coat, a blue sash slanting across his white, frilled frontage, having motioned everyone to remain seated, perhaps to relieve pain, was now standing, though markedly stooping, one hand behind his back, the other occupied with a cigarette. He too was wearied, traces of white showing through his thin brown-tinted hair, his eyes scarcely visible within their swollen pouches.

Seated on a crimson chair on his right, the Empress, in black – 'widow's black', Canrobert had mumbled – had sat through the long, argumentative session, saying nothing, though her feelings were at times obvious, over-obvious.

Ollivier, mollifier, bridge-builder, had been dispatched to the Assembly, on reports of 'troubled waters', with instructions to plug the dike until Sovereign and Council had reached decision. Doubtless he had confided his own opinion to the former.

Leboeuf's decision to mobilize the reserves had been ratified, but by now the debate, issuing from depleted faces, mostly bearded imitations of their master, had sunk to the ragged and repetitive, the Emperor surveying them all as though he were not personally concerned, Eugénie following the voices, frowning, as if over a difficult musical score. At this juncture her beauty had lapsed; she too was tired, fretful, perforce holding beauty and charm in reserve. Only her eyes were intact, blue, direct, and, as Morny had once said, dogmatic or fearless, make your choice.

'In the interests of dynasty . . .'

The voices, sharp, irritable, impatient, seemed chasing each other.

'We cannot, either in political or military terms, disregard the unpopularity of Prussia, not only in Europe, England excepted, but in the German-speaking world. Where else can the southerners look for succour save to France?'

'His Majesty the King of Bavaria will accompany his troops only on the piano. By permission of the Wagner person.'

The joke passed unnoticed, and the Emperor, almost creaking, resumed his seat. Persigny, in a baroque uniform of no known army, was present though without office, a sun-god on half-pay, the brass voice cracking. His red, grooved face was set in perpetual grievance, and he now spoke for the first time, heard with the scrupulous inattention due to a distinguished, rather absurd nonentity whose right to address such a gathering was questionable, the deposit of a bygone age. He was urgent, throaty, attempting to sound magisterial.

'Their Majesties were first to know the view of that Viennese crab, von Beust, that Austrian goodwill is by no means assured and will operate only after six weeks and a decisive French victory. I ask, no, I implore . . .'

'Austria!' Leboeuf, army chief, was contemptuous. 'Austrian help would assure our defeat. Since when has she ever conducted any war without catastrophe? His Majesty thrashed them in '59, von Moltke at Sadowa . . .'

'But support, even from Württemberg, must surely . . .'

'There's Italy to consider. She's already discontented with her new Prussian friends. Though without us, there would have been no Italy. And who else secured her Venice, though Bismarck took the credit?'

'To surrender Rome, for whatever assistance, would betray our most stable hope in France. The Catholic vote . . . they'll accuse us of surrender to Jews, Protestants, Freemasons . . .'

'Our colleague rests his case on the assumption that gratitude is a recognizable factor in politics. I, on the contrary, recognize no such factor. The Bavarian monarchy was created by Napoleon I, as His

Majesty created the Italian. But such gifts incur more resentment than gratitude. And remember, Bavaria joined Austria in '66 and will not have forgotten her indignity before the Prussian boots. She will risk nothing now. Moreover, King Ludwig . . . The Empire has given outstanding benefits to France, but France merely demands more. The Italian nature is such that we can expect . . .'

Interruptions made the moment feverish. The Emperor, whose head, as so often, appeared too heavy and who had remained either detached or sleepy, was roused to speak. 'Gentlemen . . .' His low voice not commanding but appeasing.

The silence was brief and the debate resumed, swaying to and fro, lurching like a drunken pendulum, wavering between peace and war. The Empress still uttered no word, though her choice was scarcely disputable, and Hermes could have seen, probably did see, impatience in the slightly slanted sapphire eyes, anger in hands very small, very delicate, rings twinkling against her funereal dress, frustration in her unnatural stillness. Could she be nagged by her collection of relics, those of the broken Queen whose last months of freedom had been in this very palace? Perhaps too she was remembering Hortense's half-complaining, half-admiring view of her son. Sweetly obstinate, she had said.

Gramont, younger than most, more ambitious, had throughout been impatient with the Peace Party.

'The Empire, that is, France herself, could not survive passive acquiescence to Prussian arrogance. That is the voice of the pavement, the farmsteads, the barracks, the workshops. You have all heard it. I have reason to know that Bismarck speaks for himself alone. The Royal House, the Parliament, the populace distrust or hate him. The generals . . .'

'De Gramont, what am I hearing? Are you envisaging Prussian mutiny? Nonsense! This chatter about German defections, or civil war . . . more nonsense. I tell you . . .'

The Peace Party looked in command. The clock ticked on. From wide mullioned windows a yellow sun-shaft lay across the table like a scabbard, abruptly withdrawn as the Empress raised her hand against the sudden glare and a minister hastened to lower a blind.

From somewhere, a third suggestion was revived, the good offices of London, St Petersburg, Turin, an international conference. A growl of approval was weightier than the murmurs of dissent. Behind his bluish cloud the Emperor stirred. International conferences were his favourite solution, the secrets of which he knew so well. He himself had suggested it at the start but, fair-minded pupil of Le Bas, was a trained listener. He at once sat straighter, and several thought they saw tears on the face parched by anxiety, ravaged by sleeplessness and worse.

Gramont began to rise, flushed and angry. 'What business has French dignity to do with foreigners? It is we ourselves . . .'

He was stopped, not only from the table but by a wholesale outburst from the crowds at the gates towering above the gardens, closed today, a detachment of troops ranged before the Palace, defiant signal of French might. Throughout, Parisians had incessantly, passionately, belaboured Prussia and queasy talk of peace.

A flunkey marched in, explaining the sudden clamour and laying before the Emperor a silver platter, on which lay a message from the Assembly.

He stared at it, calculating the imponderables, then slowly, almost gingerly, picked it up, as though it were leaden, the tension, as all waited, scarcely bearable.

Ollivier had not yet spoken, but by almost unanimous vote the demand for guarantees had been renewed, backed by threat of force.

Napoleon was again on his feet. Short, still hunched, he uttered a mirthless, gently nasal laugh. 'I doubt whether we have yet done justice to the opinions of the Chambers and the Nation. Meanwhile, we will adjourn. Madame and I will retire. You will find refreshments for you all . . .'

His words trailed away, he bowed, moved aside, for Eugénie to allow them the curtsy renowned throughout four continents. Even when perfunctory it was a spectacle perfected without theatricality: an inclination of the head, small flutter of hands, then swift ripple of silk and light, pure line of descent, tiny pause, not in humility but climax, before the rising, effortless, soundless, complete, lingering after it vanished.

Behind a tall brocaded screen, she faced her husband. 'Louis . . .' Distorted by feeling, she was hoarse, very foreign, in appeal, demand or despair. 'Louis', or was it Loulou? Admonition, or reminder of the sacred. Her beauty again faltered, strained by apprehension, but she did not continue.

The clock moved to eight thirty. Few had eaten well, and, reassembling, the notables saw that Gramont had departed to grapple with the Senate. Further missives revealed that he had already spoken, implying, never precisely stating it, an alliance secured with Austria and Italy. In the Assembly, Thiers had brazenly attached the Empire for slackness in army reform, which hitherto he had relentlessly opposed. Nothing was yet known of Ollivier's performance.

Another chair was empty. The Emperor had withdrawn from the table and now sat apart, head tilted a little sideways, in an armchair alongside the wide, curved Louis XIII fireplace, gold stars fiery within the marble, cherubs kneeling on scallop shells, clutching the twin pillars, clumsily moulded, as if added in hasty afterthought. Sunk deep in cushions, he appeared intermittently asleep.

During the recess, the balance had apparently shifted, the Peace Party in retreat.

'Italy will demand the impossible, our withdrawal from Rome . . .'
Everyone was startled by a near shout from the youngest present,

a general so newly promoted that almost nobody knew his name. He had pushed back his chair so violently that it had overturned, and now stood, aloft, above them all, as if rehearsing a heroic pose. Lamps had been lit, illuminating his decorations, his sword hilt, his furious mouth.

'Schleswig-Holstein has gone, Hanover has gone, Austria is stricken by this ravenous Prussia. We could have taken Luxembourg and absorbed Belgium but have done nothing. No one forgets that Blücher, that Prussia, won Waterloo for Wellington. I ask His Majesty to crush without further prattle-tattle this otherwise uninteresting country. No one could call it a nation.' His excess of anger ignored expostulations, calls for order, the restoration of his chair and invitations to use it.

'I beg . . . centuries of French honour and prowess be not thrown away . . .'

His lumpish hands clenched were thrown up in challenge, then relaxed, and, overcome by embarrassment or further stress, he sat down, fumbling with papers.

The silence was prolonged, all waiting on the Emperor, who remained impassive, face half hidden. Eugénie was in shadow, scarcely present. Persigny, sergeant and duke, always ill at ease in ceremonial clothes which never quite fitted his stout, irregular figure, his face in the dull air coloured like old burgundy, looked choked by angry frustration, tortured by protocol, inability to use language habitual to him. Oldest, most faithful of Bonapartists, he no longer had a role. Gazing along the files, portfolios, cigar-cases, he compared the faces, morose, ill-tempered, vehement, to those of rival surgeons eyeing each other above an unconscious patient.

An antic outsider, unseen, unknown, but with influence perhaps decisive, could be reminded of Tragedy, badly staged and imperfectly understood. To Eugénie, the figures propped, receding, might have become spectres tinged by the green table.

Before arguments were recharged, yet another message reached the Emperor. He glanced at it, his features unchanged, then handed it to the nearest, Marshal MacMahon, Duke of Magenta. Thiers was still speaking, pleading for reason, conciliation, magnanimity. Even the Peace adherents were stung by this, several looking at the Marshal as if for leadership.

At such a pause, evoked by an abyss ignored by the map, one realized the distinction between minutes, swift, continuous and of equal length, and moments, rarer, critical, of unpredictable duration.

Leboeuf, however, was equal to both. In all the accoutrements and dominion of a Minister of War, word perfect, he repeated what, to fearsome delight, he had earlier informed the Assembly.

'The Army, my oath upon it, and the honour of the Staff, has never been in better shape, the reserves never in higher spirits, the general disposition more loyal. Should the unthinkable occur, and a war last two years, we should not have to buy, I should say purchase, a button for a single trooper.'

To defy a capital city in its wrath or agony, a Marius, Sulla, Caesar would have deployed half a legion in savage temper and quelled danger with a flash of metal. Danton would have pulverized opposition, like an earthquake, Robespierre have contented himself with a quiet stare through tinted spectacles before signing a few deadly papers, and Bonaparte would station several cannon in strategically selected sites.

None of these exemplars were immediately appropriate. With the clock hands, intricate filigree, climbing towards midnight, the voices gradually stilled into exhaustion, ground down by words that had lost currency, overcome by crude images of pageantry and epic, leading to a healing draught of decision. There must be a final ultimatum, no, already time was too late for ultimatums and guarantees;

the commotion from across the Rhine was almost audible, and all France demanded more. This was the consensus awaiting only the Jovian nod.

The Emperor's pale blue eyes strove against further. His Swiss-German tones were so soft, so slow that all had to strain forward to hear. The Empress, very pale, affected composure, though her hands were trembling and her eyes were closed. Against over-exaltation? Against wild Paris? Against horror?

'Gentlemen, I think I have heard you aright. And even had we no case for war which we could avow, we should be obliged to obey the will of the People.'

When they had departed, and Eugénie had soundlessly slipped away without a glance, he moved, almost stumbling, to the dishevelled table, littered with scribblings, ash, chewed pencils, soiled blotters, the scraps of history.

Priding himself on his scholarship, he did not rejoice in a reminder of it, a long-dead voice muttering 'The Ides of March.'

A few minutes ago, the statesmen, generals, dignitaries of the Empire had been bowing, saluting, congratulating him, their words and gestures already ancient in Babylon, Tyre, Thebes. He stood, head lowered, holding the table for support. Had he now won? At such a crossroads, he was not certain. The December *coup* had gone askew. Even when victorious at Magenta, MacMahon had had to reassure him, to prevent him ordering retreat.

He waited, all Europe waited on his pleasure, until irresolution dropped away and he, commander-in-chief, at the slime-green table, prepared to write his address to the People of France.

TWENTY-SIX

HEADLINES reach extraordinary height as Hermes, in his secret box, watches comedy and tragedy expertly positioned, in telling repartee, the star performers reciting the gabble he had heard from Agamemnon and Priam, clanging across Europe in infantile play. Few would remember, fewer would understand, that line of fluent Pindar, 'the future is the wisest of witnesses'.

On one podium stands Emperor Napoleon III, in sober regalia:

'We have done all in our power to avert this war, and I may say that it is the nation to a man which, by its irresistible impulse, dictated our decisions. I am resolved to energetically pursue the great mission entrusted to me. I have faith in the triumph of our armies, for I know that behind me France has risen to her feet and that God protects her.'

On another, King Wilhelm is also speaking his lines, with identical, puppet-like motions:

'The government and myself are acting in full awareness that victory and defeat are in the hands of Him who decides the outcome of battles. With a clear gaze, we have measured the responsibilities which, before the judgement-seat of God and of Mankind, must fall upon him who drags two great and peace-loving peoples in the heart of Europe into devastating conflict. Germans and French, equally enjoying and desiring the blessings of Christian civilization and increasing prosperity, are summoned to a rivalry more wholesome than that sanguinary tumult of arms. Yet those who hold power in France have, by preconceived misguidance, found means to work on the legitimate but excitable national sentiment of our great neighbour for the furtherance of personal interests and the gratification of passions.'

A third stands high. M. Emile Ollivier lays aside his brief and, hand on heart, stock repertory gesture uncharacteristic of him, speaks on impulse, delighting Hermes, connoisseur, virtual inventor of irony, watching from the shadow of a church porch.

'I accept responsibility for the war with a light heart.' In the condescension of authority, he confides to General Maxim du Camp, hero awaiting his hour, 'We have only to stretch out our hand to take Berlin.'

Gramont acknowledges congratulations, bows to the plaudits of a distinguished audience. 'An insult has been offered. It can be avenged only by war.' Hermes nods to himself, as to an old friend, accepted but not especially liked. People swirl past him, intoxicated with nonsense, lunatics who imagine that eating newspaper will expand knowledge. Foreknowing the contents, he ignores yet another speech, from Rouher, leading a Senate deputation to address the Sovereign in the Galérie de Diane.

'The Guarantees demanded from Prussia have been spurned, the dignity of France disregarded. Your Majesty draws the sword and the nation is with you, trembling with anger at the excesses which an ambition, over-stimulated by one day's good fortune, was certain to produce, sooner or later. Your Majesty was able to wait but has spent the time since Sadowa perfecting the armament and organization of the Army.'

In general's ceremonials, Napoleon responds, his bearing sombre, thanking them but foretelling a struggle long and arduous, the speech chilling the hot, almost stifling noon. Hermes yawns, the constant display of human folly prompting renewal of *ennui*. Nevertheless, he considered the ongoing plot, pleased with his own handiwork. Perhaps the most pernicious human attribute is memory. Today, all Paris is swallowing the poison of history, its grievances, hatreds, misunderstandings, its threat.

Aphrodite had fled, chaste Wisdom was nowhere, an Academician remarking that Reason, gift of horse-loving Athene of Many Counsels, had taken flight, but this was largely taken as praise for the delicious courage of youth. Glaring Mars was ascendant, wafted aloft by clarion calls from *Moniteur, Figaro, Journal des Débats, Patrie* and by jubilation in avenue and square, round Arc de Triomphe, Notre-Dame, Tuileries, even at the old Revolutionary lair the Hôtel de Ville. Life was simple as an egg. A streaming pageant of voices, coloured by the dementia that hangs over crowds, was hailing the green plumes of the Chasseurs. The day was perpetual anthem, *To Berlin* replacing *guarantees* as the ruling theme. Huge bets were being laid on the date of the initial French victory. At the Bourse government stocks clambered to the exceptional, steel shares doubled overnight. Gaming-rooms were deserted as blinking, yellowing players, strangers to their own pavements, joined processions which, swift and luxuriant as tropical growth, blossomed everywhere. Spirits were wild as Mexican suns, Algerian sandstorms, engulfing all classes. Refugees from back-street *estaminets* dipped withered souls into magic; 'ether frolics', where addicts hopped and flapped, screeched and barked, and opium seances in rue de Maintenon, in which figures lay supine in dazed paridisia, were alike abandoned. Terrible hospitals in eastern suburbs seemed to have emptied themselves into a new population, continually swelling.

All Paris recalled Bismarck's mastiff face, an excuse for execration and boasts. *To Berlin* was chorused with the resonance that had inspirited the salutes to Victor Noir, to Baudin, which had routed Louis-Philippe, Charles X, Louis XVI, which had stirred Danton into magnificence and escorted the Prince-President to the Elysée. *To Berlin.*

Peace talk was dangerous, though at the Assembly little Thiers was emboldened, not Thersites but a Gracchus in miniature, irrepressible. 'Do you want all Europe to declare that, though the quarrel has been settled, you have decided on pouring out torrents of blood, on the score of a trifling formality?'

Left and Right joined in howling him off stage. A single-page pamphlet from the Paris Section of the Workers' International was ripped apart whenever detected, and several printers' works were pillaged on suspicion of having produced it, with its traitorous beginning: 'War for Empire or dynasty can be regarded by working people only as criminal absurdity.'

The Emperor and the Prince Imperial had already departed, unostentatiously, from an inferior railway station, to join the staff at Metz, leaving the Empress as Regent. In the palatial Jockey Club, secured by protective railings, thick marble pillars, substantial walls, where Morny had once established the tone, gentlemen sat in the sedate reading room, quietly, sensibly, serene in their opulence, discussing what they called, without immoderate convictions, the events of the day.

'Victor Hugo says . . .'

'But when does he not?'

London newspapers had arrived, and a duke and a Provençal baron were reflecting on a speech in London by a German Jew, Herr Marx. 'The fact is, that at a moment when official France and Germany are plunging headlong into fratricidal war, the workers of both countries are exchanging messages of peace and goodwill. This great fact, unparalleled in history, opens the perspective of a better future. It proves that in the face of the old society with its economic miseries and political furies, another society is rising, an order whose international relations will be Peace, because its lawgiver will everywhere be the same: Labour!'

One grey beard turned to the other, an eyeglass glinted. 'I am unwilling, my dear colleague, to confess any inclination to subscribe to messages, either of peace or goodwill.'

Nearby, on a leather sofa, others had ordered brandies. A white-gloved hand picked up the London *Spectator* with the careful delicacy with which a bower bird selects colours to attract a mate. Over the editorial, lips tightened but composure was maintained.

'The real cause of this war, the vote of 50,000 soldiers against the Empire, is, of course, not mentioned, but Paris has gone mad with patriotic pride, the French Army is moving towards the Rhine, and Europe must pass through a year, perhaps years, of misery in order that one single man may secure the career and position of one single child. This war has not cause, no motive, no justification, save the fear of Napoleon Bonaparte that, without it, his boy's succession would not be clear.'

The Viscount de Rambuillet, slender, almost emaciated, though in but his early thirties, with grey, tired eyes had been reading the *Pall Mall Gazette*. He looked up, fastidiously touched his brow with a handkerchief lightly perfumed, then, glancing about him to see that no servant was near, raised a hand at his companions. His voice rose and fell, melodiously, as if conducted, as he read:

'Partings are at all times painful, but it would be difficult to conceive any farewell more tinged with sadness than that of the Emperor and the Empress on his departure from Paris. There are no two people in Europe who have played so prominent a part as the royal couple whose fate hangs upon the present war. When they meet again, if indeed they ever do meet, what an eventful story will have been told, and each line written in letters of blood! To France, though the issues are great, the war is but one chapter in her history; but to the Emperor and the Empress it may be the last chapter in the records of their career. For him at least, there is no future but in success; in drawing the sword he has thrown away the scabbard, he has burnt his boats. That great and glorious city which, as with an enchanter's wand he has remodelled and rebuilt, will either close her gates to the fugitive or welcome the return of a victorious leader. Bold as the Emperor may be to beard Bismarck in his power, it will require more boldness still to reappear at home without his army.'

The Viscount ceased. He surveyed the group from beneath immaculate brows. 'Well, gentlemen?'

Save for the tiny hum of a gnat, the silence was complete, that felt during an inquest following a witness peculiarly inconvenient or damning.

Etienne was amongst thousands in place du Temple, in reservist's uniform. At home he was a one-man parade, watched by loving wife and docile, if slightly disappointing son. In the office he was a conduit between ministerial orders and clerks' obedience, though occasionally he felt he did not exist.

To face ox-brained Prussians would demand less manliness than to mention the Countess to Amélie, affectionate, with a mind like an air-pocket and a soft trust in himself, and who would collapse for ever if she discovered it violated.

He had heard, or thought he had heard, a whisper directed straight at him. 'Life rewards. If there is not someone else, there is always something else.' For perhaps no Lisa would read of him picking up a Prussian head in Berlin, galloping to a frontier with a vital message, raising the flag over a bastion.

Amélie, unwillingly, somewhat fearfully, had allowed Emile his two hours outside, she herself too scared of the noise and feet to accompany him. It was as though Paris was being swamped by the great wave which he had told her would one day crash over it. Tired from the stamps and unflagging noise, she grieved for something long lost, indescribable but gentle as healing fingers on an injured bird.

She would pray for the Prince Imperial, though of the Emperor's magic she had no doubts. God, moreover, succours the righteous.

Emile was blindly pushing forward, a digit in this city which played so many tricks on him, with its false doors, unfinished staircases, magic mirrors and breathing statues. He was part of an enormous, surging something, of songs and shouts, strange kisses and unpleasant jokes, which forced him to remember that when M. Havet first used his rod on him he had felt not quite pleasure, not wholly pain but a curious thrill shot through with both. Meanwhile, he constantly paused, gaping at bearskins and shakos, lances, dragon-helmets, Pioneers' axes. His moods foundered. Jostled by a hard shoulder, laughed at by a ragged girl, pushed aside by a shouting gang, joining in cheers for the Emperor, once fancying he heard his mother's voice, he several times had a sensation which books called uncanny, that was once caused by looking up and, startled, seeing a vast blood-red balloon hanging over Paris absolutely motionless, three man in a basket beneath, also still, like waxworks. He had shivered violently and now, at a smashed window and crocked lamp-post, he wanted Suet Oozing Apple but could only imagine a lump of horse-shit.

An anthem sounded from Notre-Dame. Gramont, leaving the Senate, was surrounded, a glitter of hands and chants by the Sorbonne radicals. He flinched, but no, they were giving him an ovation. 'Vive la guerre.' 'A bas la Prusse.' Ollivier too had never been more loudly acclaimed, even Persigny, driving to Turkish Baths, took his bow. Uproar only diminished, catcalls dwindling to a tolerant, somewhat pitying sympathy, as von Westler, Prussian envoy, made his exit.

Though 'Partant pour la Syrie', Hortense's 'Chant du départ', was heard on training fields and outside barracks, the 'Marseillaise' was omnipresent, sung from balconies in theatres by mighty basses, in cafés by young chanteuses, from beneath the Column, from Café Printemps. Thousands in place de Bourse waved hats and sticks as Victor Capoul, from the Opéra, led the singing from the top of an omnibus, the diva, Marie Sassé performing from Madeleine steps. Elsewhere, more of the famous – Ristori, Christine Nilsonn, Carvalho – were tireless in their voice.

In his Chapel the Pangs of the Messiah preached to the world, his sermon, much quoted, several times referring to a new entity, undefined but impressive, faintly protecting, the Exterminating Angel.

Tramp. A rattle of arms. A blur of uniforms and feathers. Bacchic frenzy, Dionysian mirth, purposeless yet ruthless, troupes at one with the beat and wail of Africa, the flash of a Spahi burnous, the red trousers of the Line, converged at the crossroads of boulevard de Montparnasse and boulevard Raspail, discharging emotions that leapt beyond words into toxic heavens and hells. Orpheus, escaping from the Underworld, ruled in the light, and, throughout, hummed, strummed, chortled songs from *Gérolstein*, mocking those Teutonic absurdities, the very ladylike Prince Paul von Steis-Stein-Steis-Laper-Bottmoll-Schorstenburg, the ludicrous General Boum, the young ranker Fritz, capriciously ennobled as Baron de Vermont-von bock-bier, Revellers chorused the strains of the Grand Duchess declaring war, only to amuse her Chancellor, Baron Puck, a farce which set Paris yelling 'Vive Puck' while children chanted 'Boum, Boum', gesticulating to imitate guns that could change the world. Again and again, whistled, crooned, warbled, croaked, you heard 'Oh how I adore the soldiers!'

Hermes too murmurs 'Boum', seeing streets as verses. Etienne heard it, louder, from drunken, arm-locked conscripts, as he stood on Pont Neuf, momentarily alone, staring at the river very slow, in loops of silver, greenish, golden, controlled by the clouds of high summer, bleached, though down west rimmed with fire. Words like Beauty, Devotion, Miracle drifted into him, keeping pace with the river.

Earth thudded and trembled. Even in outer suburbs, far from the parades, entrainments, processions, the tread of marching men, sometimes imaginary, was inescapable, a persistent undercurrent making strangers link arms, shout 'It's happened.' Street-sweepers positioned their brooms like rifles and, grinning but humourless, demanded cash from whoever passed. Itinerant hurdy-gurders ground out the melodies that underpinned, *guaranteed* the salvation of France.

Newspapers of all persuasion joined hands in a *galop infernal*. *Siècle*, *Temps*, *Soir*, *Réveil*, Right and Left, stamping out Prussian infamy, insolence, pretentiousness and inventing new stories. Wilhelm was threatening abdication unless Bismarck resigned, two regiments had mutinied, the Crown Prince and his wife, Victoria's daughter, had fled to Windsor, Munich was in turmoil. Each paper carried a particular headline. 'Emperor takes Supreme Command.' Of course. A Bonaparte can do no other. He rides victorious between blue and silver praetorians or is nothing. Habsburgs, even Hohenzollerns, can repeatedly lose, yet deep-set loyalties will hold, amongst peoples who love kings in their tragic defeat, the quintessence of primitivism. In the New Paris, however, the *vives* inadequately conceal howls for sacrificial blood, preferably Prussian. Failing that . . . enough. Meanwhile, boulevard de Sébastopol, boulevard Magenta, Pont de Solferino, place Algiers . . . bedecked, beflagged, blazed the glories of the Second Empire.

Another catchphrase plunged thoroughout the capital. *God Is Danger*, sometimes, with similar effect, *God Is in Danger*, repeated like an imprecation, password or rallying cry, from Notre-Dame and quai des Célestins to the jewellers, couturiers, fashionable restaurants in rue de la Paix, from place de la Bastille to rich, cosmopolitan Hôtel de Meurice on rue Rivoli and to the latest emporium in rue Royale, repeated by Bon Marché shoppers, Les Halles fishmongers, by loungers in kiosks, tourists in Hôtel du Rhin in place Vendôme, the Column so dense with petal and leaf, the exhalation of a superb summer, that flower-sellers at the Madeleine had emptied their baskets by noon. Vying with flowers, the tricolour hung from balconies, windows, garden poles and park obelisks. Only in certain grandee mansions in Faubourg Saint-Germain were blinds and shutters drawn, gardens silent. Driven along in the tidal flow were cocodes, drab or gaudy, pawnshop dandies, English milords, reeling bargees, Left Bank professors, youths on French leave from houses of correction, girls from loom and counter, market-stall and brothel, clinging to escorts of either sex, all dedicated, merry, in love with the hour. A devout horde congregated in hymnal quietude outside the Invalides where lay dead Hercules, whose spirit would drive the phalanxes over the Rhine; the invincible N, soul of France, with the old *élan*, under the gigantic eyes of the dead.

Drums had returned, banging mongoloid rhythms from circus earth to emblazoned sky. Fathers explained the sights to volatile children. Green epaulettes of Chasseurs à pied, red and blue of the Zouaves. Stacks of hastily produced prints of the Empress had been distributed in barracks, to be slipped into forage caps. With them were simple maps of the Rhinelands and, for officers, German dictionaries.

People were coalescing, in a single marvellous dream, exhilarating as a frilly cancan. Hawkers were selling caricatures, Bismarck as a novice matador shrinking from a priapic Gallic bull, the Emperor with Hercules' lion skin and club, Eugénie, haloed, in blue robe, Queen of Heaven. A parrot was known to have squawked 'To Berlin', which babies were now whispering from prams.

A crowd swiftly degenerates to a pack, so that nervous jewellers were pulling down shutters on pretext of necessary redecoration. A news vendor near place du Palais-Bourbon who had forgotten to remove a *Charivari* cartoon of 'Badinguet', crookbacked, neckless, top-heavy, sucking a pipe upside down, one hand outstretched for a tip from contemptuous Bismarck, had his stall demolished, a tailor with a foreign name, actually Swiss, was chased between quays, then ducked in the Saint-Martin Canal, spies were reported, suspects' windows gleefully or savagely smashed, on avenue Wagram a woman was arrested for speaking German.

Above the din and confusions foreign ambassadors were conferring over wartime protocol, substantially as to whether neutrality would be breached if embassies, legations, consulates were illuminated at Prussian defeat. A tiny paragraph in *Temps*, muffled like the cry of a foundling thrust into some fetid asylum, announced that the Imperial representative at Washington had shot himself but elicited only a few grimaces at cowardice or treachery. From some fairground, rockets were ripping the twilit sky to tatters, with showers of bloodshot commas, sprinkles of white fire, whorls of demented stars.

'I remember our friend Louis Blanc remarking that only the dead return.'

The Madrid, despite the tumult, remained very full, the atmosphere disconsolate. Dirty gas pendants were already lit, though outside all was luminous with flags, uniforms, weaponry.

Rigault had departed, breathing defiance, secreting threats, but those at table and bench were resigned to the prolongation of the Empire, doubtless to Napoleon V. The covert manoeuvres of union leaders, civil rights philosophers, the gallant manifestos of the International could not enliven them. Every news sheet was gloomily taken, almost immediately crumpled. At best, an indecent oath was managed. Earlier reports, buzzing like hornets, had not aroused desire to resist, though troops were said to have refused to board trains, a scandal had left the arsenals half empty. Perhaps more hopefully for the revolution were fresh rumours that masterpieces were being smuggled from the Louvre, trees were being felled in the Bois, orders had been issued to destroy houses nearest the outlying forts. Could the government, for all its bluster and cock crows, be secretly preparing for a siege?

All this, of course was kept from the Press. Truth from above, from anywhere in this hysteria, was as likely as a statue of Napoleon III accepting an invitation to supper with Rochefort. The *Soir*, just delivered, reserved its front page for pictures of that hag Eugénie presenting ceremonial swords for a victory parade.

Following the reference to Louis Blanc, conversation attempted revival, though drinking remained listless, stale apricot turnovers were nibbled mechanically.

'So Napoleon the Little tries to change again, though from tyrant to generalissimo is not an outstanding transformation. His self-deceptions chase each other in no very convincing purpose, unless you call it the Rhine. Though anyone who served under him in Italy . . .'

'Well, at least war saves us from him redesigning the Seine, shaving it to straight lines and strict corners.'

'I'd scarcely be too sure of that.'

'A cry from Cain.' With this, an aspirant and bitter novelist, whose father's wealth had removed him from the conscription lists, attempted to sketch a vision of bloody knives, smoking flesh, unearthly paeans, orgiastic nakedness, discarded panther skins, then, discouraged by the other's shrugs, failed his muse.

Emile had lost himself in the roaring night, hemmed in by figures now larger, noisier, yet indistinct scarcely human. Paris was showing another face: like jam which, hours later, tastes quite different to the way it had at breakfast. It was stinking, hellish, he had never felt so black a loneliness, as though protection had been altogether withdrawn. Longing for home, he no longer knew the direction. Smaller, scared, he was gulping upheavals of dust, suffocating and ghostly. A hand touched his cheek, but no, his collar had flapped as youths surged past. He realized, without being able to find words, that this must be part of what Maman called the hardships of growing up.

TWENTY-SEVEN

MAKE us amiable in words and deeds was the prayer to
Aphrodite, who seldom listened. Prayers very seldom sufficed
for Hermes, debonair bringer of useful changes and guide for the
dead.

Mortals, like any mammal or insect, fight for space, are wary of
tide, wind, shadows, predators. Moreover, they are pursued by furies
in the blood, injected by having bred with Titans.

Hermes inhales a thick smouldering brownish substance proscribed by all European chiefs save the Turkish. Infected by the
Parisian vaudeville, he hums a few bars of an Offenbach lullaby, 'A
Blue Cloud Is His Chariot', then sees ice crystals gather into cloudy
towers and citadels. Only after they dissolve does he, as if from
Cretan height, again gaze down, barely concerned, at this enflamed
morsel of Earth. Blood, fire, clamour, decorated victims. For the
young, old age is fearful, death is not, and now they gibber for it,
infants bored with their toys, tiros hypnotized by Dionysus, he who
prefers to wander eternally amongst men, smiling, mysterious and
cruel.

Again visible through steam are Paris and Berlin, Troy and
Mycenae, for, in this sight, where the sea is a platter of blue-green
marble, all cities are identical, beehive hut merging with Versailles,
Ajax's face stamped upon Mussolini's, doomed, recurrent chief of
men, as if in cinema montage.

Such a simile is permissible, a god fuses hindsight and foresight, immediately perceiving what humanity needs aeons to fathom.

In apparent lunacy, bowing to tribal ancestors, Paris is enacting inescapable rituals, entangling challenges, oaths, names. Regulus, obeying his oath, returning to Carthage for torture and death, is part of a design which, in a later age, will be called the July Plot, knightly conspirators planning to sacrifice the chief for the tribal good. Forswearing one's pledge, dishonouring one's name, can be catastrophic. Nemesis is everywhere: the curse uttered by ruined Carthage ultimately destroys Rome, the Prince-President's violation of his oath invites retribution.

Despite his nose for the trivial, Hermes remains detached. Gods belie themselves if they love humanity too well: mortals immolate themselves in Promethean efforts to reach heaven, complete history, avert *moira*, fate. These flag-waving Gauls, slaves of time, are rebelling against teachings to love the unlovable and seek the illusionary. They flee from *metis*, intelligence, into *theia*, a luminosity, flowering of soul, sought by the élites, by poets and athletes, harpists, wild orators who harassed rulers, but devoid of irony and paradox. Empires prevail less than some nameless woodland elf, imaginary yet outliving them all.

Hermes' slanted smile is fading, a pale eyebrow lifts in courteous disdain at the saturnalia, the myrmidons frantic to thrust lances into the infinite, unaware of another drama, that of Earth spinning towards irresistible heat, the last survivors clambering for salvation on some moon still undiscovered. They have forgotten the gods; the gods have not forgotten them.

AFTERWORD

Within six weeks, the French armies had been defeated. Tortured by the illness that was to kill him, Napoleon III had vainly sought death in battle, before surrendering with his 'Army of the Rhine' at Sedan, 'betrayed by fortune, or fate as he believed, but pursued, others might say, by the natural consequences of his own marvellous adventures, and a strange neglect of the one source of strength on which he relied, the Army'. *

Led by Thiers and Gambetta, the Third Republic was instantly proclaimed in Paris, the Empress-Regent fleeing to England. Napoleon III died in exile at Chislehurst, Kent, in a house once owned by his mistress-financier Emily Rowles, today a golf club. Eugénie survived until 1920, regularly revisiting Paris, where she met Jean Cocteau. Allegedly, she read aloud over the tombs of her husband and son at her foundation, Farnborough Abbey, the outline of the Versailles Treaty, the French vengeance for Sedan. The Prince Imperial, accompanying the British troops in a Zulu war, 1879, was killed in circumstances which disgraced his companions.

'The Second Reich', Bismarck's unification of Germany under Kaiser Wilhelm I, was established at Versailles, while German troops still occupied France, beneath the massive painting A *Toutes les*

---

* Moritz Busch, quoted by George Hooper in *The Campaign of Sedan,* Bell, 1916

gloires de France. The Republic hopelessly continued the war, until finally capitulating it was forced to allow a ceremonial parade through Paris by the triumphant Germans.

Protests by the radical Paris Commune against the peace terms, and its fury with the national elections which returned a 'legitimate', anti-Bonapartist royalist majority, led to it claming the independence of the capital. Paris was then besieged by the Thiers government, watched by the amused or indifferent Prussians. The brief reign of the Commune, which contained anarchists and Jacobins – though not, despite Marx's opportunistic assertions, Marxists – witnessed shooting of hostages – the archbishop, generals – and scores of 'suspects', 'traitors', 'class enemies', the burnings of the Tuileries, the Hôtel de Ville, the attempted burning of Notre-Dame, the overthrow of the Vendôme Column – for which Courbet was later, though vainly, sent the bill for restoration – followed by the atrocities of Thiers' suppression, perhaps twenty thousand men, women and children shot or bayoneted without trial by the enraged soldiery.

Military disaster, the Commune and its fearful aftermath, contaminated French politics for generations, breeding desire for revenge on Germany and the recovery of the 'lost' provinces, Alsace and Lorraine, which helped promote the First World War. Political hatreds remained, certainly until another collapse, defeat and occupation, 1940.

Of those mentioned in my novel, Ollivier, driven to resignation by the first French reverses, abandoned politics but published *The Liberal Empire*, a defence of his career and of the regime, in seventeen volumes, before dying in 1913. Thiers resigned from the Republican leadership in 1873 and died in 1877. Rochefort served briefly in the provisional government, 1870, though without administrative ability. For associations with the Commune he was transported to

New Caledonia, escaping in 1874, eventually, after the 1880 amnesty, to resume his career as editor and polemicist, becoming increasingly anti-socialist and anti-Semitic, a spokesman for the nationalist Right and denying the innocence of Dreyfus. Though outliving his celebrity, he published his entertaining *Les Aventures de ma vie, 1895–6* and died in 1913. Rigault served the Commune as a particularly ruthless Police Prefect and was executed at its defeat. Gambetta, as Republican Minister of War, vigorously though unavailingly resisted the invaders and in peace was foremost in overcoming attempts to restore the Bourbon monarchy. Less capable in government than in opposition, he was premier in 1881–2, but died from a gun accident the same year. Clemenceau won world renown as 'the Tiger', dynamic war leader during 1917–18, and as an architect of the Versailles Treaty, living on until 1929.

I envisage both Tacitus and Emile, in Hermes' last joke, making one street journey too many and being shot, Etienne perishing at Sedan, Amélie mournfully living out her widowhood until French victory over the Second Reich and its downfall in 1918.

I append two professional assessments of Napoleon III:

It is only in recent years that Napoleon III has come to be seen as a precursor of the Common Market. His intentions were partly political – he wished to strengthen his alliance with England – but mainly economic, to stimulate agriculture and industry in France by competition and to benefit the masses by lower prices . . .

He had a strange charm for those with whom he came in contact. He could flatter without seeming hypocritical; he was generous, he was a good listener. But there was always something opaque about him, so that it was no easy matter following his lead.

His silent meditations and his mystical communion with public opinion made him – when he was successful – a kind of wizard.

– Theodore Zeldin, *France 1848–1945*,
Oxford University Press, 1974

Marx supposed that the class war would be fought to a finish, that one side would win. And since the bourgeoisie could not exterminate the proletariat, the proletariat would exterminate the bourgeoisie. There has been a different outcome: someone has slipped in between, played off one class against another and exploited both. This, not his ragbag of ideas, was the great historical innovation of Louis Napoleon. He appealed to the fears of the middle classes when he made the *coup d'état* as 'the Guardian of Order'. But he was also, in his muddled way, a socialist; he did more for the French working classes than any other French government before or since and when he died a trade-union representative was the only man to come from France for his funeral.

– A.J.P. Taylor, *Europe: Grandeur and Decline*,
Penguin, 1967

Praise for Peter Vansittart's fiction

Aspects of Feeling
'Hugely enjoyable. It is also ambitious, eccentric, comic and complex; but to pile on the adjectives makes it sound indigestible and, although it is a rich dish, it slides down easily.'
– Nina Bawden, *Daily Telegraph*

A Choice of Murder
'Extraordinarily vivid with startling flashes of beauty and drama. Vansittart's vision of the ancient world is ferociously convincing.'
– Isabel Colegate, *Daily Telegraph*

The Death of Robin Hood
'Extraordinarily written with power and craft, sensitivity and dry wit . . . Those who fail to read this book will miss a significant and renewing work of art.' – Andrew Sinclair, *The Times*

Landlord
'Finely focused and grotesquely comic.' – *Financial Times*
'Brilliant in its pictures of London moods.' – *Evening Standard*

Parsifal
'Delightful; every page is gripping. It also has a serious intention: to look at the mythological arguments behind the rise of Hitler. It's very ingenious and extremely well written.'
– V.S. Pritchett, *Sunday Times*

Pastimes of a Red Summer
'Those who like to see their history as a bright assemblage of ghosts, fugitive and crowded, will delight in these packed pages.'
– *Guardian*

A Safe Conduct

'The work of a fine novelist in his prime.' – *Sunday Telegraph*
'Wonderfully evocative of a cold and mysterious age.'
– Roy Hattersley, *Mail on Sunday*

Three Six Seven

'A wonderful book, a haunting, many-coloured dream of
murderous splendour, an evocation of the past which no other
historical novelist now writing in England could rival.'
– Michael Wharton, *Spectator*

The Tournament

'Sumptuous, evocative, strange and appalling. Such resonance
and sensuality and myriad curious detail have not been found in
the novel since Flaubert's *Salammbô*.'
– Andrew Sinclair, *The Times*

The Wall

'Extraordinary, as well read as it is well written, his finest yet.
– David Hughes, *Mail on Sunday*

All these titles are available from Peter Owen Publishers